Changeling Press LLC

ChangelingPress.com

Hawk/Riot Duet
A Bones MC Romance
Marteeka Karland

Hawk/Riot Duet
A Bones MC Romance
Marteeka Karland

All rights reserved.
Copyright ©2026

ISBN: 978-1-60521-957-8

Publisher:
Changeling Press LLC
315 N. Centre St.
Martinsburg, WV 25404
ChangelingPress.com

Printed in the U.S.A.

Editor: Jean Cooper
Cover Artist: Marteeka Karland

The individual stories in this anthology have been previously released in E-Book format.

Table of Contents

Hawk (Kiss of Death MC 3)
A Bones MC Romance
Marteeka Karland

May God have mercy on Carrie's enemies, because I have none.

Carrie -- When I stumble out of the fog into a motorcycle club compound, the guys seem more freaked out over my name (something about an old movie?) than the fact that I'm covered in blood and asking for a jug of sulfuric acid. Not my best moment. Then Hawk steps in. His smile and the careful way he takes care of me steal my heart. I'm asking for heartache, but my whole life has been nothing but pain and disappointment. Just this once, I want to take control, take what I want. And I want Hawk. No matter what happens when my family finds me.

Hawk -- I knew Carrie was trouble the second I laid eyes on her. Of course, she was covered in blood, so, easy call. What I didn't count on is how completely and quickly I fell under her spell. I might not be ready to admit it, but my brothers know and plan accordingly. Carrie is mine. Even though she's proven she can take care of herself, whatever trouble she has coming for her will have to go through me.

Chapter One

"This is gonna be good." I popped the top off my beer as I watched the scene about to unfold. Me and Chains sat at a table in the common room in steel folding chairs. Chains was leaning back with his booted feet on the table while I slouched with one ankle crossed over the opposite knee.

"Yep."

Knight hurried to us from where he'd been snagging his own beer at the bar. Three club girls were in tow, all with tits out, wearing only thongs. I grinned, raising an arm to welcome the brunette with pouty lips onto my lap.

"We placin' bets?" Knight looked gleeful in a maniacal kind of way. It was a little creepy to be honest.

I shrugged. "Might as well."

"My money's on Gunnar." Knight high-fived Oktober as the big man walked up to us. Everyone was waiting eagerly. Pippa, Gunnar's woman and Knuckles's daughter, had already met and welcomed Hannah, but Gunnar and Cain had yet to confront Knuckles. Cain, the former president of Bones MC in Somerset, Kentucky, was Hannah's father. I wasn't really concerned for Knuckles. Especially after he'd attempted to beat the fuck out of Gunnar when he'd caught him and Pippa in bed together. So a beating was definitely going to happen.

"What's goin' on?" Oktober hadn't been home long. After practically crawling back to the compound and into his room half dead from fatigue, I really thought he'd sleep for a fucking week. Bastard stumbled to bed for a couple hours and now looked fresh as a daisy. I hated the man on principle.

"Gunnar and Cain both pulled up outside the compound." Tiny, our road captain and not tiny at all, pulled up a chair and flipped it around backward to straddle it. He crossed his arms over the back of the chair, resting his forearms there. "I told the guys not to let them in yet, but Gunnar pulled rank." He shrugged. "I mean, brother outranks officer any day of the week, I suppose." Tiny didn't look the least bit upset. In fact, I was pretty sure he was looking forward to this as much as the rest of us were.

That got chuckles from us all. Knight clinked beer bottles with Inferno as the other man walked by. The second he sat down, two club whores descended on him. He didn't let them undress him but had one on his lap with his hand cupping a tit while sucking on a tit of the other woman. Made me give the tit of the woman in my lap a squeeze. She promptly giggled and arched into my palm. Yeah. Tits. Gotta love tits.

The door burst open and Gunnar stalked in, an intent look in his eyes. "Where the fuck is he?" The bite of demand in Gunnar's voice was unmistakable. He was a man looking to do violence.

"You know..." Tiny nodded in Gunnar's direction as he took a pull from his beer. "I do believe he's good and pissed."

I grinned as I raised my voice to be heard over the low din in the common room. "Where's who, Big Gun?" I'd started calling him Big Gun the second he came to the club. Just 'cause I liked fucking with him. My way of showing affection. And honestly, any man who would go to prison to protect his sister was definitely a big gun.

"The Goddamned motherfucker who made my sister his old lady without permission!"

That got a hoot from everyone.

"Better be careful takin' on the big boss, Gunnar."

"Fixin' t' get your ass handed to ya, boy."

"I got fifty bucks on the kid."

"Never happen!"

"Prove me wrong?"

"Oh, I'll take that action."

And the betting was on all across the room up until the moment Knuckles descended the stairs into the big room. The club compound was like four city blocks of abandoned four- and five-story warehouses the club now owned. We'd walled it off so there was no entry into the compound without our say-so. Each warehouse had been renovated so the bottom two floors were for various things that fell under club business, while the top floor, or floors, were made into suites and apartments for all our members. We had all this because of Knuckles, despite him being in prison. Once Knuckles entered the room, the betting and excess chatter stopped.

"You got somethin' to say to me, kid?" Knuckles crossed his arms over his chest. The pose was intimidating because Knuckles was a big-ass, strong motherfucker. His pecs and arm muscles all bulged with the effort, straining his black T-shirt. Only man in the club bigger than Knuckles was Tiny. More than one club girl had drooled over him since he got home, but Hannah had managed to shut them down. I'm not sure what exactly happened and none of the whores were saying, but to a woman, they left Knuckles alone.

"You're Goddamned right I've got something to say to you!" Gunnar stalked toward Knuckles like a jungle cat getting ready to pounce.

As one, we all leaned forward in anticipation. I could practically feel the tension in the room. I know I was coiled tight as a banjo string. Gunnar stopped a few inches from Knuckles, neither man giving an inch. Both of them looked ready to kill.

"The next couple minutes should be fun." Knight murmured the comment so softly I could barely hear him "But I think Gunnar can take him."

I would have rolled my eyes, but Gunnar lunged at Knuckles. We all sucked in a breath.

Knuckles flinched back slightly, bringing his hands up into a defensive stance but Gunnar didn't attack. Instead, he laughed and clapped Knuckles on the shoulder before pulling the other man into a welcoming embrace.

"You cocksucker," Knuckles muttered, his tone disgruntled. The whole place roared in laughter.

"If only you could see the fuckin' look on your face, man." Gunnar continued to wale on Knuckles's back so hard it probably felt like the beating Gunnar had refrained from giving him.

"It wasn't like I could fight back." Knuckles sounded disgruntled but was grinning. "Especially after I barged in on you and Pippa."

"Exactly. Just know things can change if you don't treat her right. You're my brother, but she's my sister."

"And I'm her fuckin' daddy." The booming voice came from the man in the doorway with a fierce scowl on his face. Cain Gill was the owner of one of the largest paramilitary companies in the world, as well as the former president of Bones MC. Our current president, Torpedo, was vice president at Bones before he came to be with us. Bohannon, our vice president, was the enforcer in the same outfit. Cain was also Gunnar and Hannah's father. And one tough-ass son of a bitch. "Which also makes me *your* daddy now."

The look on Cain's face was a mixture of amusement and I-will-totally-fuck-you-the-fuck-up. "Gunnar may be younger than me, but I have bigger guns and better torture devices. You displease my little princess in any way" -- he pointed a finger at Knuckles -- "and I will remove your balls. With fire ants."

Both Gunnar and Knuckles winced even as the rest of us hollered with laughter. Soon after, Cain and Knuckles shook hands and everyone carried on.

Such is life.

The club whore in my lap turned to straddle me. Giving me a coquettish grin, she slid her panty-covered pussy over my lap, rubbing my cock. I wasn't hard, but there wasn't a man alive who could resist Ruby when she was in the mood to fuck.

"Been waitin' for you, Hawk. Got somethin' special for you in my room."

"Oh, I bet you do, darlin'." I slid my hands around to cup her plump ass. I squeezed, then smacked one fleshy globe. Much as I loved playing with Ruby -- or any of the club whores, really -- I wasn't feeling it tonight. For some reason, I was wound too fucking tight to let my guard down enough to enjoy the experience. "Got shit to do tonight. Next time I'm at a party, though, I'll fuck the shit outta ya."

Ruby pouted prettily. "Promises, promises." She leaned in and fed me her breast, encouraging me to latch on to the jutting nipple. Of course, I did. Her breasts were large, full, and obviously enhanced. I loved banging her from behind while gripping her hair in my fist. Watching that sight in front of a mirror never failed to get me off. Despite even thinking about one of my favorite erotic images, my cock barely twitched.

"I'll give you my cock another time. And if

you're good, I might even let you come." I gave her a smile, but my attention was only half on her. Something felt just that little bit… *off*.

When Ruby tried to push the issue, I lifted her off my lap and set her on her feet. "Enough. I said no. Go find one of the other brothers. Plenty here who'd love to fuck you." I turned her around and smacked her ass to get her moving, trying not to be too much of an asshole while still getting my point across.

Club whores were here for one reason. To fuck. Since most of us had spent time incarcerated, we knew what it was like to go without a woman for extended periods. That shit wasn't happening again. Every woman we let in knew the score. She could put out or get out. Problem was, we'd created monsters. Because when most of the women started with us, we spoiled them rotten. We were good to them as we could be, protecting them and making sure they had food and shelter. Still were. The women knew how we were and did their best to take advantage of it. "No" wasn't a word they heard often, and as a general rule, they hated the word and would push back every time we used it. It was cute.

Until Knuckles and Gunnar came to Kiss of Death with old ladies. Now, we were all waiting patiently for the explosion. The club was Knuckles's. Everyone knew it. The guys from Bones were here at his request, from what I'd heard. Knuckles would be president again. I wasn't sure what role Gunnar would play, but he was a new fish -- which all but guaranteed the club whores would be on him like stink on shit. It would happen. Only a matter of time.

The family reunion continued. Unfortunately, the women weren't here. "Unfortunately" because I really wanted to see some fireworks tonight. Probably just as well, because that feeling I had before was becoming an itch between my shoulder blades I couldn't ignore.

I stood, acknowledging my brothers as I passed them on the way to the door. I stepped outside and took a deep breath. It was barely summer and already the air was humid and thick with moisture. I welcomed it, though. Inside our little corner of the city we'd created a haven of sorts. One whole city block in the center, we'd turned into a small forest. In the center of that, was a park of sorts where we had a couple of vegetable gardens and several flowerbeds. Wasn't a very "biker" thing to do, but it was peaceful. At one time or another, after getting out of prison, we all needed the relative quiet and solitude.

"What's goin' on, Hawk?" I looked over my shoulder to find Chains. He'd been my cellie for a while, and after I'd gotten out, he found me and brought me to Kiss of Death. We'd helped clean out the trash in the club when they'd picked a fight with the wrong club.

"Don't know. Somethin'."

Chains nodded as he stepped beside me. He leaned against the rail in front of the main clubhouse. Crumbled concrete, gravel, and dirt lined the paths that made up the "roads" in our territory. It looked exactly like what it was. A prison of our own making. Only this one was to keep the rest of the world away from us instead of the other way around.

"You got that feelin' again?" Chains lit a cigarette, the flare of his lighter briefly illuminating the hard planes of his face. He'd been with me long enough to recognize when my instincts kicked in.

I nodded, scanning the perimeter of our compound. "Yeah. Like somethin's comin' our way."

"Something or someone?"

"Fuck if I know." I rubbed the back of my neck, trying to shake the sensation. My instincts had saved my ass more times than I could count, both on the inside and out. When they started screaming like this, shit was about to go down.

We stood in silence for a few minutes, Chains smoking and me just watching the night. Our guard posts on top of each building were manned. Security lights flooding lights flooding the area close to our fencing provided a little extra protection for the buildings around us. If nothing else, the extra lighting made it easier for their own security cameras to get good imaging of whomever was trying to rip them off.

The sound of laughter and music drifting from the clubhouse behind us usually filled me with contentment. Tonight, it was an irritation. I needed to hear the night around me, to get an idea what was about to hit us.

I ducked under the railing and walked down the gravel path, not sure where I was going but needing to get away from the noise and light. Though the area around our compound was well lit, the interior was dark except for inside the various buildings. The paths between buildings and everything other than the center garden were covered in camo netting. We were as protected as we could be here. So why were my instincts screaming at me? The feeling got worse with each passing moment.

"Hawk?" Chains fell into step beside me, his gaze sweeping the area above the fence line. "You see somethin'?"

I didn't answer. Wasn't sure I could because with every second ticking by, my anxiety increased. It wasn't late, but the high humidity and milder temperatures made the fog coming off the Cumberland

River roll in thick as pea soup. Every breath in was heavy and wet, the water vapor tickling my nose. The security lights reflected back, making visibility very far outside our walls nearly impossible.

The moment I saw the small figure emerge from the thick mist, it felt like all the hair stood up on my body. It was definitely a woman, but there was something off about her. I took a step forward. Then another. I was stopped when Chains grabbed my arm.

"Easy, brother. That's creepy as fuck and I don't fuckin' know…" He trailed off. Which is when I got my first good look at the woman, courtesy of the flood lights as she came closer. No mistaking she was heading straight for us with a purposeful stride. "Why's she covered in mud?"

"Don't think that's mud, Hawk." Chains puffed his chest out and called out to the would-be intruder. "Stop there, little miss. Private property and all that."

She stopped directly in one spotlight so there was no mistaking her appearance and physical state. "That your blood?" Private property or not, need for secrecy and privacy or not, I absolutely would not deny a woman help who'd lost that much blood.

"What?" She had a confused look on her face, then looked down at herself. "Oh! That. Nah, not my blood. I'm good." She gave me a bright smile and a big thumbs up. "But I'm kind of in a bit of a bind?" She actually looked like she was genuinely sorry to take up our time. Like she wasn't covered in blood looking like something out of a horror movie.

I glanced over at Chains. His fists were clenched at his side, his eyes wide. Guy was superstitious as fuck, but I'd never seen him like this. Looking back to the woman, I started to answer when a light flashed over her blood-splattered face and I had to fight off a shudder. *Never show weakness.* It was a mantra that had served me well. Yet, here I was about to piss myself because of one tiny woman with a little blood on her. OK, so a lot of blood, but how did I know it was even blood? Might be fake blood. Might be animal blood, which was disturbing in itself. Maybe it was mud after all, and the lighting and mist were distorting the colors.

"Yeah, small bind." She winced and held her thumb and finger an inch apart. "Very small. Almost nonexistent, except it's not." Her expression fell slightly. "Um, anyway. I gave the guys every chance to walk away. I swear." Her eyes were almost comically wide. Like she was a kid trying to talk her parents out of a punishment for something she'd done.

"Gave who a chance to walk away?" The question tumbled from my lips without my consent. I didn't need to know. Didn't *want* to know. The less I knew the better. Ex-con and all. I saw Chains out of the corner of my eye. He gave me a sharp look, but didn't say anything, either unwilling to show division or to stop the carnage he knew would follow. Yeah. We were sick bastards like that.

"Oh, the guys I stabbed." She gave a slight, nervous laugh. "I wouldn't have hurt either of them if one of them hadn't pulled the knife after I broke the other guy's leg. And I wouldn't have broken his leg if he hadn't tried to hit me."

"Tried to hit you." Could I sound any more stupid?

"Yeah. They were trying to rob me, and I took exception." This time her voice was prim and proper, but she still looked nervous as shit. Which, I guess I understood. No, Goddamnit, I didn't understand! Why was I freaking out like this? Why was she *not* freaking out?

"What the fuck?" Knuckles and Gunnar approached. Fuckers had either snuck up on me or I was officially a pussy because this girl was seriously freaking me out. I was going with losing my edge. I was getting older, after all. Because no way I was that big a pussy. I wasn't even sure which one of them spoke.

"Uh, hi." Creepy Girl gave us all a little wave. "Can we... I mean, I'd like to get out of the light, if you don't mind? Makes me kind of nervous."

"Yeah," Chains muttered. "I bet."

Knuckles made himself front and center while Gunnar stood at his left shoulder. I like that the pup had the boss's back. He was an excellent addition to the club as far as I was concerned. "What's your name, girl?"

"Carrie."

"No way, man." Chains took a step backward, shaking his head. "No fuckin' way."

"Shit." I thought that was Gunnar. A quick glance and the man was scrubbing a hand over the back of his neck. "That's just fuckin' creepy."

"Strange," she muttered. "I didn't expect this reaction." Then she spat, making a face, disgust evident. "Gross."

"You do this kind of thing often?" Why wouldn't my mouth stay shut? I wanted to bang my head against a wall, but I was making a big enough ass of myself as it was.

"What?" She spat again, wiping at her mouth with her fingers and the back of her hand.

"Show up at a gated compound full of strangers, covered in the blood of your enemies." Nope. Still couldn't shut up.

Then the damnedest thing happened. Little Carrie smiled. Like I'd said the funniest thing ever. And I knew I was doomed. Because my cock hardened so fast I was certain every ounce of blood went straight to my groin. I groaned and had to fight to stay on my feet. For a man who never showed weakness, I was showing an awful lot of weaknesses.

"That's a cool description." Her smile was beautiful. Except for the fact it kind of looked deranged. I wasn't altogether certain she *wasn't* deranged. Which would make this attraction I had to her complicated.

"Where's the bodies?" Knuckles took another step forward, putting the attention squarely on himself.

"Um, back that way? Between the buildings." She pointed in the direction she came from. "If you've got some sulfuric acid or something, I could fix it. I'm pretty sure there are several abandoned buildings I could use to store them for a couple days until they dissolve."

"I'm outta here," Chains muttered, turning and jogging back to the clubhouse. He had to go through a couple of the guys who'd wandered out here when Knuckles and Gunnar joined us.

"Sweet baby Jesus in the manger." I winced as Torpedo, our current president and his VP, Bohannon pushed their way through the gathering crowd. "No one's dissolving a body."

"Oh, I know." Carrie said brightly. "There's two." There was something hanging from her lip and I took my finger, mimicking wiping the corner of my lip. She gave me a confused look, so I did it again. She lifted her hand to her face and came away with whatever gore was around her mouth. She immediately gagged once, shaking her hand to sling the… I cringed to think of what exactly was clinging to her finger, but she tried to shake it off.

She stopped and turned her gaze back to Torpedo. The big man gave her a death stare for several seconds. Most men I knew might have thought twice about crossing Torpedo when he got that particular expression on his face. To my surprise, Torpedo looked away first. "Christ, I'm too fuckin' old for this shit. Bohannon."

"Don't look at me, prez. I'm just as old as you are." Bohannon actually chuckled, though he looked as shell-shocked as I felt.

To be clear, it wasn't the situation had us all spooked. Violence was a way of life for me in and out of prison. It was the whole surrealness of the moment. If this was one of my brothers at the gate, I'd have already gotten the materials he needed, and we'd be out there taking care of business. But this woman was five foot nothing and maybe a hundred pounds. If she ate a sandwich.

And she was still spitting blood.

And her name was Carrie.

"You get hurt? Your mouth's bleeding." Bohannon, bless his heart, was braving the waters. I'd wondered the same Goddamned thing, but there was no fucking way I was asking that shit.

"No." She made a face then spit out more blood. Then she kind of gagged a little. "Gross." She kept spitting until she was finally satisfied. "That's not my blood."

"What did you do? Drink their blood? How the fuck did you get that much blood in your mouth?" Bohannon looked morbidly curious and I knew he was just as freaked as the rest of us. He also looked like he regretted the question the second it left his mouth. I know I winced. Pretty sure more than one of the other brothers witnessed the spectacle.

"No." She spat again. "But one of the guys grabbed me in a bear hug from the front and I couldn't move. So I bit his ear off. Then the other guy? He got behind me and put his hand over my mouth when I screamed. So I bit a chunk out of his hand. I think it's the ear I'm having trouble with. Cartilage. Or something." She went pale, her breathing growing ever more rapid. "I'm so s-sorry!" she sobbed out. Carrie collapsed on the ground in a heap looking so broken and terrified it made my heart ache. I actually rubbed the middle of my chest trying to soothe the hurt. Then she looked up at me. Not anyone else. Me. "I-I'm so s-sorry. Please help me."

"Well, fuck." Christ, my life!

Chapter Two

Carrie

I was really surprised I managed to hold out this long before I completely lost my shit. It was the whole gristle in my teeth thing, knowing it was a person's flesh that tipped me over, I think. All the men were looking at me like I was a complete lunatic, and I didn't blame them. For some reason, though, out of all the men there, despite knowing I needed to fear every single one of them, the big man who'd first met me at the gate held my gaze, and I did the only thing I could think of.

"I-I'm so s-sorry. Please help me." It was pathetic and miserable. "I did it." I sobbed out. "I killed them."

"I think I know where she's talkin' about, Bohannon."

"Take a crew," one of them ordered. "See what you find, then let me know what's going on."

"I found the incident, Torpedo. It happened just like she said." Another guy, his gaze drifting to me once before shoving a tablet in front of Torpedo's face.

The other man -- Torpedo, who seemed to be in charge -- viewed it and nodded his head crisply. "Back it up. Follow everyone's movements." Torpedo gave me a hard look.

"She needs looked over to make sure she's not injured." The big man stepped forward and knelt in front of me. "I'm Hawk, little lady."

"Carrie," she said.

"Yeah, honey. I got that." He smiled.

"Are you going to turn me in to the cops? That's what happens when you kill someone. Right?"

Hawk glanced up at the one called Torpedo, then at one of two other men who seemed to be part of the group but also standing apart. Torpedo turned to those two men and raised an eyebrow.

"What do you think, Knuckles? This is your outfit."

"Take her in. Let her get cleaned up and get Pain to check her over. Knight, I want you to examine every second of footage you can find. If she's on the up and up, we'll take care of this... uh, how did she put it, Gunnar?"

Gunnar held up his thumb and forefinger an inch apart. "Little bit of a bind, I think. I wasn't close enough to hear much."

"I didn't do it on purpose." I sounded whiny even to myself. "OK, so I did do it on purpose, but only because they were gonna hurt me. And I didn't kill them as a first resort. Only when the one guy brought out a knife, and I knew things were serious."

Hawk's brow furrowed as he studied me. I couldn't tell if he was horrified or impressed, and honestly, at this point, I didn't care. My hands were shaking so badly I had to sit on them.

"Let's get you cleaned up," he said, his voice surprisingly gentle for a man who looked like he could bench press a motorcycle. He reached out, hesitated. I swayed slightly, the adrenaline crash hitting me hard. "Your story checks out, everything will be fine."

"And if it doesn't?" It was embarrassing, but my voice shook. My dad would be so ashamed of me right now. He'd raised his only daughter to be as strong as her brothers. Not even one of my brothers would be on his ass in the gravel while men stood over them. They'd be on their feet ready to fight for their lives. Me? I just wanted to go home and hide for the rest of mine.

He raised an eyebrow. "Is it going to?"

I shrugged. "It's a matter of perspective, I guess."

"Relax, uh, Carrie." He stumbled over my name, and I didn't understand why. "We're gonna look at all the footage we can find, but Knight seems pretty satisfied with the fight."

"I think I'm gonna be sick," I mumbled, then promptly vomited on the ground next to Hawk's boots. Thankfully, I missed his actual footwear.

"Christ," someone muttered behind me.

"Oh, like you've never blown chunks after a fight, Noose." Gunnar shoved Noose backward. Not hard, but enough that the younger man got the message.

"I'm a sympathy puker, all right?" the younger man grumbled. "Meant no disrespect." Several of the remaining guys laughed and clapped Noose on the back as they passed.

Hawk didn't even flinch at the mess near his boots. "It's the shock, honey. Happens to everyone the first time." He looked over his shoulder. "Gunnar, can you get a prospect to get her some water?"

I wiped my mouth with the back of my hand, which was pointless since my hand was as disgusting as my face. "I didn't want to kill anyone," I whispered, only for Hawk's ears. "But they wouldn't stop."

"I know, darlin'." I was surprised at the confidence in his tone, but as I looked up at him, he seemed sincere. Not like he was humoring me to get me to do what he wanted. "We'll get to the bottom of this, but I believe Knight's assessment. He's never wrong. Besides, self-defense is a thing, you know? Ain't no one here gonna judge you for defendin' yourself."

"But I stabbed him in the chest. Multiple times." I emphasized the last part by jabbing my finger in the air. "And I'm pretty sure I broke the other guy's windpipe after I broke his leg."

I looked up to find all the men staring at me with varying expressions of shock, amusement, and something else I couldn't quite identify. Hawk seemed to be fighting back a smile.

"Jesus," Torpedo muttered. "How'd a little thing like you manage that?"

"I had six older brothers and a dad who wished I was a boy. It was learn to fight or be crushed by the weight of all the testosterone." I wiped at my face, probably making more of a mess. The thought made me want to gag again. "I panicked. I just…" I sucked in a breath as my voice hitched. "I just wanted to get away."

Hawk stood up and extended his hand to me. "Come on, let's get you cleaned up. I'll see if we can round up a toothbrush for you. Might have to send one of the guys to get you a few things, but I'll get you comfortable."

I hesitated for a moment before taking his hand. His palm was warm and calloused, his grip gentle but firm as he helped me to my feet. The world tilted briefly, and I swayed.

"Whoa, there." Hawk's arm came around my waist to steady me. "Easy, killer."

I nearly laughed at the nickname, but it came out more of a sob as the reality of what I'd done crashed over me again. I had killed someone. *Two* someones. I trembled so violently I could barely stand.

"I've got you," Hawk murmured against my ear. "Just breathe." He guided me forward, his large frame sheltering me from the curious stares of the other men. When I stumbled again, he simply lifted me into his arms and strode past the others toward another big

- 22 -

warehouse in a field of them. I was vaguely aware of the other men parting to let us through, their voices a low murmur around us. Some of them looked impressed, others wary. I couldn't blame them.

"Where are we going?" I asked, my voice small.

"Clubhouse first. Get you some privacy so you can clean up, then we'll figure out what happens next." His voice was matter of fact, and somehow that steadied me more than if he'd tried to be comforting.

The clubhouse, as he called it, was massive and surprisingly clean. The interior had an industrial vibe going on. Basically, there were steel posts and lots of concrete. Furniture consisted of several tables, couches, and chairs, none of which were in the best of shape, but didn't look dirty. While the place smelled of beer and pot, it wasn't disgusting or anything.

The place had twenty or thirty men, as well as at least the same number of women. Probably more. I heard the whispers as Hawk walked in carrying me. It was mostly the men, but the women picked up the lead of the guys, whispering among themselves. I caught snippets like, "Carrie, like the movie?" and "Batshit crazy" and "Tiny little thing to cause that much havoc," and cringed. *Great first impression, Carrie.* Show up covered in blood and vomit on their property. And now I really needed to Google the movie *Carrie,* because there was obviously something I was missing.

Every fiber of my being screamed to hide my face, but there was nowhere to go except to bury myself against Hawk's chest. I'd never been more mortified in my life. And the real shit of it was, now that I was coming down and I wasn't so hyper-focused on simply surviving, I was very aware of the man who carried me. And, sweet God, he smelled good! The inappropriate thought made me even more ashamed.

Maybe I was weak, like my father always said. If I was this distracted by a man when I should be planning my escape, then it made me weak *and* stupid.

"Jesus, Hawk. What'd you drag in?" A woman with platinum-blonde hair stepped in front of us, blocking our path. Her eyes were heavily lined with black, making the blue pop even more dramatically.

Hawk stopped, his grip on me tightening slightly. "Outta the way, Silk."

"But who is she?" The woman, Silk, pointed a long, red nail at me. "And why is she covered in blood?"

"None of your business," Hawk replied, his voice clipped. "Now move."

Silk's eyes narrowed, but she stepped aside, her gaze following us as Hawk carried me through the crowd. I could feel dozens of curious eyes on me, and I wished I could disappear.

"Sorry about that," Hawk murmured as we headed down a hallway. "Club whores can be territorial."

"Club whores?" I asked weakly, my shaking getting worse. "Why am I so cold?"

"Shock. Part of it. A hot shower would do you good. Maybe make you feel human again, yeah?"

I looked up at him and knew my eyes were wide and wild-looking because it was how I felt. My dad always said I could never hide my feelings worth a damn. He said it made me vulnerable, and I needed to learn to guard myself. Instead of disappointment when I met Hawk's gaze, though, I saw only kindness and understanding.

He carried me up two flights of stairs, then down a long hallway. It looked like there were several apartments. Hawk took me to the end of the hall and set me on my feet long enough to open the door with a key. I thought he might invite me inside, but instead he picked me back up and carried me inside himself, going straight to the bathroom.

"Here ya go." He set me on the vanity of a surprisingly spacious and clean bathroom. The place didn't actually look lived in. The main area was a little messy, but the bathroom was near spotless. "There's a bench in the shower. Sit there and wash until you feel better. I'll be just outside if you need help. Don't fall." He delivered his instructions in a crisp, no-nonsense voice.

"Are you always this bossy?" The second I said the words, I regretted them. I opened my mouth to apologize, but Hawk only chuckled.

"Yeah, Killer. I'm always this bossy."

"You might want to get that looked at," I muttered, which got another laugh out of him.

"Tell you what. When Pain comes to look you over, if you don't give him too much shit and let him make sure you're OK physically, I'll see if he'll look at my bossiness while he's here."

"I really am sorry I got you guys involved. I didn't intend to. I was just trying to get out of the area and got lost in the fog."

"Don't worry about any of that. Get clean. Take a few minutes to sit in the hot water and just be. I'll leave you some clothes outside the door, then I'm going to see what Knight finds. I'll come check on you in an hour." He moved to a wooden cabinet in the corner of the bathroom. "Towels and washcloths. Use all you need. Knuckles says his woman is gettin' you a few things together. I'll have her set them just inside the door. Throw your dirties in the corner and I'll take care of it later."

My gaze snapped to his. "Will everyone be able to get in here?"

"No, honey. I have a key. I'll give that key to Hannah, who will give it back to me once she gets your shit together. You're not gonna be locked in or anything, but I wouldn't advise leaving without an escort. You saw how pushy the club whores can be. Hannah or Gunnar's woman, Pippa, will be happy to take you wherever you want to go."

I tried not to wince at the term "club whores" but wasn't sure I pulled it off. "They're here because they want to be. Right?" Of all the questions I needed to ask, that wasn't any of my business.

"Yeah. Every woman here knows the score before she comes in."

My stomach clenched and I took a step backward. "I didn't agree to anything like that." My heart pounded in my chest. Had I made a huge mistake? Had I escaped one bad situation only to fall into a worse one? I was under no illusion I'd fare as well with this man, or any of the other men I'd seen on their property. Every single one of them looked sturdy, strong, and more than a little mean.

"Relax, Carrie. You're not here for the same reasons they are, and this is not a permanent situation for you. Now, if you decide you want to live here, that's different."

OK, that was funny. If it weren't for the fact I actually needed a home, his words might have been amusing. But the fact was, I was desperate. It's how those guys had found me in the first place. Because I wasn't very good at finding safe places to sleep, and they'd tried to take my last five bucks. When they'd realized that was all I had, they'd decided to take other things from me.

"I see," Hawk said, sounding like he really did see. "It's like that is it?"

"Like what?" My whisper was soft. I wasn't even sure I could speak louder.

"Do you have a place to stay, honey?"

"Sure." I tried to smile.

"Don't lie to me, Carrie. You're shit at it."

"Yeah. So I've been told." I took a breath. "No. I don't have a place to stay. I was sleeping in one of the warehouses and apparently didn't hide well enough."

"All right. Enough of this. I will take care of everything. I'll help you get back on your feet."

"I can't pay you. And I'm not sure what being a club whore entails, but I'm betting it's just what the name says. I don't judge, but I can't do that."

"Never said you had to." He scrubbed a hand over his face. Probably exasperated with me. "Do what I told you. Take a long shower. When you get done, if you want to, lie down and take a nap. I promise no one will bother you. And, Carrie..." He waited until I met his gaze and held it. "I don't expect payment. Just let me help. That's payment enough."

Chapter Three

Hawk

I was in so much trouble as to not even be believed. I think I'd rather go back to prison than have to deal with the shit show in front of me. And I didn't mean cleaning up the dead bodies. I mean that fucking girl and her fucking big eyes and trembling lips with an apparent streak of badassedness that was off the fucking charts. My cock was so hard right now the fucking room was spinning. And I felt like a fucking giant-ass prick.

Carrie was... ethereal. In some ways, she was so very innocent and timid, but after watching that fucking video feed Knight showed us? That woman was lethal. And a huge fucking question mark.

"Ain't never seen nothin' like that in my whole Goddamned life." Tiny sounded equal parts awed and terrified. "You found the third guy yet?"

"Yeah." Knight did something on the tablet in his hand and we watched as the third guy she hadn't mentioned stumbled through the fog. She'd sliced a wide arch over his abdomen with the knife she'd taken away from his buddy but hadn't been able to finish because one of the others had grabbed her again. He made it about a hundred yards before he was grabbed by someone out of the mist, his neck quickly and efficiently broken.

"Guy's done that a fuckin' time or two," Knuckles muttered. "Were you able to identify the bastard?"

Knight sighed. "I managed to blow up one image. Luckily, it was on the one HD camera in this whole place other than ours."

"That's a good thing. Right?" I didn't like the

look on Knight's face. It meant whatever he found we weren't gonna like.

"You'd think, huh." He shook his head as he tapped on the tablet again. A picture of the guy pulled from the cameras popped up. "Guy's a ghost. Not in any database I've run it through. And I got access to the FBI and INTERPOL."

"How'd you do that?" Noose sat up straighter, taking interest when not much ever made him look up from whatever handheld video game he was playing. Guy had spent the majority of his childhood in juvie before finishing out five years in a federal prison for the big boys. Once he got out and came to us, he buried himself in technology. Specifically, anything that made whatever game he was interested in at the time run faster and better.

Knight gave him a look. "Not for you, Noose. Fucked up as the system is, I like the world in a semi-stable place."

Noose narrowed his eyes. "What're you tryin' to say?"

"That I'm not letting you anywhere near anything where you can cause havoc." Knight pointed at Noose. "Got my eye on you, brother." Knight was only half joking. The rest of us chuckled. I thought the whole thing served as a way of breaking the tension. I couldn't be the only one wondering what kind of killer we'd brought into our midst. Suddenly, the nickname I'd given her earlier wasn't nearly as funny. Hadn't really been funny then, but sometimes you just gotta poke fun.

Knight continued. "Anyway, the point is, his image isn't in any criminal database. On Torpedo's orders, I reached out to Bones. Data, Zora, and Suzie were all over it, just like Prez said they would be."

"And?" Torpedo crossed his arms over his chest, his feet apart. He looked every inch the grizzled biker president. Torpedo had earned his respect with me and everyone else when he'd first come here. He was hard but fair, and had a vicious streak when it came to protecting those he considered family. But he wasn't my president. For me, Knuckles would always be the leader of Kiss of Death MC.

"And, they got a hit. I didn't ask where or how, but the guy you see on the screen there doesn't exist on paper. Anywhere."

"Shit." Gunnar scrubbed a hand over his face then the back of his neck. "Ain't likin' this."

Knight looked from Knuckles to Torpedo. "Data suggested we talk to Rocket at Grim Road MC."

"Black ops." Bohannon muttered. "Rocket might be able to help. Every one of those fuckers was black ops."

Bohannon and Torpedo stared at each other for a long time. The rest of us shifted nervously. I thought they'd make the call themselves, but, surprisingly, they both turned to Knuckles.

"What do you think, brother?" Torpedo's gaze was steady on Knuckles.

There was a pause before Knuckles shook his head and took a breath. "Never hurts to have all the information." He nodded to Knight. "Follow Data's instructions. Let him put you in touch with Rocket. Were you able to find this guy before he took out the third attacker?"

"No." Knight didn't look happy about that either. "Not even a shadow."

"Fog?"

Knight shrugged. "Maybe. Or the guy's just that good."

Knuckles looked at me. "I want your girl to see this guy. And I want to be there when you show her."

That got my attention. "She's not my girl, Knuckles. I just met her. Same as you."

Knuckles snorted. "Right. She chose you and you let her. Now you're stuck with her." That got some chuckles all around.

"Look, I'll protect her while she's here. I'll help her get on her feet or get somewhere she's safe. I'll even be her guard if you think it's necessary. But I don't think she's a threat, Knuckles. She wants to feel safe, and I'm a big fucker." I shrugged. "That's why she chose me."

"You ain't as big as me." Tiny grinned at me. "And I was standin' pretty close to you, Hawk."

"No one is as big as you, Tiny." More chuckles.

"Look," Knuckles continued over the ruckus. "I'm not telling you to hurt her, Hawk." He gave me an exasperated look. "Make her feel safe. Let's find out what happened to her. See if we can help her."

"Hawk, in order to keep her safe, we need to figure out why a professional killer was tailing her. Seems like a hell of a coincidence that three random thugs attack her and a ghost appears to keep them from hurting her." Torpedo's voice was uncharacteristically soft, but I knew it was because the man was trying to manage me. To get me to do what he wanted. Truth was, I hadn't considered Carrie might still be in danger. "You think she's being followed?"

"I think it's worth finding out," Knuckles replied. "Because if she's got trouble on her tail, I want to know what kind before it lands on our doorstep."

I nodded, understanding his concern. This wasn't just about helping a woman in distress anymore. If someone was after Carrie, it could mean trouble for the club. "I'll talk to her," I promised. "After she's had time to clean up and rest." I kept my face neutral, despite the fact that my brethren were eyeing me with varying levels of amusement.

"Get back to her. Make sure she's comfortable. If she's homeless like she indicated, she's probably in need of a meal and some actual rest." Knuckles gripped my shoulder. "Also, I'm pretty sure she *is* your woman."

"Knuckles --" I stopped myself. There was no point in arguing, especially when I wasn't entirely sure he was wrong. Something about that girl had gotten under my skin immediately. I couldn't explain it, and I didn't like it. I also wasn't entirely sure I could fight it. "I'll get her settled and find out what I can."

Gunnar laughed. "Man, you should see your face right now. Like you swallowed something sour."

"Fuck off," I muttered, which only made him laugh harder.

Knight tapped the tablet again. "I'll update you when I hear from Rocket. In the meantime, maybe we should increase security around the compound. Just in case this ghost decides to pay us a visit."

"We have to be careful here." Bohannon glanced at Torpedo. "I've already doubled the prospects on guard, but this place isn't secret. Every parole officer in the state knows about this place."

"The local authorities seemed to like that we're keeping to ourselves." Noose shuffled uncomfortably. "No one else wants us and no one from here has ever been rearrested."

"I'll keep a lid on everything," Knight offered. "Main thing is to keep the noise down and control the camera feeds. I'll keep an ear out on the dispatch center. If anyone is headed our way, I'll know about it in plenty of time."

"Go take care of your girl, Hawk. Get as much as you can before she goes to bed. Maybe while she's eating." I could tell Knuckles didn't like having someone interrogate a woman who'd been hurt, but the fact was he had a whole club of people to worry about.

"I'll get anything important from her, and I'll be careful doing it."

Knuckles gripped my shoulder. "Come with me." Odd, but I followed him inside. Where the party had been in full swing before, now the place had quieted and all the club whores had gone to the basement of this building to the panic room. All the security, the compound, all the shit we had for Kiss of Death and ourselves -- all of it -- was because of Knuckles. Even from prison he protected us as best he could. The club had taken a dark turn those first few years, but Knuckles came through for us.

He led me to his office, and I took a seat in front of his desk. Knuckles braced himself on the edge and stared at me. He was the one who'd brought me here, so I wasn't breaking the silence.

"Look, man. I'm sorry." Knuckles popped his neck, looking uncomfortable.

"What for?"

"I'm going to need you to look after Carrie's best interests until we're sure of what happened and who that fourth man was."

I narrowed my eyes. "What do you mean?"

"I'm not cruel, Hawk. Not unless someone really deserves it. But my instinct is to protect the club. I need you to make sure I consider Carrie in any decision I make after we get all the information."

That surprised me. "That's why you said she was my woman."

Knuckles shrugged. "Fewer complications if there are problems. I don't like deceiving my family, but I'm pretty sure I'm not far off the mark, so I'm not gonna feel too bad."

"And if Knight finds something on her? If she's deceiving us for some reason?" I was surprised at how much my heart rebelled at the mere thought of Carrie betraying us. Not for the reasons I thought, though. Much as I loved my brothers, we could take care of ourselves and our women. Carrie didn't seem to have anyone. And a betrayal of my brothers would forfeit her life. I wasn't sure if I was capable of sitting back and letting that happen.

"You think he will?"

"My gut led me to her, Knuckles. That instinct has never let me down. Not in prison. Not in life."

"And?"

"My gut says she's exactly what she says she is."

"That's good enough for me. She gets every benefit of the doubt. But I still want you to watch out for her. Don't let any of us run over her if there's trouble."

"*If* there's trouble? You know Goddamned good and well there's gonna be trouble."

"You got me there." Knuckles held out his hand to me, which I stood and took immediately. "Go take care of your girl. Let her know she made a good choice of a protector."

"All over that, brother."

"Hey. Before you go, I need your opinion."

"Name it."

"How would you feel about being sergeant at arms again?" That got my attention.

- 34 -

"How should I feel?"

Knuckles shrugged. "Completely up to you. Just know that you're one of the few men left here I know and trust. You were exactly what we needed then, and I believe you still are."

"You takin' the reins back?"

"Up to Torpedo. That was the deal. But I don't think it will be long."

"Put me where you need me, brother. This is my family. I'll go where you tell me to go."

He clapped my shoulder and grinned. "Get on with you. Be careful with that one. I don't think she'd stop at takin' your balls if you got fresh and she didn't want you to."

"I know it makes me more than a little crazy, but watching her kill those guys tipped me over the edge, Knuckles."

"You mean it wasn't her being covered in the blood of her enemies?"

I winced. "Heard that, did you?"

"It was a memorable exchange all around." I wanted to wipe the smug look off the bastard's face but was on the verge of grinning my own damned self.

"Are we all gonna take our women the second we see them?"

"Kinda looks that way, but my advice is to not fight it. Roll with it. Make her want to keep you around."

"I'm all over that shit."

Chapter Four

Carrie

I stayed in the shower until the water ran cold, scrubbing my skin raw trying to remove every trace of blood. The hot water had helped ease some of the tension in my muscles, but my mind was still racing. I'd killed two men tonight. Two human beings who had lives and families and... I shook my head, trying to dislodge the thoughts.

They would have killed me. Or worse.

After drying off, I wrapped myself in one of the large, surprisingly soft towels and cracked open the bathroom door. True to his word, Hawk had left a small pile of clothes just outside the bathroom door. Women's clothes -- a pair of sweatpants, a T-shirt, underwear still in the pack, and socks. The sweatpants were a perfect fit, but the shirt was miles too big. After pulling it over my head, I inhaled deeply. Then I pulled the collar up to my nose and inhaled again. Definitely a man's. Didn't matter. I was grateful I had something clean. The soft fabric felt like heaven against my skin.

The bedroom just outside the bathroom was sparsely furnished but clean. A king-size bed dominated the space, with plain gray sheets and a black comforter. There was a dresser against one wall and a small desk in the corner. No personal touches that I could see. Was this Hawk's room? It didn't feel lived in.

My body felt like it weighed a thousand pounds as I sank onto the bed. It didn't feel right, sitting on someone else's bed without their express permission. Maybe he meant I should sleep on the couch? I left the small bedroom to a larger living room where an old sofa sat along one wall. There were no pillows or a blanket or anything, but I honestly didn't care. I was too beat to care.

Since I had to get up anyway, I dug through the bag of stuff Hawk had left and found a toothbrush still in its packaging, so I took that and went to the bathroom to brush the gunk out of my mouth. The thought brought on a whole 'nother bout of anxiety.

I slumped against the vanity as I struggled to open the toothbrush and glanced at the mirror. Huge mistake. The face that stared back at me from the mirror was nearly unrecognizable. I was pale, with haunted, wild eyes. Lingering panic still had my pupils blown. My light brown hair was a tangled mess, but at least all the blood was out of it. I had avoided the mirror at all costs until now so I could only imagine what I'd looked like before.

"Oh God," I whispered, reality crashing down on me again. "What did I do?" I glanced at the clothes in the corner where I'd tossed them. They'd been torn and bloody and I'd tried not to look at them much before, but now I couldn't take my eyes from the pile.

I shook myself. "Get over it, Carrie. It's all over and done with. You'll never have to do something like that again because once you get home, you're never leaving." Except I didn't have a home. I'd left. And my father told me if I left, never come back.

A quiet sob broke free before I could stifle it. Two tears slid down my cheeks and I angrily dashed them away. This would not break me. It would *not*!

As the adrenaline continued to fade, exhaustion hit me like a ton of bricks. My body felt like it weighed a ton. I kept seeing the bloody clothes on the floor.

I gripped the toothbrush tightly in my hand, squeezing until my knuckles turned white. A faint voice rang in my head that sounded suspiciously like my father's whispered, "Weak," but I pushed it away.

"Bastard." I didn't hate my father, but he wasn't an easy man. And he was definitely not easy on his children. Except for me. At least, that's what he said. It never felt like he went easy on me, but I suppose, compared to my brothers, he had.

I shook it off. Had to. Just getting through the next few hours was going to be more than I could handle without hearing my dad's voice in my head telling me how inept and disappointing I was.

Brushing my teeth helped me feel more human again, the mint taste replacing the coppery flavor still lingering. I shuddered, trying not to think about where that taste had come from.

When I finally made it back to the couch, I curled into a ball at one end, not even bothering to look for a blanket. Sleep claimed me almost instantly.

I jolted awake to the sound of the door opening. Disoriented, I shot upright, my heart hammering in my chest.

"Easy, Killer. Just me." Hawk's deep voice cut through the panic. He stood in the doorway, his massive frame blocking most of the light from the hallway. "Sorry I woke you."

I blinked, trying to get my bearings. "What time is it?"

"Just after two a.m. You've been out for about three hours." He stepped inside, closing the door softly behind him. The room was dim, the only lighting coming from the kitchen area over the stove.

I swung my legs over the side of the couch to sit properly. Not sure what to say, I gestured over my shoulder to the bathroom. "I, uh, my clothes..."

"Don't worry. I'll take care of them."

"Do I..." I cleared my throat. "I mean, should I keep them? Like for evidence or something?"

Hawk snorted. "Nah. I can disappear those if you'd like. Probably the best idea anyway." He crossed slowly to the couch and sat on the other side from me. "You up for a little talk?"

Instantly my hackles rose. I pulled my knees to my chest and focused my complete attention on Hawk. "Am I in trouble? Did you call the cops?"

"Honey, no one here is gonna call the cops on you. We avoid them at all costs."

"Even if someone deserves it?"

"We take care of it ourselves." He studied me for a moment, his gaze intense but not unkind. "You hungry? I brought food." He gestured to a bag I hadn't noticed before.

My stomach growled loudly in response, and I felt my cheeks heat with embarrassment. "I guess that's a yes."

Hawk's lips quirked in a half-smile as he stood and moved to the small kitchen area. "Hope you like burgers. Not much else available at this hour."

"Anything sounds amazing right now." I watched as he unpacked the food -- two large burgers, fries, and some cans of pop. The smell made my mouth water. "Thank you."

He brought the food over, setting it on the coffee table between us. "When's the last time you ate, Carrie?"

I shrugged, unwrapping my burger with trembling hands. "Yesterday morning, I think? Maybe the day before." Time had become a blur lately. I'd been focused on simply surviving to pay too much attention to anything else.

"Eat up, honey." He set a pop on the coffee table

in front of me. "I can get you something else to drink if you want."

"No." I grabbed the can and popped the top, chugging a good portion before swiping the back of my hand over my mouth. I started to set it down, but thought better and chugged the rest. Which was followed by an impressive belch.

I clapped a hand over my mouth, mortified. "Sorry," I mumbled. I cringed and ducked my head. I wasn't typically this rude. At least, I didn't think I was. But I was so hungry, and the food smelled amazing, and the caffeine in the soda had gone straight to my head.

Hawk just chuckled, the sound rumbling deep in his chest. "Don't apologize. Nice to see you've got an appetite." He sat back in his seat and rested one ankle on the opposite knee. "Impressive range. Better out than in."

I couldn't help the surprised laugh that escaped me. "That's what my brother Zach always says." The memory made my chest ache. Despite everything, I missed my family. Well, my brothers, anyway.

Hawk pushed the container of fries toward me. "Eat. Then we'll talk."

The burger was like ambrosia, greasy and perfect. The fries were hot and salty, the best thing I'd ever tasted. I devoured the innocent sandwich and deep-fried potatoes with embarrassing speed, barely pausing to breathe. When I finished, I wiped my mouth with a napkin and eyed the second burger.

"That's yours too," Hawk said, gesturing to a second wrapped burger. "I already ate."

"You sure?" My stomach growled again, making the decision for me. I reached for the second burger without waiting for his answer and the big oaf grinned but stayed silent. I got the feeling he had something to say, but was holding back.

As I ate, Hawk watched me with a calculating expression that made me nervous. "What?" I asked around a mouthful of food.

"Just trying to figure you out, Killer." He leaned back, his massive frame making the couch look small. "Where'd you learn to fight like that?"

I swallowed hard. "Told you. Six brothers and a hard-ass dad."

"That explains some basic self-defense, but not the skill you used on the two men we found. Also, Knight found the footage and we've all watched you fight. You gave those guys every opportunity to run. It looked like you were begging them to leave. Even after you'd already handed them their asses."

"Yeah. The harder I pleaded with them to leave, the less likely they were to go. I knew that, but I kept asking them to just walk away."

"Also, there was a third guy."

I started and I felt my cheeks heat. "Fuck. I forgot about him." Yeah, my dad would be laughing at me so hard right now. Then he'd tell me how a girl was useless to him.

Knuckles raised an eyebrow. "Forgot? How do you forget a third combatant?"

I couldn't help but cringe and all the food I'd just consumed threatened to come back up. Typically, what would have followed would be a lecture to do any drill sergeant proud. After that, an epic beating disguised as training.

"I was focused on the two guys in front of me," I admitted quietly. I put my chin up because I would not cower in front of this guy. I couldn't afford to. Because, while he was being nice now -- they all had -- I didn't know these people. Also, this guy talked just like my dad. He used the same words. I could almost recite the coming beratement word for word. I knew better than to lie, though. He already knew I'd lost sight of the third guy, but he didn't know the full breakdown. I cleared my throat, trying to choke back bile. "I'm not sure I realized there was a third guy. It's all a blur, really."

Hawk nodded slowly. "That happens in a fight. Tunnel vision. But here's the thing -- that third guy? Someone else took care of him."

My head snapped up. "What?"

"Yeah. Knight found footage of a fourth person who snapped the third guy's neck after you wounded him. Clean, professional kill." Hawk leaned forward, his eyes intent on mine. "Any idea who that might have been?"

"No," I whispered, genuinely shocked. "I swear, I had no idea anyone else was there."

"You being followed, Carrie?"

I shook my head. "Not that I know of. I mean, I've been on my own for a few weeks now, moving around, trying to stay under the radar."

"Under the radar from who?"

I hesitated, looking down at my hands. I wasn't sure how much to admit to this guy. My whole life had been about secrets. It was drilled into me from the time I could talk that I didn't ever talk about family secrets with anyone. Ever. Under any circumstance. Now that I'd made a break from my father and my brothers, did that rule still hold?

"I…"

"You don't have to tell me everything if you're not ready. But I do need to know if there is a possibility someone's comin' to the compound after you."

I bit my lip, weighing my options. I didn't want to put these people in danger, and I didn't want to lie when they'd shown me nothing but kindness, but the ingrained secrecy had me hesitating to say much. "My father might be looking for me," I finally admitted. "He's... not a good person."

"What kind of 'not good' are we talking about?" Hawk's voice was carefully neutral, but I could see the tension in his shoulders. When I didn't immediately answer, Hawk asked another question. "Your dad. The one who taught you to fight like that?"

"Yeah." I shifted uncomfortably. "Look. You're going to have to bear with me. My whole life has been about secrets, Hawk. I want to tell you everything, but my entire being is telling me to shut the hell up and leave so I don't have to tell you anything."

"Just because you don't want to spill secrets you've kept your entire life doesn't mean you have to leave. But I need to know if there's a threat on your heels. A simple yes or no is fine. For now." There was a measure of kindness in his voice and expression, but also an underlying insinuation he'd expect more later. Either when trouble showed up, or when I trusted him more. I had a feeling the former would happen before the latter.

I took a breath. I'd left the family. While I didn't want my brothers in trouble, they hadn't exactly tried to help me. OK, so they had. Kind of. They always looked out for me and hadn't allowed our father to spar with me if they could help it. If Father was trying to teach me a lesson, one of my brothers would insist on doing the teaching. Unfortunately, Father stopped giving me his "lessons" when my brothers were around a few years ago. I owed my father nothing. Anything I'd gained in being able to defend myself, I'd more than repaid in sweat and enough blood to fill an ocean. No tears. Never tears. "My dad is… intense."

"If he's the one who taught you to fight, then yeah. I'd say he's intense."

"There is a possibility he'll come for me. I don't think he'd hire someone to kill me. He wouldn't trust my brothers to bring me back. Says they're too soft on me. No, if he decides I'm worth the trouble, if there is something he needs from me, he'll come to get me himself."

Hawk handed me a photo. It was a closeup of a man as he broke the neck of the third attacker. My breath caught. The photo was a bit pixelated where it had been enlarged, but there was no denying the man in the photo was my brother looking up at the camera. "You know that man." It wasn't a question because my expression, once again, gave everything away.

"Yes. That's my oldest brother, Victor." My heart pounded. "Did he follow me here? Did you see him?"

"This is the only image Knight found, and no one has been near the walls that anyone has seen."

"You might not see him," I said quietly. "All of them are good at not being seen. It surprises me you got this photo."

"Wouldn't have except Knight pulled footage from cameras way the fuck away from where your brother was."

Slowly, Hawk reached over and put his hand over mine. "You're safe here, Carrie. No one's getting to you unless you want them to." The certainty in his voice was comforting, even if I wasn't sure I believed him.

"You don't know my father," I whispered. "When I left, he let me. That in itself surprised me, but he also said if I left, I couldn't come back. I thought that meant he'd leave me alone. I don't think he thought I could make it by myself and the shit of it is, he was right."

"I don't know about that."

"No, Hawk." I took in another deep breath, my chest tightening with anxiety. "You don't understand."

There was a knock at the door. The knob rattled as someone tried to enter. They knocked again. "Hawk? You in there?"

"Christ." Hawk scrubbed a hand over his face as he stood. He stomped to the door and jerked it open. "What." The word was bitten out with anger and annoyance. I'd heard the tone many times throughout my life.

The man at the door glanced in my direction before turning his attention back to Hawk. "We've got a situation. Knuckles and Torpedo want her in Church. There's been a development."

"Church?" I squeaked out the word before I could stop myself. This wasn't the time to draw attention to myself. I guess my dad was right. I was a complete failure. I couldn't even keep my mouth shut when it could mean life or death. Because, as I'd already told myself multiple times, I didn't know these guys.

"Club meeting," Hawk explained tersely, then turned back to the man at the door. "What kind of development?"

"Car pulled up, then disappeared. Knight says whoever it was knew exactly where our cameras were. Also managed to take a route that avoided other cameras away from the area like we caught the guy who killed her third attacker. We've got nothing except a glimpse of a dark sedan and the fact that there are no plates."

Hawk turned to me, his expression grim. "Looks like we're headed to Church. Can you walk, or do you need me to carry you?"

I stood quickly, swaying slightly as my head rushed from the sudden movement. I thought I hid it, but the look Hawk gave me said otherwise. Yeah. Complete failure. "I can walk."

Hawk nodded his head crispy and took my hand. "Stay close to me."

"What's Church?" I whispered to Hawk as we briskly walked from the room down the hall.

"Club meeting room. Usually just for members, but this is an exception." His voice was low. "Nothing for you to worry about. They have questions and will want answers. I'll be with you the whole time, but if there are any surprises, you might want to let me know now."

"Surprises." My chuckle sounded as bitter as I felt. "That pretty much describes my entire family, Hawk. My *life*."

We descended two flights of stairs and went through a series of hallways before going down one last set. There was a man at the door. He glanced from Hawk to me, then nodded back at Hawk and opened the door.

Sounds of men talking filtered through the room as we walked in. Hawk still had my hand firmly in his as he took me to a seat at one of the tables in the room. Other than big, solid steel folding chairs and several folding tables, there was nothing else in the enormous room. We sat in silence. Several of the men glanced in our direction but said nothing. A group of men were off to themselves looking at a tablet one of them had, murmuring softly.

Finally, they all moved toward one long table at

the front of the group and sat. "Carrie? Do you remember me from the gate?"

"You're Knuckles," I answered. "Hannah is your, er, old lady?"

"That's right." The corner of his lips lifted in a slight smile. "Good. Hannah told me not to give you my growly face and scare you off, so I've instructed Hawk to be your advocate since you seem comfortable with him. I tend to look at the overall picture instead of how my decisions might affect everyone and not just the club."

"I don't want to cause problems for you." I looked around at the men in the room. "*Any* of you."

Knuckles gave me a nod of acknowledgment. "We'll get to the issues facing us in a bit. Right now, let me do some brief introductions." He indicated the men sitting at the table with him. "This is Gunnar." This man wasn't as big as Knuckles or Hawk, but was every bit as intimidating. All these guys had the same hard look about them. It was kind of like my dad and brothers but more... feral? They didn't seem at home in this setting for some reason, like they were uncomfortable with the windowless walls around them, even though the space was brightly lit. "He's Hannah's brother and my closest friend. Torpedo and Bohannon" -- he indicated two men on his other side -- "are our president and vice president respectively."

Torpedo picked up when Knuckles stopped. "Knuckles is in charge of the situation as it stands." He addressed everyone, looking around the room. "Any questions, problems, solutions... anything regarding this matter, Knuckles will address." Obviously, there was more going on than I was aware of, but I knew enough to realize the less I knew the better.

My insides twisted with nerves. These men were

likely getting ready to discuss my fate and I was at their mercy. I was grateful they were at least letting me sit in to listen. Hawk still hadn't let go of my hand and he squeezed harder under the table. Encouragement or a warning to keep quiet? I looked up at him and, though his expression didn't change, he winked at me. I nodded at him, deciding my best course of action was to take my cues from him.

"Knight, our intelligence officer, has some questions for you." Knuckles gestured to a younger man with a tablet sitting next to Gunnar at the head honcho table, as I thought of it.

"Carrie, I need to know about your brother Victor." His voice was smooth and pleasant. It belied his full beard and shaggy hair, to say nothing of all the tattoos. His face was covered in them as was most of the skin on his arms I could see. Even the whites of his eyes looked like they'd been tattooed or colored in somehow. He looked eerie as hell.

"What about him?" My voice was barely a thread of sound.

"Did you know he was following you?"

I glanced at Hawk, who gave my hand a reassuring squeeze. "I... I don't know for sure that he was. I didn't know he was there until you showed me that picture."

"But you're not surprised," Knight said flatly. It wasn't a question.

"No," I admitted. "Victor and Zach always looked out for me."

Hawk stirred beside me. "More than your other brothers?"

I shrugged. "Victor was the most obvious. As the oldest he made it his responsibility to look after us all. Kind of like Father was the general, but Vic was the one leading the troops into battle. The others helped me, too, but they were more subtle. Things would just break in my favor and one of my brothers would always be there. Most of the time they still looked disapprovingly at me, but they still helped me in whatever way they could. Zach is seven years older than me, so we were kind of kids together. What little childhood we had. The others were teenagers when I was born." I stiffened, sitting up straighter and snatching my hand from Hawk's grip. That got me nowhere as he just reached over and snagged my hand again.

"Woman." His tone brooked no argument, so I didn't continue to try to get free of him. "Settle. We're not gonna use anything against you. You're not in danger from us." He rubbed his thumb over the back of my hand under the table. The gesture seemed out of place for the big man, but if he was trying to calm me, that touch was working. The tenderness of it made my heart ache when I knew there was nothing to read into the innocent touch. I had to blink back tears because how sad was it I practically melted under Hawk's simple caress?

I nodded and whispered, "OK." He squeezed my hand again but didn't let go like I thought he would. "I'm sorry." Panic was beginning to overwhelm me and before I realized what I was doing, I shifted my hand and Hawk's so I could grip his big hand in both of mine. I cringed to think about how sweaty my palms were. Another visceral reaction to my environment my dad would be disgusted about. "What I just told you about my family is more than I've ever told anyone. We don't… *share*."

"How about we start simple." Knight smiled at me. With the tats on his face and the bright red of his eyes, he looked more than a little deranged. "What's your last name."

"Yeah," I muttered. "You'd think that would be simple, huh."

"It's not?" Hawk raised an eyebrow at me.

"No."

When I didn't elaborate, Knuckles spoke again. "Why not?" The demand in his question was clear.

"Because, I don't have a last name."

Chapter Five

Hawk

I couldn't help it. I barked out a laugh. Which wasn't the smartest move because everyone except Knuckles and Knight looked at me like I'd lost my mind. Carrie flinched. She tried to let go of my hand, but I held onto the one I had laced my fingers through.

"Not helping, Hawk," Gunnar muttered.

"You don't believe me." Carrie still tried to twist her hand out of my grip, but I held on tight. No way I was losing this silent war we waged under the table. If I was going to convince her to be mine, I had to make her understand I was on her side. Even over the club. That thought was so much of a surprise I nearly allowed her to slip out of my grip. Her hands were clammy, so she was hard to hang on to, but I managed.

"Sorry." I adjusted my hold on Carrie's hand, trying to reassure her. "Just not what I was expecting you to say, Killer." The second I uttered her nickname, I knew I'd shown my hand to the brothers. They'd know Carrie was mine without me saying a fucking word. I'd have to eventually make a loud and proud statement to the fact -- like getting her a property cut -- but for now, the silent meaning would work.

"Everyone has a last name," Knight said, his voice neutral but his expression skeptical. "Birth certificate, social security card, driver's license…"

"I don't have any of those things," Carrie replied quietly. "At least, not with a real last name on them."

The room fell silent. I could practically hear the gears turning in everyone's heads. Carrie's shoulders hunched slightly, as if she was bracing for an attack.

"Explain," Knuckles said, his voice surprisingly gentle.

Carrie took a deep breath. "My father is… well, he's paranoid about leaving paper trails. I was born at home. No hospital records or anything. I don't know if it was the same with my brothers, but I'm pretty sure it was. He taught us to be ghosts. To hide in plain sight. I shouldn't have been near the warehouses because there's always so many security cameras, but it was raining and cool and I didn't want to sleep in the woods again."

"Any idea why he had you living like that?"

"Only that he said last names and medical records and such are for people who need to belong to a system. He wanted us to be self-sufficient." She looked down at our joined hands and took a deep, trembling breath. "Saying it out loud sounds so fucked up."

"Why teach you to fight like you do?"

I shrugged. "He said it was for when society crumbled. That we'd need to know how to defend ourselves and our territory, but there was more to it than that."

"How much more?" Knuckles had his full attention on Carrie, and I wanted to slide her behind me for some reason. Knuckles wouldn't hurt her. He detested harming women for any reason.

"I know he's sent my brothers to kill people for him." She imparted the information so quietly I barely heard her.

"You're gonna have to speak up, darlin'." Gunnar kept his voice gentle but insistent. "We only want to know what we're facin' if they come our way."

"I know --" she broke off and a small sob escaped her. "God, I'm so stupid," she muttered as she wiped angrily at a tear tracking down her cheek with her shoulder. It made my chest puff up a little that she hadn't tried to let go of my hand. In fact, she held on tighter.

"Look at me, Carrie." We needed this information, but I didn't want her to feel threatened or bullied. When she looked up at me, I reached out and brushed a tear from her other cheek. "I've got your back. With these guys. With the club. With your family if you need it. I will not let anyone hurt you because of information you give us. You're not your father or your brothers. We've all been judged at one time or another, so we're not gonna automatically say you're guilty by association."

"My father would kill me if he were here now," she confessed softly.

"He's not here. And if he was, I'd eliminate the threat." My reply came without hesitation. Not only did I want Carrie to understand I meant business, but my brothers needed to understand as well. And pass it on to any motherfucker who'd fallen in love with her when she'd walked out of the fucking fog covered in the blood of her enemies. I nearly smiled at the memory. She'd liked the phrasing then, but I didn't think she'd appreciate it now.

Her eyes widened. "You'd kill him for me?"

"Without hesitation. You say he needs killin', I'm all over that shit." I saw Knuckles shift, but a quick glance in his and the other officers' direction told me they were all hiding smiles. Yeah. They knew. Killing wasn't something we took lightly since every single one of us had done time and had no desire to go back, but they weren't laughing at that. They were laughing at me. Because I'd laughed at both of them, and had done the exact same thing I'd made fun of them for. I'd fallen in love with a woman at first sight. Yeah. That wasn't going away any time soon.

Carrie was silent for a long moment, then she nodded. "I believe you."

"Good." I smiled at her. "Tell me what I need to know."

She took a deep breath, seeming to gather her courage before taking the plunge. "My father trained me since I could walk. I don't know how long he did my brothers, but I'm pretty sure it was all the same. All his kids are trained to kill. He has connections. Scary connections. I don't know who they are exactly, but they're all the kind of people who can, and do, make others disappear on the regular, including my father. *Especially* my father. My brothers are his soldiers. Victor is the most independent of the bunch. He doesn't always follow orders blindly and the others will usually follow his lead. He's protective of all his siblings and always weighs his chances of success against the risks. I've heard him and my brothers planning to make changes to the strict protocols my father tried to make them follow on a mission. Vic puts the team above the mission."

"Which is why he might be protecting you instead of dragging you back," Knuckles mused.

"Yes. Maybe." Carrie's voice trembled slightly. "But if my father decides he wants me back, he'll come himself or send a couple of the others. And they might not be as gentle as Victor or Zach."

"Your other brothers hurt you?" I couldn't keep the question back any longer. I had to know exactly how many of these fuckers I was gonna have to kill.

She shrugged. "Only during training, and never very much. They always pulled their punches. At least, that's what Father accused them of. They'd get rougher on me when he pushed like that, but they still held back."

"So Goddamned many people to fuckin' kill," I muttered. Carrie stiffened. This time, she yanked her hands away from mine, meaning it. Yeah. I knew she didn't really want free earlier. If she had, it wouldn't have mattered how hard I tried to hold this woman; she wouldn't be touched by anyone she didn't want touching her. Now, I got to see her temper in the flesh.

"You're not killing my brothers." Her gaze was fierce as she stood. I watched her quarter the room, assessing the men closest to her. I'd seen that look so Goddamned many times in the yard just before a fight.

Knuckles saw it too. "You're good, woman."

Carrie's brow ruffled her brow in confusion. "What?" She shook her head. "I didn't do anything." She took another step back but hit the table behind her.

"Hey, honey," I soothed, raising my hands so she could see them both clearly. "No one's accusing you of anything."

"Well, what am I good at? What did he mean?"

I smiled. "Well, not that you're trying to deceive us, if that's where you were going. He was complimenting the way you assessed the room. You were going to go for Tiny first. Then Pain. After that, I'm not sure who you were gonna hit, but I'm guessing me, since I'd be less likely to hurt you than anyone else. What I want to know is why Tiny first?"

She eyed me warily, like she sensed a trap but was ninety percent sure the bait was a free meal, but was still skeptical. Her gaze flickered from me to Tiny and back. "Because I can't win this fight. He's big. Like *really* big. Perfect name, by the way." She gave a nervous laugh, likely trying to deflect her nervousness.

Tiny grinned, not offended in the least. "Size matters, little lady." That got a round of chuckles from everyone. It seemed to put her more at ease and she continued.

"Anyway, if I went low, I could take out a knee with a good solid kick inside. He'd go down and everyone else would hesitate just because of our size differences. The shock value would only be a couple of seconds, but I'm betting I'm faster than everyone here other than maybe him." She pointed to Knight. Though still heavily muscled, Knight was leaner and not quite as tall as the rest of us. "But I'm also betting that, though he can fight, I can take him if it doesn't matter if he's dead or alive. So, get free of the compound, disappear into the fog if it's still as thick as it was. If anyone catches me, Tiny is probably the only one here I can't take one on one." Carrie sounded so confident I had to grin. She might be timid, but she knew what she was about. "Unless I got a good jump on him, that is."

"You decide you can't handle her, Hawk, I'll take the little lady." Tiny had his arms crossed over his massive chest. The man really was huge. Like fucking huge.

"I can't kick your ass hand-to-hand, but I can stab the shit outta you." I let go of Carrie's hand to drape my arm around her shoulders. That got a roar of laughter from my brothers. I felt her exhale a relieved breath and leaned in to kiss the top of her head. I was afraid she might flinch at the memory of her killing the men she had, but if it bothered her, she didn't let on. At least, not much. Her hand went to her stomach just below her breasts, like she had a cramp right before she needed to hurl again but fought it back.

"All right," Knuckles said with a slight grin. "Settle back down. Your woman's a badass, Hawk. Get used to brothers tryin' to coax her away from you before you put your property cut on her."

"So, bottom line," Knuckles continued once

everyone had settled back down, "is that your brothers and father are badasses, and we're not exactly sure what your brother, Victor, is up to but we should assume he's here to either take you or kill you."

"You'd know it if Vic was here to kill me." Her softly spoken declaration sent chills down my spine. She believed what she was saying. "Vic is his right hand. The others are all good at what they do, but Vic is the one he sends when he wants someone to speak on his behalf and either doesn't want to go himself, or if he believes there would be a threat to him."

"And what about you?" Torpedo's question was soft, and I didn't think he was judging her, but I shot him a look just the same. He merely gave me a challenging glance before he turned his attention back to Carrie. "What did your father expect you to do?"

She shrugged. "Not much of anything, I don't think. What I mean is, I never met his expectations. If anything, I think he planned on marrying me off to one of his associates."

"To make an alliance." Gunnar drummed his fingers on the table even as he frowned. "Doesn't sound like something a man with so many secrets would want to do. Especially if you could give that associate information on him. What's your father's name?"

"His name's Flagg. At least, that's what I've heard people call him. We were never allowed to call him anything other than Father or sir. Flagg is all I've ever heard anyone else call him."

"I'll get that information to Data," Knight said, tapping on his tablet. "I've got Rocket's contact info. Do you want me to go to him directly or keep Bones in the loop?" He addressed this question to Torpedo.

The other man curled his finger over his lip,

obviously thinking hard about this. "From here on out, cut Data off. Ain't tried to stifle your game, Knuckles, but I'm not comfortable getting Bones too involved with Kiss of Death."

"You knew what we were about when you agreed, Torpedo." It surprised me that Knuckles was talking about this in front of Carrie. We weren't talking about anything sensitive, but his willingness to pick this up with Carrie here told me he expected she'd be around for a long time. Manipulative, maybe. But it was yet another way my president was looking out for me. If he accepted Carrie, the others would too.

"I did. And as long as you ain't hurtin' innocents, I could give a good Goddamn what you do. My only concern was that you not fall into the same pattern Slash and Rat Man fell into. You guys are vicious to your enemies, but you don't kill or harm needlessly." He shrugged. "I can respect that. Bones has done its share of killin', too. They've done things on the wrong side of legal, too. But with ExFil getting bigger and coming under closer scrutiny, it's best if Bones goes the other direction."

"You afraid this is gonna come to a boiling point?"

"I'm afraid there's gonna be a lot of killin'. I'll be right there in the middle of it with you. But I'd prefer not to bring the fuzz to Ice and Cyclone's front door if I can keep from it."

Knuckles nodded in acknowledgement. "Understandable. Always believed in cleanin' up my own mess."

"Now, having said all that..." Torpedo grinned. "I'm pretty sure Grim Road MC is the club you want helpin' on this."

"I hear ya." Knuckles chuckled. "Spooks to catch

spooks."

I glanced at Carrie. She looked like she was deep in thought, so I leaned in. "What's goin' on, Killer? Somethin' buggin' ya?"

"Yeah, but I don't know what."

"Tell me." I put my full attention on her while Knuckles, Torpedo, and Knight did their thing. I could hear a few of the others offering input but I tuned it all out and focused on Carrie.

"Grim Road. I've heard that name before."

"Good or bad?"

She shook her head. "I'm not sure. I wish I could tell you." She frowned, trying to remember where she'd heard the name before. "Father wouldn't have mentioned them unless they were a potential threat or ally."

"Grim Road MC is a motorcycle club made up of mostly former black ops soldiers," I explained quietly. "They're extremely dangerous and extremely loyal to their own. If Knight can get their help, we'll be in a much better position."

Carrie's eyes widened. "Wait. I remember now. Victor mentioned them once to Father. He said they were off-limits. Completely. Father was furious, but Victor wouldn't back down." She leaned closer to me, her voice dropping to a whisper. "That's the only time I ever saw Father back down from one of my brothers."

That was interesting. Very interesting. I caught Knuckles's eye and gestured for him to come over. When he approached, I relayed what Carrie had just told me.

Knuckles' eyebrows shot up. "Well, ain't that something." He turned to Knight. "When you contact Rocket, Knight, ask him if he knows either Flagg or Vic."

Knight nodded and tapped at his tablet, his fingers flying over the screen. "Already done. I've sent him an encrypted message with the names and a brief summary of the situation." He glanced back up at Knuckles. "Headed to my office to do this. I'll give you an update as soon as I have it."

"Good." Knuckles stood. "I want round-the-clock lookouts by patched members. Keep the prospects already assigned guard duty with you. We sleep in shifts until this is over. Though, honestly, if he's half as good as Carrie says, I expect he'll get in without us knowing much."

"I'll know." Knight gave an arrogant lift of his chin.

"Good." Knuckles turned back to me and Carrie. "For now, you stay with Hawk. If your brother Victor is still watching, we want him to know you're protected."

"I really don't think Victor would hurt me," Carrie insisted. "He's the only one who ever really stood up for me."

I exchanged glances with Knuckles. Neither of us was convinced, but pushing her on this wouldn't help. "Maybe so, but until we know his intentions, we play it safe."

Just as he'd turned to leave, Knight's tablet pinged. He glanced up at Knuckles who sat back down.

"What is it?"

Knight frowned at his tablet. "Rocket." He looked up, his expression serious. "He wants a video call. Now."

"Do it," Knuckles ordered, gesturing to the tablet. "Can you put him somewhere we can all see him?"

"Yeah. Give me a second."

Knight tapped out a few commands and the big screen TV along the wall flickered to life. Followed soon after with the image of a man with a closely cropped dark beard appeared. His eyes were sharp, assessing. I got the feeling he didn't miss much. The plain black T-shirt he wore molded his powerful arms and shoulders. Over his shirt, he wore his colors with his name and rank as president on the chest. Beside him, a fierce-looking blonde pixie stood with her hand on his shoulder. I noticed she also wore a vest, but instead of something like "Property Of" and the name of her man, the patches said, "Lemon" and "Vice President."

I gave Rocket a questioning look. The other man raised an eyebrow and practically dared me to say something. Right. Not on my life.

"You're on the big screen, Rocket." Knight held the tablet up so he was looking into the camera as he spoke. "Everyone can see and hear you."

"Understood." He sat back slightly, ready to start the conversation. "This is my vice president, Lemon. Any time there's a woman involved, Lemon is in on the conversation. While I know Flagg and Vic, I'm not familiar with Carrie, though I know *of* her."

"Will you tell us what you know?" Knight was soft-spoken and delicate as ever. He had an arrogant streak with us, but he was always respectful when dealing with another club. He always said his job was to make them comfortable. Despite his appearance, Knight was an expert at putting people at ease.

"First, let me meet the young woman, Carrie."

Knight brought the tablet to us and I took it from him, holding it so Carrie and I were both in frame. "I'm Carrie's protector," I said by way of introduction. "This is Carrie." Carrie gave a small wave but said nothing.

Rocket stared at us for several seconds. Then his expression changed subtly. Had I not been watching so closely, I doubt I'd have seen the slight widening of his eyes or the tightening around his mouth. "Well, shit," he muttered. "You're Flagg's daughter."

"Yes." Carrie's chin went up and she put her shoulders back slightly. An expressionless mask fell over her face as she met Rocket's gaze calmly. "I am."

Rocket took a breath, closing his eyes as he held it in. Then he exhaled and put his hands flat on the surface in front of him. Lemon glanced his way before putting her hand over his. Rocket turned his hand over and grasped her hand in his. That told me I wasn't going to like what he was about to say.

"Carrie, did you know your mother?"

I didn't want to take my eyes from Rocket, but I needed to see Carrie's face. That mask was still firmly in place, giving nothing away when before she'd been an open book. "No. She died shortly after my birth."

"Your mother was the daughter of a mafia boss named Seth Miles. Flagg made a deal with him years ago that was supposed to unite his army and the Miles Syndicate. I knew her when my father was still alive and a patched member of Grim." He glanced at his VP and she nodded at him. "One of my first missions as team leader was with Vic."

"You know my brother."

"I do. But your father doesn't know. If he did, he'd be furious. Vic was supposed to kill me on that mission. Something about closing a trade route and rerouting it to another port to shift the flow of money. I honestly didn't pay much attention past he was supposed to kill me." Rocket shook his head as he chuckled. "The point is, I don't think Vic is there to hurt you, honey. I also don't think your father knows where you are or Vic wouldn't have let anyone catch even a glimpse of him."

"I did think it was odd Vic got caught." Carrie's expression still gave nothing away. This was the woman who'd been so open before. Now it was like she'd closed herself off.

"It's exceptionally odd," Rocket agreed.

"Unless he intended for you guys to see him and show me."

"Carrie trusts her brother, Rocket," I said. "Should she?"

Rocket nodded his head crisply. "Absolutely. He might not show himself if her father was on to where she went, but he would always look out for his sister."

"What does she need to do?"

"I suppose that's up to you, Hawk." Lemon took over the conversation. "You said you're her protector. What's your gut tell you?"

I shook my head. "Well, I'm not gonna meet him on neutral ground. If half the shit Carrie's told us about Vic and the rest of her brothers is true, I'm not sure I'm comfortable meeting him at all."

Lemon raised an eyebrow, a grin tugging at her lips. "But?"

The chuckle bubbled up from my chest. I liked this woman. "But I think it's better to meet him now and figure out what the deal is."

"It's what I would do." Rocket leaned back once more. "I'll reach out to him, assuming my information's still good. I'll tell him to show himself at the front gate, if that's OK?"

Knuckles nodded. "Yes. We can work something out from there."

"Good. If there's anything else we can be of help

with, let me know."

"Appreciate it, Rocket. Good to meet you."

"Same, Knuckles. Torpedo, Tell Venus and Piston we said hello when you see them."

"Will do. Venus said to tell you she'll call you in a few days, Lemon. Something about getting a ride together for the women from Evansville to Lake Worth and back."

"Bitchin'!" The smile that split Lemon's face was just shy of maniacal. "Pink Harleys unite!"

Everyone groaned. "Pink" and "Harley" should never be mentioned in the same sentence. Unless it had to do with pussy. Then they could be in the same sentence.

Knight broke out laughing as he ended the call. "I bet she creates more than a little havoc."

"All right." Knuckles stood again. "Got a feelin' it won't be long before we have company. Hawk, do you want a buffer between Vic and Carrie?"

"Might be nice. She's not had much sleep. I could use a few Z's myself. I'd like to be on top of my game when we face him."

"Fine. Assuming he contacts us in the next couple of hours, me, Torpedo, and Bohannon will talk to him before we get you and Carrie. I'll send someone for you when we're ready. Until then, I suggest the two of you decide what you're gonna tell him when he gets here."

"What do you mean?" Carrie looked from me to Knuckles and back.

"If we tell your brother I've claimed you, I'll need to get you a property vest ASAP. If you don't want to do that, we need to come up with an excuse for you to stay here."

She gave me a thoughtful look. "Yeah. I guess we

need to get that straight." Kid looked almost resigned, like she wasn't sure her new life was going to be better than her last. I had news for her. If she let me make her mine, I'd treat her like a fuckin' princess. And kill any son of a bitch who tried to take her from me. Including, but not limited to, her father and brothers.

Her willingness to discuss the topic was more than I expected. I kind of thought she'd balk at telling her brother she was going to be a biker's old lady, and she might still. Also, she needed to know what I'd done to earn my place in Kiss of Death. We'd get to that. First, she needed sleep. And I needed to really think this through. Because if she decided she wanted to be my old lady, it had to be all the way. I'd done things in my life I wasn't proud of, but I prided myself on keeping my word. If I pledged myself to her, if I took her as my old lady, I wasn't letting go. I couldn't. Because, for some fucked-up reason I couldn't even imagine, the few hours I'd known Carrie were enough for me. This woman was my destiny, and I didn't want to fight it. I wanted her to be mine. Once she was, I'd fight to the death to keep her.

Chapter Six

Carrie

As Hawk led me back upstairs, it felt like we were descending into chaos rather than rising from the basement. And yeah, my metaphors were all over the fucking place, but, dammit, none of this had been on my fucking BINGO card. I thought I was entitled to be a little discombobulated.

My hand was firmly in Hawk's as we headed into the main room. I let him lead the way and I retreated into my own thoughts. Which was my first mistake. Never take my mind off my surroundings unless I was sure I was safe. And definitely not when I didn't have both my hands free. So when the big-titted bleached blonde stepped up to me and lashed out with a stinging slap to my face, her long, pointed nails raking my flesh more than the blow, it caught me completely off guard.

I sighed, closing my eyes in humiliation. "My father was right."

"What the fuck, Kat?" Hawk was immediately between me and the other woman. The next thing I knew, he had his hand around Kat's throat as he slammed her against a nearby steel column. The other woman cried out, her eyes wide with shock and fear, her hands around Hawk's thick wrist as she struggled to keep her feet under her. Hawk turned his head to find me. I knew he was looking for me specifically because his gaze was wild until the second it collided with mine. "Are you hurt?" His tone was gruff and more than a little urgent. Like he actually cared if I was OK or not. Like I *mattered*. I'd never mattered before. Though some of them were protective of me, I always knew I was a weakness in the family. I never mattered to them. Not really. Certainly not to my father. The only reason he kept me around was in case he needed to trade my body to gain something he wanted.

"Only my pride," I grumbled. I pointed at Kat. "You get that one for free. I blame myself for not paying attention." I touched Hawk's arm and pushed, needing him to stop touching the other woman. When he refused, his grip remaining stubbornly around Kat's neck, I gave a huff. "If I'm gonna be your old lady, I'm gonna have to insist you not *fucking touch other women*."

"She hurt you," he bit out. "She dies."

"Goddamnit, Hawk," I snapped. "If you don't stop touching her, you're gonna be the one I stab."

That worked. He dropped her like he'd been scalded, stepping back several paces. It was the only thing that cooled an ire I'd only been faking moments before. Yeah. Seemed I was a possessive bitch and I hadn't even been sure I wanted the life he was offering, especially since I knew absolutely nothing about my surroundings other than the men here were all fucking huge. Seriously. If there was a place on earth that grew men this big, I had no idea where it would be.

The second Hawk moved away from the bitch, I stepped forward. "Hi, Kat. My name's Carrie. I'm told my name suits me. Something about a movie and a woman named Carrie. I've kind of lived in a movie void most of my life so I have no idea what they mean. But it had something to do with me being... How'd you put it, Hawk? Covered in the blood of my enemies?"

"You're full of shit, bitch," Kat snarled, but I noticed she took a step to the side along the way and away from us. She rubbed her throat where Hawk's hand had been, letting me know he had been serious about killing her.

"Maybe." I shrugged. "But here's the thing. I've had a really long day. I killed two men tonight. I stabbed them and broke bones and I even bit off a couple body parts." Not completely accurate, but sometimes it's the implication. "I'm tired, hungry, and not a little bit horny. All of which add up to me not being in the mood for bullshit of any kind." I stepped closer, lowering my voice. "I understand territorial behavior. You thought you'd mark what you considered your territory. I respect that. Since it was my bad judgment to not be aware of my surroundings, I'd go as far as to say I fucking deserved the attack. Unfortunately for you, even if he was yours to mark, he's mine now. And I promise I'm a bigger fucking Alpha than you are." When she swallowed, I took a step back. "I don't repeat myself, Kat."

Hawk's hand settled on my lower back, a possessive touch that sent warmth through my body despite the confrontation. "Kat, you're out. Go pack your shit."

"What?" Her voice went shrill. "You can't do that!"

"Already did." Hawk's voice was cold. A crowd gathered, watching the drama unfold.

"Goddammit," I muttered under my breath, not believing what I was about to do. As the seconds ticked by, I decided maybe it wasn't the worst idea. "Hawk. Stop." I turned so that I faced him directly. "Don't throw her out."

"Give me one good Goddamned reason why not."

"Because I don't have a fucking property... *thingie*." I glared over Hawk's shoulder when I heard snickers from the men and women watching on.

"Property thingie." He looked startled, like he

was in a daze or something.

"Yeah. The thingie you guys said I needed so the club would recognize me as yours. This would have been avoided if we'd done something like that. Right?" More snickers.

"Thingie."

"I think you broke him, Killer." Knuckles gripped Hawk's shoulder, chuckling as he pulled us away from Kat. I looked over my shoulder to find the other woman hurrying away. I honestly didn't care if she left or not, as long as she didn't touch Hawk.

"Jesus, honey." Hawk picked me up so that I had to wrap my legs around his waist. He stomped to the stairs and didn't break stride as he went up them, taking a few of them two at a time the closer we got to our destination.

He took me down the hall, back to the same door as before. I was surprised when he shoved the door open, marched inside and kicked it closed behind him. Then he turned with me still wrapped around him and pressed me against the door.

"A thingie." His lips curved up in a smile that had my stomach doing flips. "I've got a thingie for you, all right."

I opened my mouth to respond, but his lips crashed down on mine. The kiss was fierce, possessive, and had me melting against him. His hands gripped my thighs, holding me up as he deepened the kiss. I moaned into his mouth, my fingers tangling in his hair.

When we finally broke apart, both of us breathing hard, he pressed his forehead against mine. "You claimed me," he whispered. "In front of everyone."

"I did." My voice was breathless even to my own ears. "I don't know why. I barely know you."

"You know enough for now. Besides, does it really matter?"

I found myself smiling. "You know what? No. It doesn't matter. But there is something I need to tell you."

"What's that, Killer?"

I sighed. "That's not going away any time soon, is it?"

"Honestly, Killer or Carrie. Either one will strike fear into the hearts of your enemies."

"You're laughing at me." I tried to scowl at him but I couldn't really commit. Had I ever had fun like this? This was the lightest conversation we'd had. Hell, it was the lightest conversation I'd ever had with anyone. Any small talk I'd done in the past had been to the benefit of my father and it hadn't happened often. Because, as he said, I was shit at small talk and just made everything more awkward.

"Nope. I'm laughing at how fuckin' much you turn me on." He fastened his mouth on my neck, sucking until I squealed, squirming against him. The shock of the sensation made me thrash, and I tightened my legs around his waist.

"Fuck!" I sucked in a shocked breath. This was… unexpected.

"Carrie?" Hawk rumbled his question vibrated against my lips. "Tell me what you need, baby. You know I'm not gonna hurt you. Right?"

"I know." My fingers in his hair clenched and unclenched, my body so tight with tension I could barely control myself. "I'm not scared. I wasn't lying when I told Kat I was horny. But the thing is, while I know how to please a man, I've never had sex myself."

"Your father intended you to be a virgin until he decided what to do with you."

"Pretty sure I was supposed to be a negotiation tool."

"You know we don't have to have sex if you don't want to. Right?" Hawk continued to feather his lips up and down over my neck. "Just let me taste you."

"Oh, no, mister." I moved my hands to frame his face and forced him to look at me. "You're gonna fuck me. Because you're who I choose."

Surprise flared in his eyes. "I've got an insane attraction to you, Carrie, but if it doesn't go the other way --"

I cut off his shit with a kiss, thrusting my tongue into his mouth and taking what I wanted. One hand slapped against my ass before he gripped and kneaded both cheeks with both hands. Then he slapped the other hand down on the other cheek.

"Fuckin' perfect ass," he growled against my mouth as his hands gripped my buttocks in a tight hold. "Can't wait to fuck it."

I was so fucked. I'd known Hawk would be more than I could handle, but I hadn't counted on how much the difference would turn me on. He knew all the words to say to make me mindless and could be using it shamelessly to humiliate me or get something from me, but the sad fact was, I simply to God *did not give a fuck*. If Hawk could make me feel like this with just his kiss, the brush of his lips, and a bit of dirty talk, when he got down to business I was going to lose my fucking mind. Worth it. Totally worth it.

He carried me to the bed, laying me down with surprising gentleness given the fire in his eyes. The mattress dipped under his weight as he crawled over me, his massive frame caging me in a way that made me feel safe rather than trapped.

"You sure about this?" His voice was rough, strained with restraint. "Once I start, I don't think I'll be able to stop." In answer, I pulled my shirt over my head, then unfastened the front clasp of my bra, baring myself to him. His sharp intake of breath sent a thrill through me. My nipples pebbled to tight peaks under his gaze and a glaze of sweat erupted over my skin. "Fuckin' perfect," he murmured, his gaze devouring me. He lowered his head, his mouth finding my breast, and I arched off the bed with a gasp.

It seemed like his hands were everywhere, rough and calloused yet gentle as they explored my body. Each touch sent sparks of pleasure racing through me. I tugged at his shirt, wanting to feel his skin against mine, and he pulled back just long enough to strip it off.

The sight of him, all muscle and tattoos and raw masculinity, stole my breath. That phrase had always seemed stupid ridiculous to me, but I understood now. When he let his weight settle over me and the light dusting of hair on his chest abraded my already sensitive nipples, my body clenched and I actually cried out, arching against him.

"Shhh, I've got you," he whispered against my breast before taking my nipple into his mouth. The wet heat of his tongue made me whimper. I'd never known I could feel this way. Desperate. Needy. Like I would die if he stopped touching me.

He held me to him with an arm around my back while he feasted on my breast. I loved the feeling of being tied to him, as if by keeping me so tightly against him, I could never get away from him. The strength with which I wanted this man was at once intoxicating and so very frightening I wasn't at all sure I should let him continue. But the sad truth was, even if he killed me or, worse, ridiculed me later or hurt me in some other way, there was no way I was missing out on what my body hinted was yet to come. No fucking way in hell. I wanted this, even if it was just this once. I was going to take this memory and cling to it as one perfect moment in my life.

Hawk slid his hands down my sides to the waistband of the pants. "Let me see all of you," he murmured, his eyes dark with desire as he slowly peeled them down my legs. I lifted my hips to help him. The look of hunger in his gaze as it traveled the length of my body was strangely powerful despite my vulnerability.

When I was completely naked beneath him, he sat back on his heels, just looking at me. "Christ, you're beautiful." His voice was reverent, almost awed. Then he frowned, tracing his fingers over a sore spot on my side, and I glanced down my body. A reddish bruise was darkening my skin, but aside from a slight soreness there was no pain. "Can't say I like this sight." He leaned down and kissed the discolored area, trailing his lips all over it before moving back up my body. "Or this." Hawk moved his lips over the scratches on my face. I had no idea how bad they were, but there was a slight sting as he brushed my cheek.

"They're nothing, Hawk. I swear." I arched my neck, wanting him to kiss me there, to lick and suck me. And yeah, I was a total pushover because the thought of Hawk putting his mark on me for everyone to see made me all kinds of hot. "Please don't stop."

I reached for the button of his jeans, suddenly impatient. "Your turn." I fumbled with the button, brushing his cock. It jumped against my fingers and I jerked back, looking up at him, afraid I'd done something wrong.

He chuckled but didn't move to help me. "Eager, aren't you?"

"Of course I'm eager! You aren't?" It was a stupid question, but the second I asked it, I had to know. Did he want this encounter as much as I did? "I told you I was horny," I reminded him as I went back to fumbling with his zipper. My inexperience made me clumsy, but he didn't seem to mind.

"Oh, I'm definitely eager, Killer." Hawk moved to his knees and shoved his jeans down his hips. He gripped his cock and gave it a couple of strokes. Moisture beaded on the head, and I knew I needed a taste. I had never actually had sex, but I'd learned what men liked. Usually in the form of porn. It was one reason I'd made the decision now to leave instead of earlier. My father had decided I needed more hands-on training, and I wasn't interested in going through anything like that. "So fuckin' eager I'm afraid I'm gonna blow before I even get inside you."

The gruffness in his voice and the way his gaze roamed over my body so possessively brought me back to the here and now. I licked my lips, my mouth going dry at the sight of him. He was huge, his cock standing proudly from a nest of dark hair. Nothing I'd watched to learn about sex could possibly have prepared me for the raw masculinity of Hawk's body or the way my own responded to him.

"I need you." My whispered plea was filled with an urgency I didn't even try to disguise. "Come here," I whispered, reaching for him, trying to make him cover me with that deliciously muscled and heavy body of his.

Hawk shook his head, a wicked smile playing on his lips. "Not yet, Killer. First, I'm gonna to taste you."

Before I could process his words, he moved

down my body, his mouth trailing hot kisses across my stomach. My muscles jumped under his lips as he settled between my thighs, pushing them wider with his broad shoulders.

"Hawk --" My protest was cut off abruptly on a gasp as he pressed his mouth against my pussy. The first swipe of his tongue across my clit had me arching off the bed with a startled cry.

"That's it, baby," he murmured against my flesh. "Let me hear you."

His tongue circled my clit before flicking across it, sending jolts of pleasure through my body. I'd never experienced anything like this feeling. The sensations were overwhelming, making me whimper and writhe beneath him as he devoured me like a starving man. His large hands gripped my thighs, holding me open and in place as his tongue worked magic between my legs.

"Oh God," I gasped, the tension coiling tighter and tighter in my belly. "Hawk!"

He hummed against me, the vibration adding to the intense pleasure. When he slid a thick finger inside me, I nearly came off the bed. He worked it in and out slowly, stretching me even more by adding a second finger while his tongue continued its relentless assault on my clit.

"So fucking tight," he growled. "Gonna feel so good around my cock."

The combination of his words, his fingers pumping in and out of my pussy, and his mouth on my clit sent me hurtling over the edge. My body convulsed as waves of pleasure crashed through me, my inner walls clenching around his finger as I cried out his name.

Before I could fully recover, Hawk was moving

up my body, positioning himself between my thighs. The blunt head of his cock kissed my opening and rested there as Hawk kissed me over and over, sharing the taste of my weeping pussy with me as he thrust his tongue inside me over and over.

I grabbed at the bed sheets, needing to anchor myself against the onslaught of sensations. When he slid deeper inside me, the burn of invasion so intense it bordered on pain, I stiffened slightly, waiting for the pain I knew would come.

"Oh God, oh God," I chanted, my hips moving of their own accord, meeting him as he slid inside me with shallow pumps. The pressure building inside me again was unthinkable. I'd thought my first orgasm had sent me soaring. The one building inside me now threatened to permanently tweak my gray matter. My entire body tightened, straining toward an all-consuming pleasure just out of reach.

"That's it, Killer. Let go for me," Hawk urged, his lips at my ear so his breath tickled my sensitive skin. "Come for me again. Let me have you."

The orgasm hit me like a freight train. I screamed, my body convulsing as waves of pleasure crashed over me. Hawk didn't let up, continuing to fuck me through it until I was trembling and sweating in his arms.

"Hawk," I gasped, not even sure what I was begging for.

"I'm gonna fuck you now, Carrie. Gonna put my cum inside you. Then you're mine. No going back."

"I don't care! Take what you want, just please don't stop." I hated how out of control I sounded. No doubt my father would add it to the long list of failures on my part, but I couldn't find it in me to care very much. The only thing that mattered was taking as much as Hawk would give me. And doing my level best to make him feel as good as he was making me feel.

He pushed forward, burying himself to the hilt in one powerful thrust that had me gasping and gripping his shoulders, my fingers denting the corded muscles I found there. The momentary pain faded quickly, replaced by a fullness that made every nerve ending in my body sing. Hawk stilled above me, his massive frame trembling with the effort of restraint.

"You okay?" he asked, his voice strained.

Was I? I took stock of my body. There was still an intense burn, but there was no real pain. Besides, the little bite made the pleasure all the more intense. I nodded, clutching his shoulders. "Yes. It wasn't as bad as I thought it would be. Please don't stop."

That was all the encouragement he needed. He began to move, slowly at first, then with increasing urgency. Each thrust sent sparks of pleasure radiating through me. I wrapped my legs around his waist, urging him deeper by digging my heels into his ass. I wanted everything he had to give.

"Fuck, you're perfect," he groaned, his face buried in my neck as he pounded into me. "So fucking tight. So fucking mine." God, he sounded so out of control and consumed in his own pleasure! Was there anything sexier than a man who'd just rocked your world taking his own pleasure from your body? If there was, I was hard pressed to think of anything.

The possessiveness in his voice triggered something primal in me. I raked my nails down his back, marking him as he was marking me. "Yours," I said hoarsely. "And you're mine."

His rhythm faltered at my words, and he lifted his head to look into my eyes. The raw emotion I saw there stole my breath. "Never seen anything so fuckin' sexy as the look on your face when you confronted Kat. I wanted to kill the bitch, but it was worth it to see her back down. You looked like a fuckin' biker's old lady."

I wanted to smile but was sure it was strained. "That's exactly the look I was going for."

"Fuckin' hot as hell, woman."

I nodded, unable to form more words. Any lingering discomfort was already subsiding, replaced by that fucking ever growing need that seemed to have taken up residence in my body and refused to leave. I rolled my hips experimentally and we both groaned.

"Fuck," Hawk hissed through his clenched teeth. Sweat dotted his brow, and he shook his head with a growl. "You fuckin' do that again and this'll be over, woman."

I grinned, feeling powerful despite being pinned beneath him. Tilted my hips this time, resting my feet on his calves. "Then fucking move, Hawk! I want all of you. I want your cum inside me like you said."

That was all it took. Hawk growled deep in his throat and began to move in earnest, his powerful hips driving his cock into me with a force that had the headboard slamming against the wall. I clung to him, unable to do anything else, my body building toward another release.

"Fucking hell," he groaned, his movements becoming more erratic. "I can't... fuck, Carrie!"

I felt him swell inside me, and then he was coming, his hot cum flooding me as he buried his face in my neck with a guttural moan. The feeling of him pulsing inside me triggered yet another orgasm, and I shattered beneath him, my inner walls clenching around his cock as I cried out his name.

He collapsed on top of me, his weight a

comforting blanket as we both struggled to catch our breath. We lay tangled together, both of us trembling and panting as we came down from our high. I wrapped my arms around him to keep him close when he would have moved off me. He nuzzled my neck, pressing gentle kisses to my sweat-slicked skin.

"You okay?" he murmured, his voice rough with spent passion.

"Better than okay," I whispered back, trailing my own kisses over his neck and shoulder. I loved his weight pressing me down after what was the most intense experience of my life. Even more than the killing I'd done earlier. Probably because there was nothing negative about this experience. The way Hawk was looking down at me now, like I was the love of his life and he never wanted to let me go, was a heady high.

"You're fucking amazing," Hawk murmured against my skin, his weight shifting slightly to the side so I could breathe easier, but he didn't roll off me completely and I didn't want him to. "Never felt anything like that before."

I laughed softly, running my fingers through his hair. "I'm pretty sure that's my line. You're the one with experience."

"Experience doesn't mean shit when it comes to this." He propped himself up on one elbow, his eyes searching mine with an intensity that made my heart stutter. "What we just did? That wasn't just fucking, Carrie."

I swallowed hard, suddenly nervous. "What was it, then?"

"Something I can't explain." He traced my lips with his thumb. "But I know I'm not ever lettin' go. Not lettin' *you* go. Not ever."

The conviction in his voice should have terrified me. We'd known each other less than twenty-four hours. This kind of instant connection only happened in movies or books, not in real life. Certainly not in my life. But instead of fear, all I felt was a bone-deep certainty that I was exactly where I was supposed to be.

"Good," I whispered. "Because I don't want to go. Not ever."

Hawk smiled down at me, leaning in once more to kiss me. "I think that about covers the proper thingie, then."

I groaned, burying my face against his chest. "Are you ever going to let me live that down?"

"Not a chance, Killer." He laughed, the sound vibrating through his chest. "Not a chance. That's a story I'll be tellin' the grandkids. All fifteen of the little rug rats."

"Fifteen grandchildren?"

"Yep. Gonna have at least five or six kids, by the way."

"Do I get a say in this?" I couldn't help but laugh, the thrill of this new life he dangled in front of me enough to sweep me up into a fantasy I wasn't sure could last. Not that it mattered. I was going to hold on to the fantasy until it evaporated.

"Sure. It's my job to get you to say yes."

"And you think you can get me to say yes to six kids?"

He frowned down at me, but there was mischief in his eyes. "Hell no! What woman would actually agree to that right off the bat?" He shook his head. "Nope. My job is to get you to beg me to come inside you." A slow smile spread his lips and the man looked positively wicked. "Over and over until you can't help but get knocked up."

I laughed until tears streamed from my eyes down my temple. Hawk had this satisfied smirk on his face like he'd won the best prize in the world. I cupped his face in one hand, stroking his beard. Hawk, the big gruff biker, leaned into my touch, practically purring in contentment.

"Never get tired of that sound," he murmured as he kissed me once more. "Get some sleep." He did a slow roll and brought me on top of him, his cock still firmly inside me. "I got a feelin' Knuckles will send someone for us sooner rather than later."

There was so much to think about, so much to plan. I needed to think about what I wanted to say to Vic. Would he try to take me home? Would he try to kill me? Those are the things I needed to consider, but all I found myself thinking about was how wonderful Hawk smelled. About how I loved those strong arms holding me tightly against him.

Fuck it. The future would take care of itself. I was living in the moment. That meant cuddling with the biker beneath me. Were the words "biker" and "cuddle" even supposed to be in the same sentence together? I had no idea. But this biker cuddled the hell out of me.

And I cuddled the hell out of him.

Chapter Seven

Hawk

I held Carrie against me as she slept, keeping her tucked securely against my chest. Her breathing had evened out quickly after our lovemaking, and now she slept deeply, occasionally making little sounds that tugged at something primal inside me. My woman. Mine to protect. Mine to cherish.

The thought should have terrified me. I'd never been the settling down type, not even before prison. But something about Carrie felt inevitable. Like I'd been moving toward her my whole life. I still had to tell her about my prison stint. I admit to being slightly nervous when I'd always given a big ole "fuck you" to anyone who'd looked down at me for my past.

My cell phone vibrated on the nightstand. I reached for it carefully, trying not to disturb Carrie.

Knuckles: *We got company at the gate. Your woman's brother is here.*

I glanced at the clock. We'd been asleep less than an hour. Shit.

Me: *Need 10. She's sleeping.*

Knuckles: *Take 15. But no more. Dude's making me nervous standing out there.*

Me: *Pussy*

Knuckles: *Asshole*

I set the phone down with a grin and gazed at Carrie's sleeping form. She looked peaceful, vulnerable in a way she hadn't allowed herself to be since I'd found her. I'd be a Goddamned liar if that thought didn't make me feel ten feet tall and bulletproof. This woman trusted me. *Me.* I was determined to prove myself worthy of her faith. No matter who I had to kill.

Carrie stirred against me, her eyes fluttering

open. For a moment, she looked disoriented, then recognition dawned. She smiled sleepily. "Hi."

"Hi yourself, Killer." I brushed her hair back from her face. "Your brother's here."

That woke her up. She sat bolt upright, her eyes wide. "Vic? He's here now?"

"At the gate. We need to get dressed." I watched her carefully, trying to gauge her feelings, but she'd closed herself off. At least, partially. I thought I saw a hint of anxiety in the tight line of her mouth. She couldn't lie worth a damn, but there were times when she was very adept at guarding her expressions. "Honey, if you don't want to do this, I'll take care of him."

"No." She sat up and smiled over her shoulder at me. I couldn't resist brushing my fingertips up and down the line of her back just to feel her tremble, and watch the chill bumps pebble her skin. The woman was the most responsive lover I'd ever had. "I'll talk to Vic." She hesitated a second, looking like she was debating with herself whether or not to say something else. "I admit, I'm more than a little nervous. I don't believe Vic would harm me unless he thought I was a threat to the rest of the family, but I also don't know what my father told him or what he believes."

"You mentioned you were the youngest of your siblings. How old are you, Killer?"

"Twenty-three. Older than I should be to be a virgin." Her smile was soft and full of amusement. "Thank you, Hawk."

I shook my head, frowning. "For what, honey?"

"For making my first time so wonderful. You can't imagine how long I've dreaded that act. But I chose you. And you let me." She stood then, not trying to cover herself. "It was glorious, Hawk. More than I ever imagined it could be."

My chest swelled with a satisfaction so deep I'd never felt anything like it. I'd gone from an angry, grizzled ex-con to a love-struck idiot in the span of a few hours. I knew my brothers would razz me unmercifully, but I couldn't give a fuck. Let them laugh. I was the one with this incredible woman in my bed. Besides, Knuckles and Gunnar knew. They'd gone through the same sprint to the finish line with their women. So, yeah. Fuck 'em. They'd get theirs. If they were lucky.

"I'm glad you enjoyed it, Killer. Because that was just the beginning." I rose from the bed and pulled her into my arms, kissing her deeply. When she pushed me back, we were both breathing hard.

"Shower first," she said with a wide, satisfied smile. "We both smell like sex."

"Part of me likes that idea." My grin was unrepentant. "Let your brother know you're mine."

"Are you sure about that? All you know about my brother is that he's a better killer than me. What I've told you is the watered-down version. Mainly because that's what Vic gives me. Whatever he does I don't know about, you can bet your ass he's in a league all his own.

"Fine." I sighed dramatically. "Shower it is." Her merry laughter was the sweetest music I'd ever heard.

I followed her into the bathroom, unwilling to let her out of my sight. If this was all a dream, I was playing it out until she called off. The bathroom was small but functional. It did have a large, comfortable shower. Most of us refused the bigger, fancier top floor apartments simply because we didn't trust too much comfort, but large, private showers were a luxury none of us had on the inside and swore never to do without on the outside. Personally, I found myself rethinking not wanting one of the bigger, fancier apartments. I wanted to give Carrie every comfort I possibly could, even if I was an ex-con with nothing to his name. Literally. I turned on the water, letting it heat up while I watched her move around the space, gathering the towels and shampoo Hannah and Pippa had thought to bring. God knew I didn't have that girly shit. Give me some good, clean Irish Spring or something and I was more than good.

"You're staring," she said without looking at me.

"Can't help it. You're fuckin' beautiful."

A blush spread up her neck to her cheeks. When she turned to look over her shoulder, I saw that the blush painted the tops of her breasts almost to the nipples. I had a moment to wonder if her skin would be hot to touch. "I'm not used to compliments."

"Get used to it." I stepped into the shower and pulled her in after me. "Because I'm not gonna stop telling you how perfect you are."

"I thought we were in a hurry?" She raised an eyebrow, a teasing smile playing on her lips.

"We are. That's why I'm offering to wash your back." I gave her my most innocent look, which probably wasn't very convincing.

To my delight, her face brightened into a glorious smile. "I think I'd like that." Instead of turning around, however, she stepped into my arms and laced her fingers behind my neck. With those absolutely magnificent breasts mashed against my chest, her body mashed against my cock as she leaned up to kiss me, I was about to come against her soft belly. "How long do we have?"

I groaned. "Not fuckin' long enough." I wrapped my arms around her and urged her to kiss me again.

"Knuckles said fifteen minutes, but I can probably push it to thirty."

"You cannot push it to thirty, you asshole." Knuckles's voice boomed from outside the bathroom. Carrie squealed and let me go, taking up a defensive stance on instinct. I moved my body in front of hers as I stuck my head around the glass enclosure of the shower.

"The fuck, Knuckles? I told you we'd be down!"

"Fifteen minutes," Knuckles repeated. "You have three left."

I couldn't help but chuckle. Carrie looked like she wasn't sure if she should be angry or amused. "Guess I can't push it to thirty."

"Damned straight you can't! Move it!"

"What crawled up your ass, Knuckles?"

"Your woman's brother. Water's still runnin'. You're down to two and a half minutes."

"I never pegged you for the mother hen type, Knuckles." Carrie raised her voice to be heard over the water and through the door, but I could almost see Knuckles's face as if he were standing right in front of us.

There was a long pause and I thought Knuckles had left, then I heard him grumble, "That was cold, woman. Really fuckin' cold." Then his heavy boots thudded as he left our apartment.

"Tell me I'm wrong and I'll apologize!" she called out again, louder this time.

Knuckles hollered back, "Nobody likes that person, Carrie."

Carrie burst out laughing as she turned me so I faced her. Her lips found mine, and she kissed me again, continuing to laugh.

I chuckled against her lips. "You're gonna fit

right in here, Killer. Come on, let's get rinsed off before Knuckles comes back with reinforcements." When we stepped out, I wrapped her in a towel before grabbing one for myself.

"I don't have any clean clothes," Carrie said, suddenly looking uncertain.

"Hannah must have sent something with Knuckles." I nodded toward a small pile on the bed that hadn't been there when we got up.

Carrie's cheeks flushed again as she picked through the clothes. Simple jeans, a black T-shirt, and underwear. And her property vest. "Are you sure?"

"You ain't backin' out on me now, woman. I'll still honor your decision if you don't want to put this on, but I will do everything in my power to change your mind. Even if I have to crawl on my knees through broken glass."

Her smile softened and she looked up at me. "That was beautiful." Then that same, gorgeous, intoxicating smile turned positively wicked. "I can't wait to tell Pippa and Hannah how poetic you are." She leaned in on her tiptoes and kissed me once more before rushing to get dressed.

"I ain't fuckin' poetic. What the fuck, woman?"

I dressed quickly in clean jeans and a fresh T-shirt, pulling on my cut over it to the sound of Carrie's laughter. The familiar weight of the leather vest with Kiss of Death MC patches settled on my shoulders, grounding me. As I watched Carrie dress, a sense of possessiveness washed over me. I needed everyone to know she was mine.

I picked up the cut Knuckles had brought for her. I'm not sure how he'd got it made this fast, but I was grateful. "Turn around, honey." She did and I helped her into the vest. "This will let everyone in the compound know you belong to me. It'll also clue the club girls into the fact I'm taken.

"So this is what Kat was talking about."

"Yes. This is the property thingie."

"Revenge for the whole poetic comment?"

I just grinned.

Chapter Eight

Carrie

I'd spent the majority of my life hiding behind baggy clothes and an invisible persona, so the idea of wearing something that so blatantly proclaimed my connection to Hawk made my stomach flutter with equal parts excitement and terror. The vest was black leather with "PROPERTY OF HAWK" emblazoned across the back in bold white lettering above the Kiss of Death MC patch. The front had my name on one side with "OLD LADY" on the other.

"How does it feel?" he asked, his voice rough with emotion.

"Like armor," I replied honestly. And it did. Despite the possessive wording, wearing this vest made me feel protected rather than owned. It was a declaration to the world that I belonged somewhere, to someone, and that I wasn't alone anymore.

"That's my girl." Hawk beamed at me like he was the proudest man in the world. And he was looking straight at me.

"When this is over, remind me to thank you."

"For what, honey?"

"For that look." I reached up and stroked his beard.

"Not sure what look you're referrin' to, but I'll do my best to give it to you all the time if I figure out what it is."

I couldn't stop the smile tugging at my lips, but it faded slowly. "Hawk."

"What is it, baby?"

"Please tell me you're real? That this shit between us is real?" I hated how small I sounded. I wasn't as good as my brothers or as smart as my father, but I wasn't weak. I could hold my own in a fight, I could think on my feet, and I was generally a decent person.

"Honey, what's this?" He brushed his thumb over my bottom lip. "We take a property cut seriously. You don't get one unless a brother's serious. I'm dead fuckin' serious, Killer. You're my woman. I will protect you with every fuckin' thing in me." Hawk framed my face with his hands, his eyes dark and intense. "You're mine, Carrie. Ain't lettin' your father or your brothers take you away from me."

"It's just gonna suck really hard if you decide this is more trouble than I'm worth and kick me out." I tried to smile and be flippant about it, but the thought really hurt.

"Never, baby. And I see it now."

"See what?"

"The false humor. How you keep your face blank when you're facing someone you're unsure about." He shook his head. "You don't do it with me, though."

"I don't?"

"Don't look so puzzled. I noticed it when you first came to the compound, but you were pretty quick to let me in. Once you did, you didn't try too hard to hide from me."

"I did, actually." I shook my head. "Yet something else my father would be disappointed in me for."

"Honey, I'm telling you, there's a difference. When you're facing someone other than me, your face is completely blank. There is nothing to read because you lock everything down. You look almost serene, but when it's just us, you're an open book." Hawk kissed me once more. "Now. Let's go meet your brother."

Hawk took my hand, giving it a reassuring

squeeze as we headed downstairs. Each step felt heavier than the last. My mind was a whirlwind of conflicting emotions. Part of me was desperate to see Vic, to know he was safe. Another part feared what his presence might mean for my newfound happiness.

The main room was oddly quiet when we entered. Men stood around, their postures tense, eyes alert. Knuckles approached us first, his expression grim.

"He's waiting outside the gates," he said to Hawk. "Says he'll only talk to Carrie."

"Not happening," Hawk growled, his grip on my hand tightening.

"I expected as much," Knuckles replied. "Told him you'd be with her."

I swallowed hard. "What did he say to that?"

"He laughed." Knuckles' mouth twisted into a wry smile. "Said he'd anticipated that. He's willing to come inside unarmed."

"He doesn't have to have a physical weapon, Knuckles," I said softly. "He *is* a weapon."

"Yeah. I know. It's an inside joke."

I frowned. "Inside joke?"

"Honey, your brother's not here to hurt you. He's here to make sure you're OK."

"You know Vic?" Now I was confused.

"Yep. Didn't know I knew him until I saw him outside."

"He's not mad?"

Knuckles shook his head. "I don't think so. Your call, Killer." Knuckles cleared his throat. "Do we let the bastard in or meet him at the gate?"

"Shit," I muttered. "Little above my pay grade." I looked up at Hawk. "But no. Until you're absolutely sure what Vic is here for, don't let him in unless you're prepared to fight him to the death. Because that's what you'll get if he doesn't get what he wants."

Knuckles snorted a laugh, then looked over his shoulder. "You hear that, Torpedo, you pussy? You owe me fifty bucks!" That got hoots and high fives all around while various items exchanged hands around the large room.

"The fuck?" I looked up at Hawk. "What just happened?"

"It appears you surprised more than a few of the guys." Hawk leaned in to brush a kiss over my temple before raising his voice. "That's my woman!"

"Y'all are crazy." What the fuck else was I supposed to say?

"You get used to them." Pippa hurried to my side with Hannah following close behind. "They're all pretty gruff and wouldn't hesitate to kill a motherfucker, but they have a code."

"Which is basically, leave our family alone and we let you live," Hannah added with a smile. The guys were still talking over each other and settling bets. Apparently, more than one of them had faith in me. The ones who didn't have that faith were taking their ribbing good-naturedly. "Family consists of everyone inside this compound. When you told Knuckles not to let your brother in, you proved you'd protect us the same way we'd protect you."

"Was it really a test?"

"No." Hannah laughed. "Knuckles knew before he asked you what your answer would be. He was just proving a point to Torpedo."

I lifted a hand to stop her. "Not my business. I'd just like to talk to my brother, find out exactly why he's here, then go back to bed."

"I'm sure you're tired, considering everything

you've been through last night."

"I mean, yeah. A little. But that's not what I meant." I gave the women what I hoped was a serious look. "I've discovered that I really, *really* love sex. The last place I want to be is here talking to my brother when I could be upstairs in bed with Hawk."

Hannah choked on air while Pippa burst out laughing. "Oh my God, Hawk has his hands full with you, doesn't he?"

"I sure hope so," I replied with a wink, enjoying their reactions. It felt good to joke with them, like I was part of something. Like I belonged. This place was warm and welcoming while my own home had been cold and hostile.

Hawk came up behind me, wrapping an arm around my waist. "You ready for this, baby?"

I took a deep breath and nodded. "Yeah. I'm ready."

We walked to the gate as a group. Knuckles led the way with Gunnar on his left and slightly behind him while Hawk kept my hand firmly in his as we followed behind the other two men. The rest of the brothers hung back, but I could feel their watchful presence. They were ready to move at a moment's notice if things went sideways.

As we approached, I saw him. Victor stood just beyond the gate, looking exactly as I remembered. Tall, broad-shouldered, his dark hair cut short, his face expressionless. But I knew him well enough to see the tension in his jaw, the careful way he held himself. The men acting as guards didn't let Vic inside. Instead, Vic stood on the other side of the fence, waiting patiently.

"Vic," I said, my voice steadier than I expected.

His eyes found mine instantly, and for just a moment, relief flashed across his features before he adopted a fierce mien. "'Bout fuckin' time, Knuckles." He turned his gaze back to me. "You good, Carrie?"

"Yes." I didn't offer any more than strictly necessary, just like I'd been taught. I could tell Vic was frustrated, but wasn't sure why.

"I said I needed to talk to her alone, man. You don't keep your word?"

"Ain't up to me." Knuckles jerked his head in my direction. "She's wearin' Hawk's property patch. He gets a say in her safety."

Vic scowled. "She's my baby sister, Knuckles. You know I ain't gonna hurt her."

"I know that because I know you, Vic. Seems your sister isn't as sure of you." When Vic opened his mouth, probably to tell Knuckles to fuck off, the other man cut him off. "She wants to trust you. Even told us how you watched out for her and that you wouldn't always follow your father's instructions if he ordered you to do something you didn't agree with."

"I didn't have much of a choice when she and Zach were little. Our relationship is complicated, but I would never hurt Carrie, or allow her to be hurt."

"She told me some about her training growing up." Hawk sounded pissed as hell. He'd let go of my hand but stayed as close to me as he could with his body between Vic and me, a barrier to what he saw as a threat.

"Did I need to be as hard on her as I was?" Vic snapped. "No. But if I hadn't pushed her, Flagg would have. Anyone he brought in wouldn't have pulled anything and Carrie would have been seriously hurt. I taught her what she needed to know while appeasing our father." Vic turned to me. There was real anguish in his gaze, something I'd never seen before. "I'm sorry, Carrie," he said, taking a step forward until he gripped the iron of the gate separating us and him. "You deserved better than you got."

"Father never wanted a girl. Girls are weak."

Vic shook his head. "Not you, honey. I saw what you did. How you handled yourself. You gave those fuckers more opportunities to attack you than you should have, but I know you. You were trying to give them every opportunity to leave you alone and walk away."

"Father says compassion is a weakness. If you let an enemy live, you're inviting him to attack again."

"I think you know Flagg is a fuckin' dick."

A small smile tugged at my lips. "Yeah. He is."

"He wants you back, but I think I can convince him to let you walk away. If that's what you want."

"I don't want to go back to him, Vic." My voice cracked at the mere thought. It wasn't that I was afraid of my father, though that was part of it. "I can't lose what I've found here. This is what a family should be."

To my surprise, Victor nodded. "I know Knuckles. He was one of my contacts inside the prison in Terre Haute. His word is unquestionable, Carrie. If he tells you something, you can bank on it. And if you're claimed by a man in his club, Knuckles will make sure you're protected. And you're right." Vic gave me a sad smile. "That's what family should be."

"I'm sorry, Vic. How mad do you think Father will be? I don't want you to take the brunt of his anger."

To my surprise, my brother snorted a laugh. "Don't worry about me, honey. I'm actually counting on him being angry with me." For some reason, that sent a chill up my spine. No one wanted to deliberately incur the wrath of Flagg.

"What have you done, Vic?"

"Nothing you need to worry about, Carrie." Then Victor looked over my shoulder and addressed Knuckles. "In return for not razing this place to the ground because you kept my sister locked in here, I'm gonna need somethin' from you."

"You've lost your Goddamned mind, Vic." Knuckles actually chuckled, though it didn't sound pleasant. "I don't owe you anything."

Victor kept going like Knuckles hadn't said anything. "You can pay me back by providing a place for my brothers to lay low if they need it in the next few days."

Knuckles stepped closer to the gate. Hawk gently moved me away and stepped in front of me.

Knuckles crossed his arms over his chest. "Ain't lettin' the enemy inside the gates like some Goddamned Trojan horse."

"On my honor, Knuckles." Victor stuck his hand through the gate, offering it to Knuckles. "I only want a safe place for my brothers if things get too hot with Flagg. I'm getting ready to bring the house down on him, and I don't want them to get the blowback. If all goes as planned, you'll never know anything's going on."

"And if things go sideways?" Hawk took a threatening step forward.

"Then the city may get a little nuts until the power void is filled. Either way, no one will be looking in your direction. No one knows about our association other than me, you, and anyone you told."

"Which is exactly no one, until today," Knuckles said.

"I wouldn't ask if I didn't think it was necessary, man. And only for my brothers. No matter what, I will need to stay as far away from anyone I don't want scrutinized as I can."

"When do you expect things to start happening?" Knuckles reached out and accepted Vic's hand.

"Forty-eight hours."

"The only phones and shit we have stays inside the compound. Give Knight your contact info. Any communication will need to go through him."

"I'll take it. Expect a call from me in the next three days. If I don't, then things really went to shit."

Knuckles stepped back. "Carrie's safe here. If you need to send your brothers, they'll be safe too as long as they don't try anything funny to get Carrie to leave."

"Unless she wants to leave," Vic added before looking at me again. "Are you sure this is what you want? I'd feel better if you let me take you somewhere I know you'll be safe."

"If you could do that, Vic, you'd have done it years ago."

Vic didn't even try to hide his wince. "Yeah, kid. I'm so fuckin' sorry for that. If I could have taken you away from him, I would have. But I was afraid he'd find you, and we wouldn't be there to protect you."

"We?"

"Come on, Carrie." Vic gave me a pleading look. "You know we all love you. You're our baby sister."

"You and Zach, yes. I was never so sure about the others."

"Flagg pitted us all against each other, but we older boys learned early on to pretend to be adversarial in front of him. But we're all really tight. We tried to keep you out of Flagg's notice as much as we could. The best way was to pretend to be annoyed with you so you stayed out of his way. The downside was, you never learned to trust us like you should have been able to."

"Father never really knew what to do with me."

"Oh, he knew. He was saving you to marry one of his rivals. To make an alliance."

"Yeah, not on board with that." I gave him a cheerful smile I didn't feel at all, but my sarcastic attitude sometimes got the better of me.

"Never figured you would be." With a heavy sigh and one long look at me, Victor finally addressed Hawk. "You don't treat my sister like the fuckin' princess she is, I will end you."

"You don't think she can take care of herself if I'm not good to her?"

"I trained her. I know she can."

"Then let me just tell you, when she came here late last night, she was covered in blood and was spitting out the remains of one of those bastard's ears she'd bitten off in the fight. Trust me when I tell you, your sister can take care of herself when it comes to me. Anyone else she needs rid of, I'll be the one to do it." Hawk offered his hand to my brother. "I'll guard your sister with my life. You have my word."

"His word good, Knuckles?"

"He was my SAA before I went away. He did his time on the inside like the rest of us, but he's solid as they come. All my men are solid or they wouldn't be here."

Vic took Hawk's offered hand. "I'm holding you to this, Hawk."

"You take care of your father. Then come back and let your sister know you're OK."

I wasn't sure how I was supposed to feel, but I had the sudden urge to hug Vic, though I'd never done so before.

I stepped forward, ignoring Hawk's attempt to

keep me behind him. "Vic." My voice broke on his name.

Vic's eyes widened slightly. He glanced at Knuckles, who nodded almost imperceptibly, then at Hawk, who reluctantly stepped aside. The gate creaked as Knuckles unlocked it, opening it just enough for me to slip through.

I didn't hesitate. I threw my arms around my brother's waist and pressed my face against his chest. For a moment, Vic stood frozen, as if he didn't know what to do with this display of affection. Then his arms came around me, holding me tight.

"Be careful," I whispered against his shirt. "I just found a family, but I don't want to lose my brothers."

His hand came up to stroke my hair, the gesture awkward but sincere. "I'll be fine, Carrie. I've been planning this for years." He pulled back slightly to look down at me. "You know how Flagg always said I was his best student?" There was a glint in his eye I'd never seen before. "He was right."

I nodded, not exactly understanding what he meant, but I knew whatever was going on, Victor would win.

Victor kissed the top of my head, and I knew it was time to let go. "Will I see you again?" The question slipped out before I could stop it, and I hated how childish I sounded.

"Count on it, honey. You'll see all of us again. Soon."

Chapter Nine

Hawk

Something in the early morning air... shifted. Every instinct I had in me said to hit the ground, but I couldn't see a threat. "Everyone inside. Now." I snarled the command before I thought better. I wasn't the SAA of Kiss of Death anymore, but the sense of urgency was so strong I couldn't stop the order.

As I turned my head, I reached out for Carrie. Her eyes widened in shock right before she launched herself at her brother. Carrie hit Vic hard enough for him to stumble back a full step. The steel post of the chain link gate next to where Vic had stood pinged with the sound of a ricochet.

"Sniper!" I wasn't sure who yelled out the warning, but everyone scattered. Vic rolled with Carrie through the gate while three prospects scrambled to shut and barricade the entrance. There hadn't been even a delayed retort so whoever was doing this had a suppressor.

Another shot hit the other side of the gate, almost like the first shot had missed intentionally when I was certain it had been meant to take out Vic. Once fully inside the gate to our compound, there was camo netting covering the alley-like streets between our warehouses. It wasn't where we needed to be, but it made it harder for our attacker to pick us off one at a time.

"We need better cover." Victor had Carrie pinned beneath him, his body shielding hers completely.

"A hundred yards behind you. Get Carrie inside the clubhouse." The interior of the compound went dark a second later.

"The fuck!" Vic crawled over the pavement and dirt deeper into the canopy cover. "Did they cut the electricity?"

"No." I led the way to the clubhouse entrance. "We did." I knew Vic would understand it was to take advantage of the darkness. Once at the clubhouse entrance, I shoved Carrie inside. "Stay here. I'll be back shortly."

"You're going hunting." Carrie looked up at me with a mixture of shock and anger.

"I am. Stay here with your brother."

"You know the sniper is Flagg, right?" Vic leveled a look at me.

"That's what I thought, too, Hawk." Carrie moved into my arms, and I couldn't help but pull her close. She'd been so close to where the bullet had hit it took my breath. I hadn't planned on holding her yet because I knew the urge to take her to the basement of one of the warehouses, wrap her up in my arms, and hide us both away from the world and any possible harm would be too strong to ignore. Spoiler alert! It was.

"We'll know soon," I said as I squeezed Carrie to me tightly. "Because I intend to bring whoever this motherfucker is back to kill him."

"Not before me, you're not." Vic's voice was calm, but his eyes were like steel. I'd seen that look on enough killers to know this wasn't a debate we were having. Vic would do what he Goddamned well pleased, and I honestly didn't blame him.

I hurried deeper into the clubhouse to the bar where Chains was readying weapons we kept locked away in a hidden locker. Several of them, actually. There was a weapons locker on every floor of every warehouse, all tucked away where they were safely hidden. All of us were ex-cons, so guns were a hard no, but we had plenty of knives and blunt instruments we could legally have on the property and not go back to prison for. And, of course, we *did* have guns; we just controlled when they were brought out and who had access to them. Again, that had been my job and it was hard not to fall back into that role when it wasn't yet mine again. I picked a large hunting knife as well as brass knuckles, then turned back to Carrie.

"I want to go with you," she said, picking her own knife as well as two push daggers she tucked into the straps inside her vest put there for just this purpose.

"Not a good idea, honey." I motioned to Knuckles who was shouting orders as he stomped through the big front room. "Let me take care of this. It's what I do. I'll be distracted if you're with me."

"We've got to go now," Knuckles said. "Knight says he has him, but he's not sure how long he can keep from losing him." He tossed me a radio. "Prospects are gettin' our bikes. Me, you, and Tiny. Bohannon too. The rest will stay here to keep the women covered."

Knuckles looked Vic up and down. "You gonna turn on us if we let you go with us? If this is your old man --"

"He's a fuckin' prick," Vic bit out. "He's getting old and it's showing, but he's still dangerous. I can, and will, help you take him down."

"I've never known him to miss a shot," Carrie said, her eyes still wide. The lights were still out in the compound, but with the blinds pulled, there were a few emergency lights we had on while we prepped for a fight. "And he used a visible red laser guide. It's why I shoved you, Vic. I saw him target you. Why would he do that? And why would he want to kill you, Vic?"

"Because I'm the glue holding the others together. If I leave him, our brothers will follow me. He sent me to find you and bring you back, Carrie. He'd still have you even after he killed me." Vic shook his head. "I led him right to you. It never even occurred to me he might follow me here."

"I'm so over that bastard," Carrie muttered. "Are you guys coming or what?" She stomped toward the door and I was helpless not to follow.

"Got your hands full with that one, mate." Griffin was one of the most upbeat men I'd ever met. He'd also been through shit. I'd been the one who'd sent him to Kiss of Death after his stint in Terre Haute. I'd been with him in the same block, but a different wing. Guy had a knack for picking fights without even trying.

"Yep." I clapped him on the shoulder and hurried after my woman.

As I stepped outside and situated the earpiece for my radio on my ear, I watched Carrie as she mounted my bike like she meant to take the fuck off. Jogging the short distance, I took the handlebar. "I got this, honey."

She snorted. "Got your ass in gear, didn't it?"

I barked out a laugh as I climbed on my bike. A prospect tossed us both helmets. We put them on and fastened the straps. "Remind me to spank your ass for that later, woman."

"Only after we put this fucker down." Yeah. Carrie was good and pissed now. I knew the feeling. But under the anger, there was a fear so bone-deep it brought me to my knees. Flagg had been aiming for Vic, but he could have just as easily hit Carrie when she lunged to push her brother out of the way.

I followed Knight's directions as we sped

through alleys surrounding our property. There were several warehouses besides ours in the area. Knight had found the bastard at the far end of the warehouses next to the shipping yard on the Cumberland River. I knew the place well because I'd told Knuckles years ago when we'd first picked up this property it would be the perfect place for a sniper ambush. He'd agreed but then life went sideways and we weren't able to build a defense against it.

"There!" Carrie pointed to a figure sticking to the shadows. "What the hell is he doing?"

We were on the guy before I could answer. I couldn't positively ID the man in front of us, but if Carrie said that was Flagg I was taking her word for it.

Just as I was about to run him down, something hit the front wheel of my bike. The machine jolted, then the back end tumbled over the front. Me and Carrie both went flying.

I hit the pavement hard, rolling to try and minimize the impact. Carrie landed a few feet away, her body tucked into a ball as she rolled smoothly to her feet, taking up a fighting stance as she tossed her helmet to the ground. The training her father had put her through was showing its value.

"Carrie!" I shouted, scrambling toward her. Blood trickled down her temple, but her eyes were clear and focused.

"I'm fine," she called back, scanning the area. "Where is he?"

A sharp crack split the air and chunks of concrete exploded near my feet. I dove for cover behind a dumpster, pulling Carrie with me.

"He's got help," Vic's voice came through my earpiece. "Looks like Gage."

"My brother." I glanced her way and saw a deep

sorrow etched into her face. This was hurting her in ways I couldn't imagine.

Knuckles and Vic continued on after the man on foot while Bohannon stopped to help us. The vice president fired his pistol back in the direction the last volley of shots came from. "Either of you hit?"

"We're good." I leaned around the dumpster, peering over the edge to get a fix on our attacker. Movement on the rooftop of the warehouse to our left caught my eye. A figure in dark clothing moved position to take another shot. "East side by the river. The weak spot, Knuckles."

"I see him."

"Don't hurt him!" Carrie screamed. "Not yet!"

"Fuck," I muttered. I'm sure Carrie needed answers, and I was going to give her everything I could. "Don't kill the bastard yet, Knuckles. We need to know who it is. Carrie will have questions."

There was a pause on the radio before Knuckles came back with, "No promises."

"Carrie!" Our attacker addressed her directly. "It's me! It's Gage!"

"Vic said it was you." Carrie's voice was shaky. "You were always the rogue. Father always muttered about you being the only one he couldn't predict. But I never thought you'd try to kill me for him."

"Wasn't trying to kill you. I was pushing you guys away until I could get your attention."

"You shot at us!" Carrie yelled back, sounding as mad as she looked. "I'd say that's trying to kill us!"

"If I'd been shooting *at* you, I'd have *hit* you. You know that."

"What do you want, Gage?"

"Flagg wants you home."

"I am home." Carrie didn't hesitate with her

answer which made me more fucking proud than I could have imagined.

"OK." He stepped into the light, his hands out as he slowly lowered his gun to the pavement. "That's all I wanted to know." I glanced at Carrie. Her jaw was tight. I could tell she wasn't convinced of her brother's change of heart. Gage seemed to know she wasn't going to take his word at face value. "I swear it, Carrie. I knew Flagg had plans to get rid of Vic because he couldn't control him. He thought he could control the rest of us if Vic wasn't around."

"Then who's the sniper on the roof?"

"That'd be Flagg's brother, Zeb Randall." Gage stood there with his hands raised and out to his sides. "It's him who wants you. Flagg's just trying to get back in his brother's good graces."

"Randall." I muttered. "Flagg and Randall." Then added, "And Carrie." I let the grin tugging my lips free. "Seems to fit." If you know, you know.

"I got the bastard on the roof." Torpedo's voice over the radio surprised me. He was supposed to be back at the clubhouse, but I should have known the man wouldn't sit this one out.

Knuckles and Vic approached us dragging an older man with them while he hurled obscenities and threats at both of them. Obviously, this Flagg wasn't happy with the situation. His mood wasn't likely to improve over the next few hours either. They'd zip-tied Flagg's hands behind his back so he was already hampered. It didn't take much to stifle his efforts to get away. Knuckles shoved Flagg to the ground. Vic kicked him over so he lay on his front with his hands at the small of his back.

Knuckles snagged his radio. "I ought to kick your ass, Torpedo. I might still if you didn't bring help."

"Griffin here. I got his back, boss. We can bring our guy to the cage if Tiny's got room."

"Always got room for one more." Tiny's voice held a wealth of humor. He'd brought an old Bronco for anyone we needed to bring back. Tiny was always ready when anyone left the compound.

"Vic." Carrie stepped toward her brother. "You got him?"

"Yeah." Vic spat on the ground next to the man on the ground. "Knuckles? Got someone who can take this piece of shit back to your compound? I'd prefer to just kill him, but this is your territory. Besides, I'm sure Carrie has questions for everyone."

"She does." I moved to stand next to Carrie, putting my arm around her shoulders. I didn't miss the slight tremor running through her body. "You okay, Killer?"

"Yeah. It's time to face my monster."

"Little whore," Flagg snapped. "You had one job and you failed. Should have strangled you when you were born, just like your mother."

"That's enough." Knuckles motioned for Tiny to help Vic get Flagg in the back of the vehicle. "We can sort everything in a bit. Is anyone hurt?"

"I think everyone's good, boss." Tiny heaved out a grunt as he tossed Flagg into the back. The older man yelped but Tiny didn't apologize, a sure sign of how irritated he was. While the big man was a terror when he had to be, he was unfailingly careful of anyone smaller than he was. Well, except when he'd been my muscle on the inside. He'd killed more men on the inside than he ever would have on the outside and he'd had zero remorse.

"Meet us around the corner, Tiny," Torpedo

ordered over the radio. "You know where." Everyone knew where the blind spots were on the security cameras. We were always careful.

"On it, Prez." Tiny confirmed the order as Vic jumped into the back with Flagg along with Knuckles. "This oughtta be fun." Tiny slammed the tailgate shut, then stomped around to the driver's side, climbed in, and took off.

I turned to Carrie. She looked shell-shocked. Like none of this was what she was expecting. I wanted to get her home and away from everything to let her process, but I knew she wouldn't want to wait. Less than a fucking day and I was already in tune with her. "We need to get back. You ready to ride?"

"That was... disappointing," Carrie mumbled. "Not sure what I expected, but I thought it would be harder than this to catch him."

"Christ, baby," I pulled Carrie into my arms and held her tightly. "You took a header off the bike and you're complaining the chase wasn't exciting enough?" I kissed the top of her head. "Ain't sure I could take your brand of excitement."

Gage cleared his throat. He'd been standing on the edge of the group watching, scowling at Flagg the whole time. "Father's having a difficult time accepting that his control over us is slipping. He's been making increasingly erratic decisions." He looked at Carrie. "When you disappeared, he lost it. Started raving about traitors and how he'd kill anyone who helped you escape."

"I didn't escape. I left." Carrie's voice was firm, but I could feel her trembling against me. "There's a difference."

"Not to him," Gage replied grimly. "Look, I know you don't trust me right now, but I swear I wasn't trying to hurt you or Vic. I was trying to get you to move out of Flagg's line of sight so he wouldn't take another shot at your man. He's slipping, but I don't see him missing a shot like that twice."

Carrie was still for a moment before she nodded slowly. "I believe you, Gage."

"I'm not asking you to trust me, Hawk." Gage's expression remained neutral, but his eyes were sharp, like he was assessing every movement I made. "You don't know me. But Carrie does."

Carrie looked up at me, her expression conflicted. "Gage was always… unpredictable. Father never knew what to do with him." She addressed her brother. "Why? Why betray him now when you haven't all these years?"

"Honey, as hard as you had it, it was worse for us boys. We all learned to cope and avoid a beating in different ways. I went along with him, doing what he asked when I had to. Other times, I mitigated the damage and worked out something I could live with."

"We need to get back to the compound," I said, not wanting to be out in the open too long. "Knight will have the place locked down tight, but I don't want to take chances if there are more of your father's men around."

"There aren't." Gage said.

"Get in the back with Knuckles and Vic," I told him.

"No." Gage shook his head. "I'll get in touch with Vic later, but I've got to let my brothers know what's going on. There will be a power void in the city if we don't move to shore everything up." He paused. "I'm assuming Flagg won't leave that compound."

"No clue." He absolutely would not be leaving that fucking compound. "Come with us and find out."

"Let me check with Vic first."

"Tiny." I spoke into the radio, hoping the road captain could answer me. Should be an uneventful drive to pick up some passengers, but things were always easy until something went to shit.

"Yeah, Hawk."

"Give Vic your radio."

"Stand by."

A few seconds later, I heard Vic's voice. "What is it, Hawk?"

"Do you want Tiny to swing back by and pick up your brother?"

"No." The response was immediate. "He needs to prepare for what happens next. Otherwise, it's going to fuck with everyone's business." I knew Vic was being deliberately vague and I approved.

"He said as much. He's leaving now unless you have instructions."

"Gage knows what to do."

"Copy that."

Gage reached for Carrie, but I stepped in front of her, not wanting him near her. Carrie put a hand on my arm and stepped around me. "It's all right, Hawk. I see it in his face. Gage isn't going to hurt me."

"You're too trusting, honey." But she still moved past me and into her brother's arms.

Gage heaved a big sigh and hugged her tight, kissing the top of her head. "I'm so sorry, Carrie. We should have taken better care of you."

"You guys weren't much more than teenagers yourselves. You helped me when it mattered. All of you, though, I admit I wasn't sure what to think of you guys. Half the time it seemed like you hated me. The other half like I was an obligation you had to do right by for whatever reason."

"That was to keep Flagg from using you against us. We all adored you. Still do. But if he knew he could control us by threatening you, things would have been so much worse." He let her go and I felt like I could finally breathe again. "Go on. Your man there looks like he's about to lose his shit." I growled but Gage just gave me a half smile. "Take care of my baby sister. I know where you live."

"With my life," was all I said. Then I urged Carrie to climb on Knuckles's bike. Tiny would come back for mine and Knuckles wouldn't want to leave his here in the meantime.

The ride back was short and uneventful. Thank goodness too because I wasn't sure how much more I could take. My protective instincts had kicked in big time. I wanted to hole up in a dark room with her for several days until I was sure nothing was coming for her again. Unfortunately, I couldn't hide us away. Not yet anyway. There was the matter of her father and uncle to deal with. And I sincerely hoped I got to kill at least one of the bastards myself.

Chapter Ten

Carrie

My father glared at me from the chair the guys had tied him to. The man next to him looked bored. There was no denying the resemblance. They looked exactly alike. They could be twins. Flagg was gagged and screaming angrily behind the cloth they'd stuffed in his mouth.

"God, what a whiner," Torpedo muttered. That surprised me. He had been more of an observer the few times I'd been around him. Of course, only one day here didn't really make me the leading authority. But the lessons my father had taught me stuck more than he probably realized. I might lack physical strength, but I wasn't stupid. My intelligence was a very strong weapon. I'd learned to read people. Just like Flagg had taught me. So, I knew Torpedo was angry as fuck without looking at him. His voice was just that little bit tight, and his tone had bite where I'd never heard him anything other than calm and even.

"You're not in a position to be a dick, Flagg." Knuckles went to the restrained man and backhanded him before taking out the gag. "Before you die, we have some questions. And by we, I mean Carrie. Whatever she wants to know, you're gonna tell her. You don't, then you piss every last motherfucker in here way the fuck off."

"Do you have the least comprehension of who I am?"

"I know exactly who you are. Zeb Randall. Partner of Seth 'The Hammer' Miles." Knuckles leaned against one of the steel posts embedded in the concrete basement floor. "What I don't get is how you don't know who we are."

"You're a bunch of thugs! *I own this city!*"

"No. The Hammer owns this city. He's had you running things here, but even if you were going to leave here alive, that's changing as of about twenty minutes ago."

"Nothing's changing, Knuckles. I've already called Mr. Miles. He's on the way and he's not pleased."

"Oh, I know he's not pleased." Knuckles cleaned one nail with the top of his knife. "Not pleased with a lot of things."

"Knuckles? What the fuck's going on?" A man who looked to be in his sixties descended the stairs to the basement. He was impeccably dressed, his silver beard short and neat. His demand was delivered without heat. In fact, there was an ice-cold look in those glacial blue eyes that gave me the fucking creeps.

"I'll tell you what's goin' on, Seth. This dumb biker has kidnapped Carrie and is holding her against her will."

"Which dumb biker?" Seth "The Hammer" Miles turned his gaze on me. This was the man who was my grandfather?

"That'd be me." Hawk stepped solidly in front of me. He was always doing that when I was perfectly capable of taking care of myself.

"And you, Carrie? Are you here when you don't want to be?" He sounded so reasonable when it was obvious I'd better answer correctly or there was going to be trouble. What I couldn't figure out was how he was so confident when he had no muscle with him. Even if Miles was armed, this wasn't a fight he could win. There were too many younger, stronger men, and he was in their lair.

"I'm exactly where I want to be. With Hawk."

"He's good to you?"

"I wouldn't be here with him, wearing his property patch, if he wasn't. And if he ever stops being good to me, I'll leave his ass. Until then, though, I'm not going anywhere."

Miles stared at me for a long time. He wasn't as big as the men here, but he was tall and broad-shouldered. His appearance was striking enough that it was its own intimidation factor. A muscle ticked in his jaw as he looked down at me. "You'll forgive me, my dear. I wasn't aware of your existence until a few years ago."

That got reactions out of Flagg and Zeb. Flagg was angry, but shiftier than I'd ever seen him. The more I watched him, the angrier I got. Just not for the reasons I probably should be angry.

"You're lying!" I shouted, moving to stand in front of Flagg. Both Hawk and Miles moved to stay between me and the old bastard, but I managed to still be able to look him straight in the eyes. "You're fucking lying, you son of a bitch."

"I am not, you little whore!" He snarled. "You've ruined everything!"

"*I've* ruined everything?" The fucking nerve! "What exactly have I ruined?"

"He was going to dangle you in front of me for control of the air and seaports out of Knoxville, and with it about seventy percent of the cocaine and fentanyl traffic."

Flagg's mouth opened, but before he could say anything, Miles nodded. Knuckles swung one huge fist, connecting with Flagg's jaw. That's when I noticed the brass knuckles. Because, of course. When Knuckles stepped back, Flagg's jaw was askew. I'd never heard my father make that particular sound before. I found I liked it far more than I should.

Zeb Randall looked on in shock. Where he'd been so arrogant before, now he was sweating and trembling. "Oh, God."

"God can't help you now." Knuckles grinned as he cracked his knuckles. "And I doubt he'll be the one welcoming you where you're going."

"What did you mean when you said you didn't know about me until a few years ago?" The question was out before I could censor it, but once free I knew I had to have the answer.

Miles brought his attention to me, and I actually saw warmth there. Sorrow too. "A man I had working for Randall so he could report to me what was really going on, learned of you one of the times Flagg had to send for a doctor to see to your injuries. It took me some time to confirm you were my daughter's child, but I finally did. The same as I finally confirmed what really happened to my daughter."

Neither Flagg nor Randall bothered to say anything. I doubt they could do more than moan at this point. It was funny. My father, the man who was universally feared by his enemies and allies alike, who buried himself and his children so deep in anonymity and trained them to be assassins and elite soldiers, was whimpering, drooling and, I thought, might have pissed himself.

"You're nothing like what I built you up to be," I mused out loud.

"He's a shadow of his former self," Miles told me. "For three decades he's been my muscle. After my daughter passed, I never fully trusted him but could never figure out why. He gave me no reason not to trust him, but I blamed him for Margaret's death."

"Wait. Stop." Chains held up a hand, like a kid in

school asking for permission to speak.

"Yes?" Miles raised an eyebrow, an expression somewhere between amusement and annoyance.

"Her mom's name is Margaret? You're shittin' me right now. Right?"

"Why would I make that up?"

Chains looked more uncomfortable than I've ever seen a man look. "Uh, no reason." He scrubbed the back of his neck. "I'm just gonna, ah, I'll be in my apartment, Knuckles. I gotta…" The man was actually pale.

"Yeah," Knuckles sighed. "Go on. Superstitious little shit."

Everyone roared with laughter. Well, everyone but Miles, Flagg, and Randall. The latter two were in misery while the former just looked confused.

"I've really got to watch that movie."

Miles stiffened. "Movie?"

"Yeah. Apparently, there's a movie named *Carrie*. Chains is freaked out by it or something. I've not watched it yet."

To my utter surprise, Seth "The Hammer" Miles, criminal kingpin in charge of the region, burst out laughing. In fact, he laughed until tears rolled down his cheeks and someone had to get him a chair. He actually wheezed with laughter.

When he finally calmed down, Miles sat with his head down for several minutes. When he looked up at me, it was with such grief and pain, but also a love so heartbreakingly deep it brought tears to my own eyes. "Your mother would have loved this story. I know how you came to Kiss of Death. The men you killed. All of it. I couldn't get to you, so I drove you this way by putting people in your path who would help you get here. To these men."

"Why would you do that?"

"Because, when you left, I knew Flagg would be close behind you. What I didn't know was how he'd started to lose his mind. He was always a mean son of a bitch, but I've been getting reports he was becoming worse."

"Why would you just... give him your daughter?" I was on the verge of shattering. If this man had been so cruel as to force my mother into marriage with a monster, I wasn't sure I could handle it. The thought was too much to contemplate.

"Carrie, I swear to you, I didn't. Margaret told me she was in love with him. She begged me to allow it. I didn't want her to marry him, but I wasn't going to deny my only child what she wanted most."

"Then what happened?"

Miles looked over at Flagg, then nodded at Knuckles again. Knuckles grinned, then hit Flagg again, this time on the other side of his jaw. Flagg tried to scream, but it came out more of a strangled gurgle. His jaw now hung loosely. Next to him, watching the whole thing with dawning horror, Zeb Randall looked like he was going to be sick and was pleading with Knuckles not to hit him all at the same time.

"She had a difficult pregnancy with you. Looking back, it was probably stress and anxiety. I didn't know it at the time, but the abuse started a few months after Flagg found out Margaret was pregnant. She told me she was fine, that she was just tired from all the vomiting and swollen feet and just being pregnant.

"Two days after she was ordered on bedrest, I got called overseas to... arbitrate." He sidestepped whatever his reasons were, but that was OK. I didn't want to know about his businesses or whatever. I only wanted to know about my mother. "Are you sure you want to talk about this here?"

"Why wouldn't I? If you're trying to get me to go with you somewhere to talk in private so you can take me away, you can try something else."

"Honey, no." He shook his head. "I just want you to have the option to hear this in private. Family matters are often sensitive."

I thought about that. "Yeah. They are. But this is my family. They're the ones having to live through it with me now."

To my surprise, Miles nodded. "I suppose you're right." He scrubbed a hand over his face. "He waited until he knew I was gone. Then he called in a doctor he paid to deliver the baby, then kill Margaret and make it look like an accident. He chose insulin."

"Why didn't the coroner rule her death a homicide?"

"Because they didn't check for insulin since she wasn't a diabetic, and her doctor was at her bedside when she died. I wasn't there and no one questioned the doctor's account of what happened."

"What about me?"

"He told me you'd died with Margaret during the birth. Then he paid the funeral director and the doctor to file all the appropriate paperwork for a stillborn death, had a closed casket for the child, then buried both side by side with a nice headstone and everything." The longer he spoke, the more fury filled Miles's face. He nodded at Knuckles again who punched Flagg in the crotch with those brass knuckles with what looked like all his considerable strength.

My father squealed over and over, crying and begging. I really should have felt bad, or been uncomfortable with seeing someone so obviously suffering, but I couldn't really muster the energy to care.

"Took me years and years to find out differently, Carrie. The second I did, I reached out to Vic."

That got a gasp of outrage from Father's brother, Zeb Randall. "Vic? You betrayed us!"

"That's rich. Coming from you." For the first time, Vic joined the discussion. He reached out his hand to Knuckles who handed over one brass knuckle. Vic put it on his right hand, then hit Randall across the as yet uninjured side of his jaw. He now looked similar to Flagg. Sounded about like him too. "It was your idea to get rid of Margaret so you could groom her child to be the perfect pawn in your game. You could marry her off to create an alliance. She'd be wife and bodyguard in one. You'd program her to be subservient and obedient. Then you'd gain an ally as well as a spy in the home of your new friend."

"After Vic and I had our little discussion, we put a plan in place to get you to safety."

"Which we did." Vic grunted as he punched Randall again. "Worked pretty good too, except I lost track of you just long enough for those punks to assault you. By the time I found you, you were already fighting them. I killed the one attacker you lost track of and did it where I knew Knuckles's people would see me."

"I don't know you." Knuckles took a threatening step toward Vic. "And you didn't lead with the fact you were here with Mr. Miles's knowledge."

"I wasn't sure what your relationship with him was, and thought it better to get Carrie to safety than to play nice before I was ready."

I felt like I was in some sort of bizarre dream. All these men, killers, criminals, whatever they were, all plotting and planning around me, for me, *because* of me. I looked at Miles, my grandfather, then at Hawk, the man I'd chosen, then back at the pathetic creatures who'd made my life hell. "So what happens now?" I asked, my voice steadier than I expected.

Miles looked at me with those piercing blue eyes. "Now? That's entirely up to you, Carrie. These men hurt you. They killed your mother. They stole your childhood. What do you want to happen to them?"

Everyone in the room went still, waiting for my answer. I felt the weight of their expectation, but also something else. Power. Real power, not the illusion of it I'd been chasing all my life.

"I want to say kill them, but I'm not sure I can do that. It's one thing to not mourn their passing, but to actually say that's my wish and wait for you to make it happen isn't something I'm sure I can live with."

Miles smiled at me. "Sweetheart, you don't have to. They killed your mother, but they also killed my daughter."

I thought about that for a long moment. My grandfather simply stood there waiting patiently. Then, finally, I made my decision. "If they'd do this to my mother and me, they'll do it again. Maybe to someone who doesn't have anyone looking after her like I did. Though…" I turned my gaze to Vic. "I didn't realize I'm not your full sister."

Vic shrugged. "Honestly, who your mother was didn't matter to me. You're our sister. We protected you the only way we could until we were able to get you out."

"Where are the others?"

"Taking care of business back home. Gage went to help, but it will take all of them to put us in a position to take over for Flagg and his brother. They worked together, since they looked so much alike. No one knew they were dealing with identical twins. The family were the only ones who knew we were their private army. We kept the other families in Nashville in line for them. We also had to protect them both, so there was no keeping it from us."

"Any other questions, honey?" Hawk was behind me, one arm around my waist, the other at his side within easy reach of that big-ass knife he had strapped to his thigh.

"Yeah, but not for them. I'm done with Igg and Ook."

"What is it?"

I lifted my chin. "What's your relationship with Knuckles, Mr. Miles?"

"Before things went sideways for him, Knuckles and Kiss of Death MC were my muscle. He helped me keep the city running smoothly, and I gave him the drug highway through the prisons in the area all the way to Terre Haute."

"And this is where we take our leave." Torpedo offered his hand to Knuckles, and Knuckles grasped it in a firm grip. "You've got your club locked down tight. You're following the natural order of the land and helping keep the void filled so supply chains aren't disrupted. Any killin' you do is the same as all of us. You don't kill innocents. Having said that, I don't need to know your business now. I'm satisfied this will be what the city needs."

Knuckles tilted his head. "Are you guys leavin' then?"

"Yeah. You're ready to take over and I hate the fuckin' city." Torpedo grimaced. "We're only a phone call away if you need help, but we're headed home."

"I appreciate your help, brother."

"Any man who'd go to prison to avenge" --

Torpedo glanced from Knuckles to Gunnar -- "or to protect his sister, is all right in my book. Because, sometimes, a man just needs killin'."

"No arguments there," Bohannon said with a grin as he extended his hand to Knuckles. "You've got a solid, loyal club. You'll hear no complaints from me."

Torpedo and Bohannon shook hands with everyone as they left. I felt like I should stay. See the end of these fucks, but I was done. I simply couldn't handle any more.

I turned and wrapped my arms around Hawk's neck. "I don't want to be here anymore."

Without a word, Hawk picked me up and headed toward the stairs. I wrapped my legs around his waist and buried my face in his neck.

"You're not stayin', Hawk?" That from Knuckles. "You're SAA now, like we talked about."

My heart sank. I couldn't expect Hawk to step away from a duty he had in order to take care of my fragile emotional state.

"Yeah. I'm also Carrie's man. She's not up to the killin', and I'm not sending her to our apartment by herself." I waved a hand in the air. "Get Tiny to fill in for me. He loves shit like that."

There was a satisfying whimper from one of the brothers waiting to die. Don't know which one. Don't care.

"Go take care of your woman, you prick. She's way more important than these sick fucks."

"Yeah." Hawk looked down at me. It was all I could do to keep from crying. This man loved me. It was there plain as day for anyone who could see. "She is."

"You got a preference about these brothers of hers?" The question caught me by surprise, and I stiffened. Hawk rubbed his hand up and down my back.

"Yeah. They ain't got no prison record, but if they want in, let 'em. Otherwise, put 'em in touch with Rocket. That's my suggestion, for what it's worth."

"Any of your brothers who want to can work for me, Vic." Miles held out his hand to Vic who took it without hesitation.

"Appreciate it. But I'm pretty sure we'll all want to stick together. Once we get this mess cleaned up, we'll sit down and have a long talk about what we want to do."

"Talk to Knight before you leave," Hawk said. "He'll get you in touch with Crush and Byte at Grim Road. That way you know what all your options are."

"Appreciate it." Vic gave Hawk a courteous nod.

"Flagg's territory is yours to run if you want it." Miles waved his hand in a small gesture, like it made no difference to him what they did. "You can do so among yourselves, or join with Knuckles and work together."

Vic shook his head. "We're ensuring there isn't a void left when Flagg leaves, but we have no designs on running anything. So if you want Kiss of Death to fill that opening, we'll gladly assist with the transfer of power. I've got all the records and contacts organized. I can pass them to Knight for your officers to review when you're ready, Knuckles."

"You know my thoughts, Prez. But I'll go with the majority."

"Get on outta here, Hawk." Knuckles waved his hand in my direction. "I'll come talk to you in a few days. Get some rest. Both of you."

"'Bout fuckin' time," Hawk muttered as he took the stairs two at a time, me still clinging to him like a baby monkey. I might have looked ridiculous, but I didn't fucking care. I needed out of that basement and the smell of blood, sweat, and urine. I needed a shower. Then I needed Hawk to make me forget my own name. "Hang on for a couple more minutes, baby. Then you can do what you need to."

True to his word, two minutes later he opened the door to our rooms and kicked it shut. Everything inside me was suddenly free, and I cried out into Hawk's neck. His hand came down on the back of my neck and pressed me against him while I raged.

When the storm passed, when all I could do was lie in his arms and let the tears slowly dry, I curled my hands in his shirt and took a deep breath. Then let it out slowly.

"I love you, Hawk. I love you."

Chapter Eleven

Hawk

Once the storm passed and Carrie settled into an exhausted heap against my chest, I picked her up and carried her to bed.

She looked so small, so vulnerable. The fierce, deadly woman who'd walked into our compound covered in blood was now curled up against me, her eyes red-rimmed from crying, her body trembling with aftershocks of emotion. The instinct to protect her, to shelter her from everything, was so overwhelming it felt like a physical ache in my chest. And I would absolutely answer that call.

"I've got you, baby," I murmured, stroking her hair as I settled us on the bed. "I'm not going anywhere." I held her close, letting her absorb my warmth, my presence, hoping it would ground her.

"It's so much," she whispered against my chest. "I don't even know how to process all this."

"You don't have to do it all at once." I pressed a kiss to the top of her head. "We take it one day at a time. Together."

She lifted her face to mine, those beautiful eyes searching my face. "You're really in this with me? No matter what?"

"Carrie, honey, I was in this the moment you walked through our gate." I traced her cheek with my thumb, wiping away a stray tear. "Believe it or not, I love you, too, Killer." I tried to smile gently at her, but she was breaking my fucking heart. I never wanted anything for this woman but laughter and complete happiness.

She gave me a watery smile that hit me right in the gut. "I've never had anyone who was all mine.

Someone who chose me."

"I choose you, Carrie. And I'll keep choosing you every fucking day." I leaned down to kiss her softly, wanting to convey with my lips what words couldn't fully express. "I really do love you, Carrie. You're it for me."

Her eyes widened slightly, a fresh sheen of tears forming. "I didn't think you'd say it back so soon."

I laughed, the sound rumbling through my chest. "Baby, I think we both know this wasn't exactly a slow-burn situation. When you know, you fucking know."

"Yeah." She snuggled closer, her hand finding its way under my shirt to rest against my skin. "I think I knew the moment you asked me if I was covered in the blood of my enemies."

"For me it was when you spat out that piece of ear." I grinned when she smacked my chest lightly. "What? It was fucking hot."

That got a real laugh out of her, the sound washing over me like a cooling balm. "You're a twisted bastard."

"Damned straight. And I think you love it."

"You know I do," she murmured, her eyes holding mine for a long moment before she leaned up to kiss me softly. "I need a shower."

"You want company?" I brushed her hair back from her face, searching for signs of what she needed most right now.

"Well, it wasn't a request. I kind of expect you to just come with me." She grinned. "You know. Like a good boy."

Yeah. The sass was going to get her fucked good and hard. I got the feeling that's what she needed and I was more than willing to provide.

I swooped her up into my arms, her weight a welcome burden. "I was just waiting for the invitation."

She laughed, wrapping her arms around my neck as I carried her to the bathroom. "You never need an invitation for this. Never."

"You don't either, honey. I'm yours whenever you need me."

"You're going to spoil me."

"Good." I set her down on the bathroom vanity. "You deserve to be spoiled." I turned on the shower, letting the water heat up as I helped her undress. My hands lingered on her skin, tracing the bruises forming from our tumble off the bike. "You're gonna be sore tomorrow."

"Worth it," she murmured, her eyes growing darker as I touched her. "Every bit of it was worth it to get to *here*. To you."

I stripped off my own clothes quickly, eager to feel her skin against mine. When I helped her into the shower, she hissed as the hot water hit her tender muscles, but then sighed as the heat began to work its magic.

I took my time washing her, my hands gentle as they moved over her body. This wasn't about sex -- though my body certainly responded to her nakedness -- this was about care. About showing her that I would be there for all of it, not just the good times.

"Turn around," I murmured, reaching for the shampoo. She complied, and I massaged the soap into her hair, my fingers working against her scalp. She moaned softly, leaning back against me.

"That feels amazing," she whispered, her eyes closed.

"Good." I continued my ministrations, rinsing

her hair before applying conditioner. "Just relax. Let me take care of you."

There was a bench along the back and part of one wall of the shower. Once I'd rinsed her hair, I moved us to the bench and saw with my back against the wall, one leg stretched out in front of me along the length of the bench, while the other foot rested on the shower floor. Carrie sat between my legs, resting with her back to my chest.

She pulled me down for a soft, slow kiss. I deepened the kiss, one hand coming up to cup her face. She shifted position so she straddled me, her slick body sliding against mine in a way that had my cock hardening instantly.

"I need you," she whispered against my lips, her hips rocking against me. "Please, Hawk."

I growled, my hands gripping her hips. "You sure, baby? You've been through a lot today."

"I'm sure." Her eyes met mine, clear and determined. "I need to feel alive. I need to feel you."

That was all I needed to hear. I swiped my fingers through her pussy to find her already wet and needy. I lifted her slightly, positioning her over my cock before slowly lowering her down. We both groaned as I filled her, her tight heat enveloping me inch by inch until she was fully seated.

"Fuck," I hissed, my forehead pressed against hers. "You feel so fucking good, Carrie."

She began to move, slowly at first, her hands braced on my shoulders. I let her set the pace, watching her face as pleasure washed over her features. With her eyes half-closed, lips parted, cheeks flushed, she was the most exotic, sensual woman I'd ever known. And she was all fucking mine.

"God, you're beautiful," I murmured, watching

her move above me. The water cascaded down her body, making her skin glisten. I couldn't take my eyes off her, the way her breasts bounced with each movement, the look of pure pleasure on her face as she rode me.

Her rhythm increased, her breathing growing more ragged. I slid one hand between us, finding her clit with my thumb and circling it gently. She gasped, her inner walls clenching around me.

"That's it, baby," I encouraged, my other hand gripping her hip to help guide her movements. "Take what you need."

"Hawk," she moaned, her head falling back, exposing the elegant line of her throat. I leaned forward, pressing my lips to her pulse point, feeling it race beneath my touch. "I'm so close."

"Come for me, Killer," I growled against her skin, increasing the pressure on her clit. "Let me feel you squeezing my cock like you want my cum inside you."

Her movements became erratic, her thighs trembling against mine. With a cry that echoed off the shower walls, she came, her body shuddering around me. The sight of her coming was the most erotic sight imaginable.

I gave myself the go ahead and pulled her to me, encouraging her to move faster until I was slamming inside her to the sharp slaps of skin on skin. When she screamed again, I let loose, filling her pussy with my hot, sticky cum.

I held her close against me, both of us panting and shaking as the water continued to beat down on us. Her forehead rested against my shoulder, her breath hot against my skin. I stroked her back, savoring the weight of her in my arms.

"I needed that," she murmured, her voice muffled against my chest.

"Yeah, I think we both did." I kissed the top of her head, feeling more content than I had in, well, ever. "Water's gettin' cold. Let's get you dried off and into bed."

She nodded but didn't move immediately, seemingly as reluctant as I was to break the connection we'd built between us. Finally, with a sigh, she lifted herself off me, wincing slightly as my softening cock slipped from her body. I stood and shut off the water, then grabbed towels for both of us.

After drying her off, I wrapped her in a fresh towel and led her back to the bedroom. She crawled into bed naked, her movements slow with exhaustion. I joined her, pulling her against me, her back to my chest. She fit perfectly against me, like she was made to be there.

We lay there in silence. I was too keyed up to sleep, and I thought Carrie was drifting but not really going under like she needed to.

"Hawk?" Her voice was quiet in the fading evening light shining through the open window.

"Yeah, baby?" I ran my hand along her arm, feeling her warm skin beneath my fingertips.

"Is it always going to be like this? Dangerous, I mean."

I considered lying to her, telling her everything would be smooth sailing from here on out, but I respected her too much for that. "Sometimes. This life isn't always easy, but it's worth it for the family you get in return." I pressed a kiss to her shoulder. "The club will always have your back, Carrie. I'll always have your back. Nothing's going to happen to you."

"I'm not worried about me." She turned in my

arms to face me, her expression serious in the dim light filtering through the blinds. "I can handle myself. I'm worried about you."

That caught me off guard. "Me?"

"You put yourself between me and danger without hesitation. Every time." Her fingers traced the line of my jaw. "I don't want to lose you because you're trying to protect me."

I captured her hand and brought it to my lips. "That's what partners do, Killer. We protect each other. I know you can handle yourself. Hell, I'm pretty sure you can handle yourself better than me. But I'm still going to be between you and any danger if I can possibly help it."

"I've heard…" She stopped and took a breath. "I've heard everyone here has served time in prison at some point in their lives."

"It's true, baby. Including me."

"What happened?"

I knew this was coming and admitted to myself I'd been dreading it. I'd never been one to shy away from who I was, but with this woman, I didn't want her to think bad of me."

"Same as most of these guys. I killed someone. I was a young hothead. Got in a fight with some asshole in a bar. He got fresh with a waitress I had a crush on. She turned him down in front of his buddies. He smacked her."

"Yeah, I don't see you standing for that."

"Nope. I slapped him back. Only he lost his balance and fell. On the way down he took the corner of the table to his eyeball, then hit his head on a concrete step. Took him a couple days, but he died. I was indicted for manslaughter."

"Oh, my God! I'm so sorry!"

"I'm not. I learned two very valuable lessons. First, I had to get a handle on my temper. Second, don't get crushes on waitresses unless you actually talk to them first."

"Wait. What?"

I couldn't help but chuckle. "Yeah. I was a busboy. Right out of high school. Worked at a nearby garage too because I was a damned good mechanic, but the view at the restaurant was a sight better. Unfortunately, I wasn't always the social butterfly you fell in love with. I was terrified of talking to her."

"Wow. And you fought that guy for hitting her."

I shrugged. "Wasn't much of a fight."

Carrie frowned. "I think I'm jealous of the bitch."

That made me laugh. "Killer, you've got no cause to be jealous. Mainly because I'm so far gone on you, I turned in my man card the second I saw you. But also I saw you covered in the blood of your enemies. I'd rather you not be covered in my blood."

She stretched as she giggled, the sound so content I wanted to puff out my chest. I'd done that for her. I'd made her happy.

Yeah. I was officially pussy whipped.

"Not something I planned on doing." She smiled and leaned up to kiss me again. "You're a good man, Hawk. I'm proud to be yours."

She nestled against my chest and her breathing gradually slowed and deepened as she drifted off to sleep.

The burner phone I kept on me in the clubhouse buzzed and I picked it up. Opening it, I saw a text from Knuckles.

Knuckles: *All done.*

So, Flagg and Randall were dead.

Me: *Thanks.*

I shut the phone and laid it back on the nightstand. Carrie mumbled something in her sleep and adjusted her position before settling back into a deep sleep.

I thought about what had happened over the last several hours. The club dynamic was about to change drastically. If we took over operations for The Hammer, it would mean more money for the club. There would be risks, but we'd use every resource available to minimize those risks.

There were lots of challenges ahead for Kiss of Death, but I knew we'd come out on top in the end. I also knew that we were gaining glaring vulnerabilities in our women. I also knew those vulnerabilities were in our having so much to lose. Not our women. They were all badasses. Carrie more than the others, but they could all hold their own.

I thought it was fitting that the biggest warrior of our three old ladies was the woman of Kiss of Death's sergeant at arms. She was a fighter just like me. She'd be my biggest asset and my strongest supporter.

"God, I love you, Killer." I whispered the declaration against her hair. "So Goddamned much."

She tilted her head up and smiled at me. "I love you too, Hawk. I love you too."

I loved my life…

Riot (Kiss of Death MC 4)
A Bones MC Romance
Marteeka Karland

Violet Harrington has a haunted look about her that pulls at my protective instincts like nothing has in a long time.

Violet -- In my world, girls aren't deemed useful for much other than to be married off, creating a tie to a rival family. I did my job. I married the man my family chose, and I got pregnant right away. Now my life is a nightmare, wondering if this is the day someone will kill me, or worse, take my son. When Caleb witnesses the abuse I live with, he gives me an ultimatum. Leave his father, or Caleb will kill the man himself. That's when my lawyer introduces me to Quinn Devereaux, the man known as Riot. He asks me a question I've never heard before. *What do you need, Violet?*

Riot -- I was gone the first moment I laid eyes on the tiny woman with the suspicious twelve-year-old guarding her like a pit bull. She's my service requirement assignment -- to protect her and her kid from her husband and father. Domestic abuse is never pretty, but her story hits way too close to home. I'll watch over them, and in the end, I'll do whatever it takes to prevent history from repeating itself. Even if it means I risk going back to prison.

Chapter One

Riot

Community service. What a fucking joke. I appreciated the fact I needed to pay my debt to society. I did bad shit and deserved everything the judge gave me and then some. Knuckles pulled some strings and got me out on parole three years earlier than expected, and it had come with mandatory community service. My lawyer told me Knuckles had friends in high places and not to look a gift horse in the mouth. I understood. I also knew how to keep my mouth shut so I had no intention of finding out anything more.

I'd only been out of prison three days. Now they expected me to go back to the courthouse. Voluntarily. I didn't know why, only that it had to do with the aforementioned community service.

It was three o'clock on Friday afternoon. My instructions were to wait outside in a specific area. Which wasn't suspicious at all. I parked my bike under a tree at the back of the building and waited. As a condition of my parole, I had to carry a cell phone on me at all times. I had no trouble keeping a phone on me. The last thing I wanted was to go back to jail, so if being tied to the fucking phone meant the powers that be could track my every move, so fucking be it.

I had to chuckle. I wanted to stay out of prison, yet I was all in with Knuckles and Kiss of Death MC. An outlaw club by their own admission. Yeah, I was new and didn't know all the guys yet, but there were two things we all had in common. First, we'd all spent time in Terre Haute. Some more than others. And second, we all knew and trusted Knuckles with our lives. Knuckles had the keys to the yard in Terre Haute. He'd been the shot caller on the inside. I thought he probably had more power in prison than most people did on the outside. If he said he could keep me safe from the probation officers with an axe to grind, I'd do what he said, when he said do it, and count my blessings.

The point being, Knuckles was the one who set me up with this particular lawyer. She'd represented me at my parole hearing, and she was the one who demanded my presence at the courthouse today. Knuckles said do what she told me to the best of my ability and without objection. The details were supposed to be given to me when we met up. Apparently, this was a rush job or something. Knuckles said she'd made a point for me to wear my colors and ride my bike. Jeans, black T-shirt, motorcycle boots, and my cut proudly proclaiming I was a member of Kiss of Death MC and that we were a one percent club. I personally didn't like this idea, but Knuckles told me not to worry. He'd kept my ass alive in prison. Just like he had most of the other guys. No way would he toss me to the wolves now.

I glanced at my watch. Five after three. She'd told me three o'clock sharp, but I'm just the ex-con biker. What did I know about being on time?

At ten after, a little white Ford Fiesta pulled up next to me. I was leaning against the seat of my parked bike, my legs crossed at the ankles and my arms crossed over my chest. Classic badass biker intimidation pose. The windows were tinted on all sides except the front. I couldn't see the passengers, but I recognized the woman who got out of the driver's side.

"Ms. Thompson. Wasn't expecting to see you again so soon." I wasn't lying. Knuckles had explained everything to me on the way to Nashville from Terre

Haute, but I thought I'd have a little time to process life on the outside before I got shoved back into the legal system.

"Nothing's free in this world, Riot. You know that." Lana Thompson was an in-your-face powerhouse. She wasn't the sneak attack you didn't see coming. She was the mortar fire you heard half a mile away warning you to get the fuck out of the blast zone.

"And it shouldn't be. I ain't complainin'. I just wasn't expecting my point of contact to be you."

She gave me a superior smirk. "Oh, you and I will see a lot more of each other, I assure you. I'm the reason you're out, you know. Well…" She shrugged. "Me and my other employer. He pays me. Knuckles gets his people."

"Impressive. Do I want to know who your other employer is?"

"Probably not. In any case, I wouldn't tell you. You want to know shit like that, talk to Knuckles."

"Yeah. I'm good." I rolled my eyes and sighed. "When I asked my parole officer about my community service, he said someone would contact me. No one has. You sure this is countin' toward my community service?"

"Who told you to meet me here?"

"Knuckles."

She grinned. "Looks like you have your answer."

"I'm not sure Knuckles counts."

"You said your parole officer told you someone would contact me. He say who?" I could tell by the look on her face she knew the answer to this question, but I was committed now.

"He said to do whatever the fuck Knuckles told me to."

"Uh huh."

"You know, people would like you better if you weren't so smug." I wanted to be irritated at the woman, but really, her making fun of me was my own fault. The joke practically wrote itself. I raised my hands defensively. "Knuckles told me to be here and I'm here. I was told three o'clock sharp." I gave her a pointed glance, then down at my watch.

"Yeah," she breathed with a sigh. "Sorry about that. Poor thing's balking hard." She nodded to the vehicle and her passengers. "Her son and I had to coax her into letting him do this, and we still had to practically drag her into the car."

That got my attention. "What's going on? What is it I need to do?" Something inside me coiled tight. I knew without a doubt something was about to happen that would change my life. Every instinct I had was screaming at me to pay attention, because I was about to get knocked on my ass.

"My client is about to testify that his father beat his mother. Kid knows his mom is the underdog in this fight. His father's a big shot with a whole team of lawyers and she's got me." She grinned, but that feeling in the pit of my stomach was getting stronger by the second. "Caleb is a good kid. He's so protective of his mother it almost hurts. If his father gets Caleb alone, Caleb will do his level best to kill the guy."

I gave her a hard look for long moments, replaying her words to make sure I'd heard her correctly. The weight of everything she was saying was hitting me like a wrecking ball to the fucking head. This woman had chosen me for more than one reason. "You fuckin' bitch," I bit out. "Only reason I don't kill you right here is because it's not worth goin' back to prison."

"Good!" Bitch Thompson, as I would now refer to her, said with wide-eyed enthusiasm. "You don't want to go back to prison. That's great! But the only way you stay *out* of prison is by doing your community service, big guy, and *this* is it."

"Why? Why me? There's got to be hundreds of other people you could use for this."

"You don't even know what I want you to do yet."

"Got a pretty fuckin' good idea. Is this supposed to make me feel better about what happened and about what I did?"

Instantly, Lana Thompson was in my face. This was the side of her everyone in the courtroom feared seeing. She'd used the same expression and tone of voice at my parole hearing as she was using now. Only this time, she grabbed hold of my ear and yanked, twisting my earlobe painfully. Sure, I could have made her stop. I could have seriously hurt her. But I didn't hit women. Not for any reason.

"No. It's not supposed to make you feel better. It's supposed to keep that young man out of fucking prison. Now. What are you going to do about this situation, hmm?" Lana's voice was silky smooth as she purred in a supremely satisfied voice.

"The fuck kind of question is that? Have you lost your fuckin' mind?"

"Can't you get out of a simple ear hold from a woman half your size?"

"Lana, what the fuck's your problem? I could fuckin' break you in half and you fuckin' know it!" I felt like I was the butt of some joke I didn't get.

"Exactly!" I thought she might let me go, but she didn't. Instead, she twisted harder and I had to lean down to keep her from taking my fucking ear off.

"You'll stand there and let me hurt you rather than take a chance on hurting me." Yep. Definitely the butt of the joke.

"What the fuck do you want me to do?" I snarled my question at her. "I ain't gonna hit you. I don't hit women. Or kids. Now, let go of my fuckin' ear!"

To my surprise, she let me go and stepped back, grinning from ear to ear. "Which was my whole point." She called out to whoever was in the car. "You see? Come on out."

I rubbed my ear, trying to get blood moving again as well as ease the ache. As I was working up to a scathing remark to Lana, the doors to the car opened and a boy of about eleven or twelve got out of the back while a short, slender woman emerged from the front. She wasn't much taller than the boy, and it was a tossup as to who weighed more.

My heart thumped painfully in my chest and I froze. She had short, shaggy curls in a riot of orange around her head, and skin as creamy as milk. Her eyes were the palest blue I'd ever seen and almost too big for her face. But what had me wanting to howl in rage, what had me ready to murder some motherfucking son of a bitch, was the bruise across her cheek, the fingermark bruises on her bare arms, and the cut on her lower lip that stood out like an accusation.

I swallowed as I stood to my full height, still rubbing my ear absently. The kid moved in front of his mother but stood his ground.

"See, Violet? This isn't a man who's going to hurt you."

"What do you need?" My gaze bore straight into Violet's, trying to pull the information I wanted out of her head so I could go kill someone. *Déjà vu* but I didn't care. I'd charge hell with a water pistol and damned the consequences if this woman said to.

"I-I just w-wanted someone strong to be here to support my s-son." Her voice was melodious and soft. Like an angel whispering. She was obviously nervous, that didn't make her any less beautiful or courageous. "M-my husband can be…" she trailed off.

"Where do you need me, Ms. Violet?" Because parole or not, there was no way I was leaving this woman to deal with some asshole on her own.

"Come with us, Riot." Lana took over, ushering me forward, urging all of us toward the courthouse. "All you need to do is what the judge tells you. This is her last hearing of the day, on purpose. I wanted as few people here as manageable, and she agreed."

"Hoping to keep the spectacle to a minimum?"

"Yeah. I know Doug Harrington will have a whole legal team with him. It's what he does. Everything is about him. Everything is for show and maximum effect. He's the big man in the room. The last thing I want is to give him any more ways to intimidate this woman or her son. They need someone just as intimidating on their side." She hurried us all through the doors and to the metal detectors. All I had on me was my bike keys and the phone.

Once through security and inside the elevators she continued. "Judge Whitmore will give you instructions, but I want you to stick by Caleb's side like glue unless she backs you off. That means you escort him to the witness stand, and you stay as close to him as Judge Whitmore will let you. If she doesn't tell you to sit, you stand where she stops you. Keep an eye on as many of Harrington's entourage as you can. If you think there's someone we need to watch out for in the future, I want you to tell me."

"He harassin' them?" I needed more information,

and I knew there was no way I was going to get it all before we got inside the courthouse.

"Subtly. He's careful about what he does and who can see. Violet's filing for divorce, which he doesn't want to grant, along with full custody of their son with no unsupervised visits, which he's not willing to give up."

"She divorcin' him because he beats her?" I glanced at Violet. She winced and ducked her head. Which wouldn't do. Not at all. "Hey," I said in a sharp command. She winced again but glanced up at me. "This ain't your fault, honey. You've got nothing to duck your head about. Not to me or anybody else." I glanced at Caleb before turning my attention back to Lana. "What led up to this?"

"The kid saw." She shrugged. "Caleb forced her hand by calling her out, telling her she had to leave Doug or he was going to kill the bastard himself."

"I ain't a kid," Caleb grumbled.

"Caleb, honey, hush." God, how could a woman's voice be so beguiling? I wanted her to keep speaking just so I had the pleasure of hearing her. Violet could read the fucking phone book for all I cared.

I studied the kid closely. He met my gaze with a defiant, angry one of his own. And, God, this was hitting too fucking close to home.

"Are you tryin' to kill me, Lana?" I asked her softly. I could see myself when I looked at that kid's face. Hell, I saw that same look in the mirror most mornings.

She merely raised an eyebrow. "Maybe I'm just trying to keep history from repeating itself." Lana reached over and released the elevator. It slid smoothly to a stop and opened. A couple people looked on curiously, but no one said anything.

I let her lead the way, thinking about what she'd told me. When we got to the correct courtroom and Lana reached for the door, I put my hand on hers to stop her. "When this is over, I want to read their file."

"Not happening." Her reply was instantaneous, no hesitation.

"You'll give it to me so I can be prepared for what happens next, Lana."

She gave me an arrogant lift of her chin. "Only if you're all in."

I opened the door and stepped back for her to precede me. "You fuckin' know I am," I whispered angrily. "It was guaranteed the moment you told me their story."

She smirked as she entered the courtroom. "It was guaranteed before that." One thing Lana was good at was reading people, so there was no doubt in my mind she'd taken in every minute detail of my reaction to Violet when she stepped out of that fucking car.

Lana led us down the center aisle and through the gallery. She had me and Caleb sit in the first row of seats behind her and Violet. The boy had a complex look of fear, anger, frustration, and worry on his face. It was an all too familiar feeling.

"Your dad hit you?" I asked the question softly, for the kid's ears only.

"He tried to, but he was drunk. Has shit aim when he's drunk." Caleb didn't look at me. His eyes were firmly on his mother.

"He hit your mom?"

Caleb was silent so long I wasn't sure he was going to answer me. Then he nodded his head. "Yeah. He fuckin' hit her."

I knew I should probably correct the kid's

language, but fuck it. If the kid could testify against his father, he could fucking swear. "This the first time?"

He snorted. "First time I caught him. Mom lies and tells me she hit a door or fell down the stairs. She stopped trying to make up an elaborate explanation months ago."

"Christ." I scrubbed my hand over my mouth. I looked at Violet. I barely had a view of her profile, but I could see her trembling where she sat. Lana leaned in to speak with her several times. She laid a hand on Violet's arm in reassurance. Violet didn't say anything, only nodded occasionally.

"All rise," the bailiff commanded. I stood with Caleb as a short, round woman with a stern expression entered from the side. "Court is now in session, Judge Evelyn Whitmore presiding."

"Take your seats." Judge Whitmore waved her hand absently as she situated herself in her chair and opened a folder. When she looked up, she removed her glasses, an impatient look on her face. "We seem to be missing half of the involved parties." She raised an eyebrow and addressed the other lawyer in the room. "Counselor? Where's your client."

The guy adjusted his glasses while tapping frantically on his phone. "Uh, he should be here, uh, any minute now." He didn't stand or look up from his phone.

Judge Whitmore continued to look at the guy who was completely ignoring her. "Excuse me, Mr. Todd. Am I interrupting something important?" Any idiot could see she was heading past irritated to straight up pissed off. Everyone except for Mr. Todd, apparently.

"I'm letting Mr. Harrington know you're here. He doesn't like to be kept waiting and preferred to arrive after you did so he doesn't have to be here a moment longer than he needs to be."

"Bastard," Caleb muttered. A bit too loudly.

"Can't argue with that assessment, young man." Judge Whitmore pursed her lips. "But I'm going to have to ask you not to use that language in my courtroom." Poor lady looked like she'd swallowed a lemon.

"I'm sorry, Your Honor," Caleb said softly. "My mom taught me better."

Judge Whitmore looked slightly startled, but also studied Caleb closely, as if seeing more than just a disgruntled, angry preteen.

"Apology accepted, young man." She took a stack of papers from her desk and straightened them before laying them back in front of her. I knew the look of a person considering their words before speaking. Not that this woman cared if she broke protocol or said something someone might take offense at. No. I pegged her as a consummate professional in the face of *un*professionals. She was determined to stay above their level, even if it meant she had to ignore stupidity on occasion. "Mr. Todd?" She pointed to his phone. "Your client?"

"He hasn't answered me yet, Your Honor." He peered at the screen briefly. "Uh, as soon as he opens the message he'll know to come to the courthouse."

"I see." Judge Whitmore didn't look the least bit impressed. "In that case, I'm going to assume Mr. Harrington is unwilling to be here for… however long it takes him to get here, and we'll get started now." She raised her hand and motioned to the bailiff. "Will you please relieve Mr. Todd of his phone, Officer James. There are no phones permitted in court, as you know. Officer James will have someone check your phone with security and you may pick it up when you leave."

"Your Honor. You can't start until my client arrives. He has the right to face his accusers. Also, I have multiple important clients who need me at a moment's notice. The phone stays with me."

"Sure he has the right to face his accusers. Which is why he was called here today. If he chooses not to show up, that's his choice. If he chooses not to show up, that's his choice. Also, either the phones goes with Officer James, or you go to jail and this hearing is over. Then I'll let the young man go with whomever he chooses, which I likely will anyway given your client's conduct regarding respect for the court by not showing up. Because it's inconvenient for such an important man to wait on something as trivial as emergency custody of his own child." She raised an eyebrow. "Your choice."

When he sighed and handed over his phone, she continued. "Now. This hearing is for emergency custody of Mr. Caleb Harrington solely to his mother, Mrs. Violet Harrington, temporarily suspending the parental rights of Mr. Douglas Harrington. Is that about the gist of it?"

Lana stood, her shoulders back. "It is, Your Honor."

"Very well. Now, for ease of communication, I'd like to use first names with the affected parties. So," she addressed Doug, "Mr. Douglas." Then she turned to Violet and Caleb. "Mrs. Violet. Mr. Caleb. Does everyone understand?" When everyone acknowledged her, she continued. "Now where would you like to begin, Ms. Thompson?"

"Mr. Caleb is here today, willing to explain." Lana placed a hand on Caleb's shoulder.

"Your Honor, this is highly improper!"

"No, Mr. Todd. Your client might think he's better than everyone else, but in my courtroom, he's on the wrong side of the bench." She turned, her sharp gaze focusing on Caleb. "Young man, for the record, are you Mr. Caleb Harrington?"

Caleb stood up straight. "Uh, yes, I am, Your Honor." He added the last part as he cleared his throat, clearly nervous but trying so hard to do and say the right thing.

"Good. Who's your friend?" She met and held my gaze.

Caleb turned, looked down at me, and swallowed. The kid was trying his best, but this was an unfamiliar situation. I could relate to where he was coming from. I'd literally been there.

Slowly, I stood. When I straightened, I put a light hand on Caleb's shoulder. "My name's Quinn Devereaux, Your Honor. I'm here to support Mr. Caleb, so he knows he's got a protector for him and his mother. Someone to stand up for them." I could see Violet's shoulders slump as I spoke. The woman was… beaten down. She was expecting to lose this hearing and have her world shattered.

"That's great, Judge Whitmore." Mr. Todd waved a hand toward me. "Have a thug here to intimidate my client? On behalf of Mr. Harrington, I demand you make this guy leave immediately."

"Oh, Mr. Todd," Judge Whitmore shook her head in a way that said she was sorry for the guy when she really wasn't. "You've just earned contempt charges. The fine won't be light and there will be no getting out of paying." The guy opened his mouth, probably to protest or some shit but Judge Whitmore continued. "The next offense for you opening your big mouth and not following my rules, Mr. Todd, will be a night in jail. You might manage to get yourself out on bail before morning, but I'm willing to bet you'd love to avoid those few hours you'd be in a holding cell -- with several other men awaiting their arraignment." Then she addressed me. "Mr. Devereaux, I happen to know your current circumstances." She didn't elaborate. "I'm inclined to believe you're not here to cause trouble." She raised an eyebrow like she was an overly patient teacher waiting for the correct answer from a slightly naughty first grader. I didn't take offense.

"No plans on starting trouble, Your Honor." I tried to smile, but not very hard. This wasn't my courtroom or my problem in any way, and I was already pissed as fuck at this Doug Harrington prick. "I'm here to support Mr. Caleb and his mother. Nothing more." I paused, glancing over at the little weasel, Todd. "Though, I won't lie and say I won't be *thinkin'* about causin' trouble." I let my Southern accent out in a rolling drawl as full of sarcasm as it was geniality. "Just a bit."

"A *bit* of trouble I can handle, young man. Just mind your manners and I think we'll all be fine."

Even though my anger still smoldered, I felt my lips twitch. I liked this judge. "Yes, Your Honor."

Chapter Two

Violet

I knew the second two police officers escorted Doug into the courtroom things were going to go bad for me. The only question was how hard it would be on Caleb. Doug hadn't physically hurt Caleb, but I knew he was capable of it. For some reason, though, he'd held himself back until now. I wasn't sure what had changed, but there had been a definite shift in power dynamics. Doug was having to be more aggressive with Caleb to keep his dominance, so when Caleb laid down his ultimatum -- leave Doug or Caleb was going to kill him -- I had to leave. I absolutely believed Caleb would kill Doug if he had half a chance.

A firm grip on my shoulder had me turning to look over it. Caleb gave me a steady look. I swear to God, the kid was too grown up for my peace of mind. I should be the one giving him support, not the other way around. I smiled, reaching up to squeeze his hand.

"It's gonna be all right, Mom." He must have seen my unease as I'd watched Doug walk in. I knew better than Caleb what the look on his dad's face meant, but Caleb knew his dad was absolutely furious.

"I got your back, too." Riot's deep voice sent a shiver through me. A quick glance his way and I met his gaze for a brief moment. His eyes were piercing, like he could see all my fears and pain and thought he was ready to help me fight them. He'd soon find out he was wrong. No one took on Douglas Harrington and won.

"Thank you." I tried to smile, but wasn't sure I actually managed it. Then I met my son's gaze and I really did smile. Not so much to reassure him as because I couldn't help it. Caleb would always make me smile as long as he was in the world. I'd fight for him with everything in me, but if either me or Caleb ended up killing Doug, it wasn't going to be Caleb.

"I've got you both." Riot put his hand on top of Caleb's, as if he were shielding us by putting himself between us and everything else. I knew it was fanciful thinking, but just once in my life, I wanted someone to fight for me. For Caleb. I'd die for my son, but I knew his father wouldn't. In fact, I was fairly certain Doug would sacrifice Caleb if it was in his own best interest.

The judge had been giving Doug and his attorney a piece of her mind, but everything seemed to have calmed down now. Lana leaned into me. "Don't say or do anything. Don't move a muscle unless Judge Whitmore gives you explicit instructions. Understand?" I nodded. Lana seemed like she was looking forward to whatever was about to happen. I turned my attention back to the proceedings.

"Now that we understand proper courtroom etiquette, perhaps we can move on?" She raised her eyebrows as her gaze landed on Doug and his lawyer, obviously waiting for one of them to say something.

"Yes, Your Honor. We sincerely apologize for any offense caused the court." Doug's lawyer was always good at making any wrong he did or harm he caused seem like nothing. Like any offense was subjective and open to interpretation, and his interpretation was really the only one that mattered.

Judge Whitmore merely nodded, a small grin on her face. "I see." And I was certain the woman really *did* see. I might have lucked into the one judge in the whole district who wouldn't cave to Doug's demands. "Ms. Thompson. Tell me why we're here."

Lana stood and immediately got to the point. "Your Honor, my client is requesting emergency custody of her son, Mr. Caleb Harrington, for alleged mental and physical abuse. I'd like to add that I've brought this matter before the court at the request of Mr. Caleb himself. Not his mother."

Judge Whitmore smiled kindly as she looked over my shoulder to Caleb. "Young man, is this true?"

Caleb looked over at Riot who nodded. Caleb stood and cleared his throat. "Yes, ma'am. I-I mean, Your Honor --"

"Your Honor," Mr. Todd interrupted, "Mr. Caleb's a child. A very impressionable one who loves his mother. Violet has manipulated her son just as she tried to manipulate Mr. Doug. Poor Mr. Caleb can't see his mother's duplicity."

"That's not true." Caleb clenched his fists at his side. He hadn't yelled, but he hadn't been quiet with his remark.

Judge Whitmore raised a hand to silence Caleb. My son murmured a soft, "Sorry, Your Honor," and lowered his head.

"It's my understanding, young man, that you want to tell me everything you saw. Is that correct?"

"Yes, ma'am."

I gasped. "Saw?" My voice wasn't much more than a whisper. Lana gripped my knee hard, a warning to shut up. I hadn't realized Caleb had actually witnessed anything other than the end of the incident. He hadn't said anything to me to indicate he'd been there any longer than a few seconds.

Judge Whitmore's gaze zeroed in on me. Yeah. She hadn't missed my reaction. Then she sat back in her seat. "Very well, young man. Why don't you come up here and sit beside me." She indicated the seat next to her where witnesses would be called to give their account.

Riot was sitting on the outside of the aisle, so he had to stand in order for Caleb to get out of the row of seats. I'm not sure what I thought Riot would do. Maybe stand there? But he followed Caleb to the chair she'd indicated and kept going until he stood beside my son. Judge Whitmore held up a hand for him to stop, and Riot did. Instead of standing there with his arms crossed over his chest to intimidate, he adopted a relaxed pose with one hand over the other wrist in front of him. He stood perfectly still, not shifting his weight or even moving his head.

"Your Honor, I object to this man being so close to my client's son. It's clear he's here to intimidate the boy."

Caleb opened his mouth, then closed it tightly. He kept looking at the judge, clearly itching for her to tell him he could talk.

"You seem like you want to say something, Mr. Caleb." Judge Whitmore leaned forward slightly as she addressed him. "Is the man who followed you to the stand intimidating you? Say the word and I'll have him escorted out straight to a holding cell. You won't have to worry about him."

"No, ma'am. Riot's got my back. He's here so I don't have to be intimidated by *him*." Caleb pointed to Doug and my heart broke a little bit. Not for Doug. The man was a serious ass from the day I met him. But for Caleb. He'd known something was wrong, but the night he came home right after Doug had beaten me, something inside Caleb broke. I saw it happening right before my eyes that night. I thought he'd only seen the aftermath of that beating, but was it possible Caleb had actually witnessed more?

"I'm your father, Caleb," Doug said, his voice soft and reasonable. "You know I'd never hurt you. Or your mother." It sounded like he'd added that last almost as an afterthought.

"I *saw* you." Caleb stared at his father calmly. His voice shook slightly but that was the only obvious betrayal of his emotions. At least to everyone else. I could tell by the set of his jaw he was holding himself together by a thread. He was angry. So very angry. Every single ounce of it was directed at his father. "I heard everything you said. And I saw what you did from the beginning until *I* stopped you." Caleb didn't back down. He continued to stare his father down. Oh, this wasn't good. Caleb was done. If he had to go home with Doug, Caleb would kill him. Doug narrowed his gaze but said nothing, letting his lawyer take over. I had to wonder if he saw the same things in Caleb I did. Somehow, I doubted it. Doug might now be picking up on the fact Caleb was losing his fear of Doug, but I doubted Doug knew the extent of his son's anger.

"Your Honor." Mr. Todd stood, sighing wearily, as if this was all so much a waste of time he didn't understand why he was being subjected to the proceeding at all. "I'd like to state again, for the record this time, you simply cannot put much stock what the boy might say. He's a parrot for his mother, who is doing everything she can to grab money. She thinks she can get sole custody so she can demand a hefty divorce settlement."

Caleb looked as frustrated as I'd ever seen him, like he was warring with getting his say in and being respectful as Lana had warned him. We absolutely could not get on this judge's bad side. Ms. Thompson had said the only real way to make an enemy of Judge Whitmore was to disrespect her or her courtroom. I knew if anyone could manage to disrespect anything, it would be Douglas Harrington. Not his son.

Judge Whitmore let Mr. Todd go on for a couple minutes before he finally seemed to run out of steam, as well as running out of reasons Caleb and I couldn't be trusted to tell the truth.

"Are you finished telling me who I can and cannot question in my own court, Mr. Todd?"

"I only want it on record for when we have to go above your jurisdiction on appeal." Oh, Judge Whitmore didn't like that at all. It wasn't unexpected. Mr. Todd always had a plan. He was tough as nails and fucking smart. Not to mention all kinds of intimidating. Just like Doug. Between them, they had nearly everyone who mattered in the city under their thumbs... including a number of judges.

"Before we go any further, I want to make sure I understand something." She raised her eyebrows and looked askance at Mr. Todd.

"Your Honor?" I'd met Edward Todd on a number of occasions. Always, he and Doug were above everyone else. What Doug wanted, Mr. Todd made happen. Having someone push back and challenge their authority wasn't something Mr. Todd was used to. He would handle the issue, but it wasn't an ordinary occurrence.

"If I understand you correctly, the only people I should believe are you and your client? No one else can be trusted to tell me the truth?"

Mr. Todd gave her a confused look before he blanked his expression. "I didn't say that."

"No. You said Mrs. Violet is only here because she wants money. Mr. Caleb is only going to say what his mother tells him. Neither of them can be trusted. What about opposing counsel? Can I trust her to tell the truth?"

"I believe you've misunderstood what I was

trying to say. I was only pointing out Mrs. Violet has ulterior motives and an agenda. You should take what she says accordingly."

"So, only you and your client can be trusted," she repeated.

Mr. Todd shook his head. "I don't understand the question, Your Honor. I've explained my reasoning --"

"Your objections are noted, Mr. Todd. Now, if I could be allowed to finish my questions for Mr. Caleb, I'd be grateful."

Mr. Todd waved his hand once with a flick of his wrist. "Carry on, Your Honor." I didn't think Mr. Todd understood the level of annoyance on Judge Whitmore's face. Likely he'd already come to the decision he was going to have to go a step past this judge. It's what Mr. Todd did. He analyzed the situation and adapted accordingly.

"Now, Mr. Caleb." Judge Whitmore turned her full attention to my son. "Will you please state for the record how old you are?"

"I'm twelve, Your Honor." His voice squeaked, something I knew Caleb hated. He'd hit puberty and not only was he as tall as me, his voice was trying to get deeper. I glanced at his father's face. The slight smirk wouldn't be missed by Caleb, but I was proud of my son for not reacting.

"What did you want to tell me, young man?" The judge was kind as she spoke to Caleb, but there was that no-nonsense teacher kind of vibe she had going on. It didn't seem like he was talking to an officer of the court, but more like a school counselor was having a conversation with him. My heart ached for Caleb. I dreaded what he was about to say. I wanted to spare him this. I never wanted him to get between me and

Doug, but I was out of options if I wanted to save my son.

"Caleb," I whispered, my heart breaking. "You don't have --"

"No, Mom. I do have to do this." His voice was firm but not unkind. "He doesn't get to hurt you again. For any reason." For the first time in his young life, Caleb met his father's gaze and didn't flinch. "I'm the reason Mom's leaving him," Caleb began. "I told her she had to because..." He trailed off and I willed him not to tell the judge he'd wanted to kill his father and had threatened to do so unless I left. He swallowed and closed his eyes briefly before focusing his hate-filled gaze on Doug. "Because Mom deserves someone who doesn't hurt her all the time."

Mr. Todd stood, a sad smile on his face. "Your Honor, are you really going to allow this to be on the record?"

"Mr. Todd, I'll deal with you when this hearing is over. Not another word." She turned back to Caleb. "Mr. Caleb, will you look at me, please?" Caleb hesitated a moment, but did as instructed. "Good. Say what you came to say, Mr. Caleb. Why do you want your mother to leave your father, and why do you want your mother to have full custody of you?"

"He's a monster," Caleb said without preamble. "I thought he might have hurt Mom before, but until a few months ago she'd always make up excuses, tell me how clumsy she is and everything. But you can only trip over a non-existent stray dog, or sleepwalk and fall down the stairs, or accidentally run into someone's lit cigar and burn yourself, so many times before the people who love you have to read between the lines."

"If that's all true, Mr. Caleb, why did you not say something earlier? Sounds like you've neglected your mother even though you profess to be concerned. Seems like you're only concerned now when you're angry at your father for grounding you for bad grades." Mr. Todd stood now, moving away from his table and toward Caleb. It was an obvious intimidation tactic.

"Mr. Todd," Judge Whitmore called sharply. "You are out of line. I've instructed you to remain silent, yet you continue to believe you're in charge. You are not."

"I'm allowed to cross examine the witness."

"This isn't a trial, Mr. Todd." She leaned forward as if speaking to a child. "This is an emergency custody hearing. The two have very different functions and rules, as a lawyer of your reputation should know. If not, may I suggest you have an associate better versed in the nuances of family court handle this hearing for you." She gave Mr. Todd a smile that held little humor. "You will get your chance to speak when it's your turn. Until then, I suggest you sit down and keep your objections to yourself." She leaned forward slightly, staring at Mr. Todd and Doug. "When that time comes, if I even get a hint of a vibe that makes me believe you're trying to intimidate Mr. Caleb, you'll be in even more trouble than you're already in, Mr. Todd."

She turned back to Caleb. "I apologize for the interruption, Mr. Caleb." I liked that she treated Caleb like an adult and not a child who didn't know his own mind or was unable to accurately give his account of what happened. "Please continue."

Caleb looked decidedly uncomfortable but put his chin up defiantly before he spoke. "I didn't want to be the reason Mom and Dad split up," Caleb said, his voice steadier now. "I thought maybe I was wrong. Maybe Mom really was just clumsy, and I was wrong about what was going on. But yesterday, I saw him." His voice cracked slightly prompting another chin lift from my sweet boy. "I came home early from a friend's house because I forgot my math book and had homework. I heard yelling from upstairs and thought maybe Mom was watching a movie or something."

I closed my eyes, bile rising in my throat. I hadn't known Caleb had seen anything. I'd been so careful to keep him away from Doug's outbursts.

"Go on," Judge Whitmore encouraged, her face neutral but her eyes kind. By contrast, I could see the rage building in Doug's eyes. I'd seen that look too many times to count and it never boded well. It was hard to hold a little whimper back, but I thought I managed. Until Lana put her hand over mine and squeezed tightly, a reminder to stay silent.

Caleb's shoulders straightened. I saw Riot shift his stance slightly, moving just a fraction closer to my son. It was subtle, but I felt a rush of gratitude for this stranger who seemed genuinely concerned for Caleb.

"He was hitting her." Caleb's voice dropped to almost a whisper. "Not just once. Over and over. She was on the floor, and he kept hitting and kicking her. Calling her worthless. Saying no one would ever want her, that she was lucky he even looked at her." Caleb's voice shook with rage now, his hands clenched into fists at his sides. "He said if she ever tried to leave, he'd kill her. That he'd make it look like an accident." He glared at Mr. Todd and snorted out a humorless laugh. "He even said Mr. Todd could get him out of any legal stuff if her death was investigated."

I could feel the tears streaming down my face as Caleb recounted what he'd witnessed. The shame burned through me. Not because of what Doug had done, but because my son had seen it. He was witness to the violence I'd allowed myself to endure. There was no way he could understand that I'd kept myself in an impossible situation because I knew that if I left, Doug would either make good on his threat to kill me or make sure I never saw Caleb again. Either way would put Caleb in his sights, and I had to be my son's protector.

Judge Whitmore nodded, her face impassive but her eyes sharp. "What did you do when you saw this, Mr. Caleb?"

"I ran in and jumped on his back." Caleb's voice had steadied, pride replacing the rage. "I tried to get him off her. He threw me off, but it was enough time for Mom to get up. She got between us and begged him not to touch me." His voice caught. "She was bleeding and could barely stand, but she was protecting me."

From the corner of my eye, I saw Riot shift his weight, his jaw clenched so tightly I could see the muscle jumping. His hands were no longer relaxed in front of him, but balled into fists. I'd seen the same look on Doug's face. In fact, they showed identical expressions. The difference was, Riot let his rage show in the set of his jaw, the way his eyes narrowed, and the slight snarl of his lip. Not to mention the way his clenched fists made the veins in his muscled arms stand out in a threatening relief. Every ounce of that malice was directed at Doug.

Then Riot turned his head to look straight at me. That anger smoldered around the edges of his visage, where Doug's face was carefully neutral. Riot's gaze burned into me like acid and for the first time, I saw the man for the killer he was. I sucked in a breath. I'd seen that exact expression on Caleb's face when he'd pulled Doug off me. It was why I'd thrown myself between the two of them. I absolutely would not let

Caleb kill his father.

Riot held my gaze for several seconds before focusing back on my son and Doug. There was something in his gaze that told me I was in so much trouble, but it felt different. He was angry with me, yes. But there was no malice in his anger. Kind of like when your dad caught you sneaking out of the house to go see your boyfriend. He was always mad, but you knew you weren't in any real danger. You just hated disappointing him because you were a daddy's girl. There was absolutely no reason for me to believe Riot wasn't just as violent, or more so, as Doug. I was certain he could be if he wanted to be. But that anger wasn't directed at me. It was directed at Doug.

"What happened then, Mr. Caleb?" Judge Whitmore prompted Caleb to continue when he paused for too long.

Caleb blinked several times as if pulling himself back into the moment. "Then he turned on me. He didn't hit me. He tried to get me to..." He trailed off, his angry gaze so filled with accusation and loathing I was worried the judge would see into Caleb's very heart and know the boy was capable of killing Doug. Then Caleb cleared his throat. "He tried to get me to help him punish my mom for... something. I don't remember." Caleb turned to the judge. "I would never, *ever* hurt my mother, Your Honor. For any reason."

"Of course you wouldn't. Then what happened, Mr. Caleb?"

"He was angry, but he left. He stormed out of the house and took off. I made Mom pack a bag and we left. Mom was too hurt to drive so I called..." Caleb trailed off, clearing his throat before starting again. "I called a friend who sent Ms. Thompson to pick us up." I could see the tension in him. Caleb was choosing his words carefully, not wanting to reveal anything that could possibly get someone else in trouble with Doug. He was a powerful man in the city, and his reach was long.

"I see." Judge Whitmore looked from Doug to Caleb and back. I was sure the other woman could feel the tension from both father and son. It was something that had been building for months. Caleb hadn't known everything, but he'd known something was wrong, and whatever it was centered around his father.

"Your Honor, we would like to know who this person is so we can question them ourselves."

"As I've already told you, Mr. Todd, this is a hearing. Not a trial. There are no charges being filed, only a hearing on the appropriateness of emergency custody of your client's son. You are not entitled to anything at present."

"Again, I would like to note my objection for future appeals."

"I've had enough. Either you're too stupid to understand, or just a petty, mean-spirited person who believes he's above the law. Either way, I'm finding you in contempt of court. You were warned multiple times and refused to change your attitude so here you are."

"I'll take care of the fine before I leave, Your Honor." Mr. Todd's smile was filled with as much contempt as the charge. But so was Judge Whitmore's.

"Oh, I don't think you quite understand, Mr. Todd. You'll most certainly pay a fine, but that's not the extent of your punishment. You'll also spend one hundred eighty-six hours in jail that I will not allow to be commuted to house arrest. I'm sure at some point you'll call someone who can make this all go away for you, but until that time, I hope you'll use your stay in the county's correctional facility to reflect on your behavior today and contemplate how you could have handled things with me differently. I'd also suggest you think about how you treat others, Mr. Todd." She turned to Caleb. "Now, Mr. Caleb, do you want to stay with your mother?"

"I do, Your Honor. I don't want anything to do with my father ever again."

"All right then. I believe you're an intelligent, articulate young man and are more than capable of deciding who you want to stay with."

"I don't want to ever have to go back with him, Your Honor."

"That's between you and your mother. I'm not putting restrictions on you being able to contact your father if you wish. Assuming divorce proceedings are eventually finalized, custody will be determined at a later date. I have every confidence your wishes will be heavily considered at the appropriate time, Mr. Caleb."

"Will you make it so he can't call us? I don't want him bothering my mom, and I have my own phone."

Judge Whitmore studied both Doug and Caleb for a long moment before responding. "I think that in this situation, I'm going to grant your request, Mr. Caleb. You're not to contact your son or your wife for any reason, Mr. Doug. If there is an emergency, you will go through nine-one-one and let the authorities contact her. Failure to follow these conditions will result in a contempt charge and land you next to your lawyer in county." She addressed Lana. "Ms. Thompson, is there anything more you wish to discuss?"

"Not at this time, Your Honor. Thank you."

Lana's tone was soft and respectful. It was obvious she had seen this scenario playing out in advance, assuming her side of the table minded their manners. I thought we'd done a fantastic job. I suppose now it was time to reap the benefits of our restraint.

"Mr. Devereaux." Judge Whitmore inclined her head. "Might I have a private word with you?"

Riot looked from Caleb to me, then to Lana. "Keep them here and stay with them. Do not let them out of your sight."

Lana raised an eyebrow. "Please," she said mildly.

"Thank you," Riot said, turning to follow the judge to her chambers, but Judge Whitmore crossed her arms over her chest and stared him down.

Riot gave a disgruntled sigh before turning back to Lana. "What I meant was, will you please keep Violet and Caleb company until Judge Whitmore is finished with me?"

Lana's lips twitched, but she nodded her head with a serious expression on her face. "Absolutely, I'll keep them company, Riot. Violet and Caleb are two of my favorite people." She gave Riot a death stare. The message was clear. Fuck with Violet and Caleb at his own risk.

"I appreciate you taking the extra time out of court, Lana. Thank you." Riot gave her a slight nod before turning back to Judge Whitmore. "Better?"

She gave a curt nod. "Better, young man." Then she led him to her chambers and shut the door.

I sat forward, putting my elbows on the table and my head in my hands. I wanted to get away from Doug. I wanted Caleb away from him too. Right now, the deputies were handcuffing Mr. Todd to take him away. I knew Doug would have someone on this the second he got outside. I didn't want to make eye contact, so I sat passively and tried to ignore everyone around me.

"Hey, you OK?" Lana rubbed her hand up and down my back, trying to soothe me.

"Yeah. I just want to get out of here and lock me and Caleb in our room for a day and a half. Just forget everything."

"Mom, you know he's not going to leave us alone. Right?"

I sighed, reaching up to stroke his face with my hand. He was getting peach fuzz on his cheeks. He tried to keep it shaved off, but he'd missed a spot this morning. "That's not for you to worry about, OK? I'll figure something out. Just be aware and protect yourself. I'll protect you too. We've got each other's backs, yeah?"

"Always, Mom." He looked uncomfortable. "Look, I'm not saying I trust him just yet. But maybe we could ask Riot to hang out with us for a couple of days? Just until things blow over."

"That's a very good idea, Caleb." Lana leaned against the table next to me. "Riot's a solid guy. I wouldn't lie to you about that for any reason. Yes, he's on parole. Maybe he'll feel comfortable telling you what happened. But trust me when I tell you he didn't do anything someone in his position wouldn't have wanted to do themselves."

Caleb sighed. "Maybe I was wrong and it's not a good idea to hang out with the ex-con."

"Caleb, honey." Lana gave him a stern look. "When you hear his story -- and I don't see a scenario where he doesn't tell you his story at some point -- you'll not only understand, but you'll also remember what you said just now and realize you were wrong to judge him without knowing all the facts. Riot is exactly the person you want protecting your mother and you from a man like Doug Harrington."

Caleb hung his head. "I'm sorry. You're right. I shouldn't judge. That was wrong."

"Christ." Lana shook her head. "Are you sure that kid has Doug Harrington's DNA?"

"Very sure. Though, I agree admitting he's wrong is not something Doug does easily."

Caleb snorted. "Or at all, really."

That got a small laugh from me. Or it might have been a sob. Either way, Caleb pulled me into his skinny arms and held me tight.

"It's gonna be OK, Mom. It's gonna be OK."

Chapter Three

Riot

I could count on one finger the number of times I'd been in a judge's chambers before. It hadn't turned out so well before. I hoped this time wouldn't end with me back in prison.

"Have a seat, Mr. Devereaux." Judge Whitmore gestured to a chair in front of her desk while she took off her robe and hung it on a hook beside her chair. She wore a crisp, white blouse and a dark suit skirt. Then she removed a suit jacket that matched her skirt from a hanger next to her robe and put it on. The woman really was freakishly formal. She sat on the edge of her seat, her forearms resting on her desk. "Why don't you tell me your plans now that you're rejoining society." She phrased her question congenially enough, but there was no doubt she expected an answer.

"I've only been out three days, Your Honor. I'm still trying to get used to sleeping in an actual bed."

"I imagine there is some adjusting to do." Her smile was genuinely kind. This woman was tough as nails, but she wasn't cruel or unreasonable. "When I said I was familiar with your situation, I meant I know you were brought here today as part of your parole agreement to offer support to Mr. Caleb."

When she didn't continue, I realized she expected a response. "Uh, right. Though, I'd like to point out I had no clue what I was walking into. Ms. Thompson's instructions were to be here at a certain time."

Judge Whitmore raised an eyebrow. "And would you have come if you'd known the situation?"

I scowled at her. "Of course! I'm a killer, Your Honor, but I'm not a monster." When she continued to stare at me, I sighed. "Fine. I'll admit, when I figured out what was going on, I balked. Hard. But there's no way I'd have refused. If you know my situation, you know why."

She gave me a satisfied nod. "I just wanted to hear it from you, because I have a favor to ask."

It was my turn to give her a look. "A favor. As in I have the right to refuse to grant said favor, but you'd advise me not to?"

Judge Whitmore chuckled. "No, Mr. Devereaux. This is fully your choice. I can promise you that I'll write a formal letter to your parole officer about how helpful you were in cooperating with unreasonable requests without complaints."

"This must be some favor." I waved my hand at her. "What is it you need, Your Honor?"

"I want you to keep an eye on Mrs. Violet and Mr. Caleb. Escort her to and from work, and Mr. Caleb to and from school. Check in with her throughout the day."

"You want me to be her bodyguard?"

"No. I want you to be a friend who's concerned about her safety, given she has a narcissistic soon-to-be-ex-husband who has allegedly been violent toward her in the past and is very likely not too happy with her at the moment."

I had to replay her little speech over in my mind to make sure I'd heard her correctly. "You want me to worm my way into her life so I can protect her?"

"Exactly."

"I'm not going to pretend to be something I'm not with her. I'll tell her I can count my time with her as part of my community service or something, but I'm not going to pretend to be her friend just so I can be a bodyguard on the down-low."

"Who said you had to pretend? Have you talked to her?"

"I think you know I haven't said much to her. And I get where you're going. But I don't think a woman as vulnerable as she is right now needs a man like me in her life. Not even as a friend."

"So you won't do this?"

I snorted out a laugh. "Didn't say that. I'll keep a very close eye on her and her son. I'll protect them to the best of my ability. If she reaches out to me, I won't refuse to spend time with her, but considering what she's about to go through, are you sure it's the best idea that she associates closely with a convicted killer?"

"Considering the nature of the charges against you and the account of events from the trial transcript, I'd say you're the perfect man for her to be closely associated with."

"Puts Violet in her husband's crosshairs. I don't know much about him but sounds to me like he's got deep pockets and spreads the wealth where it benefits him. He could use me against her."

"You worry about keeping Violet and Caleb safe. I'll take care of the legal aspects of your concerns." I had other concerns but nothing Judge Whitmore could help with, so I kept them to myself.

"I'll watch over them and keep them safe."

"Good. I'll let you get to your charges. Make sure to check in with Ms. Thompson regularly. I want her involved directly, especially if you have concerns with Mr. Doug. I try to be as impartial as humanly possible. Pride myself in my ability to be willing to look at both sides of a situation with equal weight. That being said, I can't ignore basic human decency. That woman and her son need a strong support system. Not just to handle their current situation, but to survive. She doesn't have anyone to help her at the moment. What I'm asking is for you to be her support. You and your club. And yes, I know about Gavin Ferguson and Gage Bohannon. Your president and vice president?"

I shrugged. "Honestly, I just got there. But I think the men you're talking about, Torpedo and Bohannon, left to go back to Kentucky. Knuckles has taken over again."

"Ah. Yes. I wasn't sure when they'd turn the reins back over to the locals. Surprising, but not unexpected." She smiled. "A few of us are working independently together to help women and children in abusive situations."

"Are you saying you manipulate the law? Turn it to benefit you or someone you know?" I couldn't help the little dig. Old grudges die hard. Besides, Judge Whitmore was too perfect to be believed.

She didn't flinch. "If I have to."

We regarded each other for several seconds, neither of us willing to flinch. Finally, she stood, extending her hand to me. "Try to get Caleb to talk to you, Mr. Devereaux. He's holding some big feelings inside him right now and it's not good for him."

I shook my head. "I'm not a psychiatrist, ma'am. I don't want the kid scarred for life."

"He already is, Mr. Devereaux. Tell him about your experience. Caution him to think about his actions before he commits to them."

"I know what you're asking, ma'am. Not sure I'm the one to have that conversation with him because, begging your pardon, Your Honor, I don't regret one Goddamned thing I did."

She squeezed my hand but nodded sadly. "I figured as much. I'd still like you to consider telling him your story. He's an intelligent young man. Give him all the information and he'll come to the right conclusion."

I let go of her hand. "I'll think about it."

"Thank you, Mr. Devereaux."

As I exited the judge's chambers, I thought about what she'd said. I wasn't sure if I was ready to talk about my past with anyone yet. Sure, it was a long time ago, but that wound was still raw and aching. The less time I spent thinking about everything that had happened, the better.

Lana was speaking quietly with Violet, who looked shell-shocked and grief-stricken. Caleb sat next to his mom holding her hand. I zeroed in on where their hands were connected. Violet clung to Caleb, her knuckles white. Caleb patted her hand with his other one while Lana continued to speak.

Caleb let his mom take what comfort she could, but it was easy to see her tears were hurting the young man. The only other person in the courtroom was the bailiff, and he looked like he was getting ready to leave as soon as the four of us did. Harrington and his lawyer were nowhere to be seen. I had a feeling he'd turn up again sooner than I wanted.

When I approached, Lana stood, meeting my gaze. "Everything all right?"

"Yes." I did my best to smile and be as non-threatening as possible, but I was a big guy and the very reason I was here was because I was physically intimidating. "Judge Whitmore thought it would be a good idea if I stay in touch with the three of you." I glanced from Lana to Caleb, then Violet. "I agree with her."

Caleb stood and put his shoulders back. "I can take care of my mom." His gaze darted to Lana then back to me. "But I don't believe it's possible to have too many people looking out for her. I know I'm just a kid so I won't have much weight with adults, so I'd appreciate it if you'd help keep Mom safe from Dad."

OK, I could work with this. I could tell he was suspicious of me, and I didn't blame him. "You know both Lana and Judge Whitmore believe I can help you. Right?"

The young man nodded at me. "I know you were in jail and that means you did something bad."

I nodded. "Yeah, man. I did."

"Do you regret it?"

Christ! This is what I wanted to avoid. As a rule, I tried never to lie. This was the most delicate of situations and the kid had just steamrolled his way straight to the heart of the matter. If I told him I regretted what I'd done, then he found out how thoroughly I *did not* regret my actions, he'd never trust me again. Not for lying about this particular subject. But if I told him the same thing I'd told Judge Whitmore, I knew better than anyone what kind of trigger that confession could be for the kid.

Instead, I took a deep breath, taking my time before speaking. "I don't lie, Caleb. Not intentionally. So before I answer that question, will you let me think about it a while?"

He gave me a confused look. "Why would you have to think about it? Was it worth going to prison for or not?"

"I want to think about it because…" I trailed off. "Christ, I'm fixin' to sound like a fuckin' shrink," I muttered, scrubbing the back of my neck then over my face with my hand. "Because I've always thought about what happened one way, but I need to think about it… the other way."

The women both blinked up at me, then looked at each other. Violet gave her a look like "the fuck?" Lana just shrugged.

"You don't sound like a shrink," Caleb offered.

"Thanks, kid," I muttered.

"No," Caleb continued. "You sound really, really confused." He tilted his head to the side. "Are you having a stroke? You kinda look like you're having a stroke."

"What?"

"You know. Like old people do sometimes. Your words aren't slurred, but are you having trouble finding your words or something?"

"I-I'm not…"

"Mom, we might want to call an ambulance for him. I don't think he's all right."

Lana snorted, then tried to cover her laughter with a cough. Failing miserably at covering her amusement, she finally outright laughed. "I'm sorry, Caleb. It's not you. Oh, God, Riot! You should see the look on your face!"

I glared at Lana, which didn't seem to faze her at all. A quick look at the fucking bailiff caught the smile he tried to hide when I turned my gaze on him. "You'd think us guys could stick together."

"Sorry, man, but I'm looking forward to you explaining that one myself."

"Which part?" I muttered. I don't know why I set myself up like that, but there it was.

"All of it. 'Cause, honestly, you do kinda sound like you're having a stroke."

I heaved out a long-suffering sigh. Then I noticed something that absolutely sealed my fate. Violet looked up at me and she was… smiling. There were tears in her eyes and staining her cheeks, but the smile was genuine and absolutely fucking breathtaking. I had to brace myself on the court gallery banister railing or I'd have fallen to my fucking knees.

The filly was a fucking angel. Never had I seen such a beautiful smile, or such a beautiful woman. Even with tears still falling and dark circles under her eyes, likely from stress and worry, that fucking smile was more than I could take. There was no defense to mount. I'd lost the war before I even fired a shot. Hell. I'd lost before I knew there even *was* a war. The tiny woman in front of me, terrified, beaten, but determined to fight for her son, stole my heart, planted a flag, and claimed my fucking soul.

The second I acknowledged I now belonged to Violet, my insides settled and something clicked into place. This was where I was supposed to be. This place. With this woman and her son. In a way, I suppose my whole life had been heading toward this moment.

Maybe Judge Whitmore was right. I had to really, really think about what these feelings inside me meant for my future. More importantly, what would it mean for Violet and Caleb's future? I knew I'd always watch over the two of them. There was no question about that. I also knew there'd never be another woman for me. The only question was, could I protect her from afar while she lived a happy life with some stupid motherfucker who didn't deserve her and would never give his whole entire being to her the way I would?

Fuck. There was definitely something wrong with me, because there was no way this woman wasn't going to be mine. No matter what it took, no matter who I had to kill, Violet was going to be my woman.

Chapter Four

Violet

I glanced at Riot as he mounted his motorcycle. In another life, I'd have been terrified of him. He was big, tattooed, and muscled. Attractive in a bad-boy way, I was sure. I'd gotten over my parents' assertion that men like Riot were trouble. Which was kind of laughable, considering the man they picked out for me was a monster. I was also fairly certain they weren't interested in finding out, not as long as Doug continued to do business with my father.

Lana unlocked her vehicle, and I got in beside her while Caleb got in the back. She started the car, then turned to me. Taking my hand, she gave me an encouraging smile. "Riot's been through a lot, but he's a good guy. I'd have gotten someone else if I didn't believe he'd protect you with his life."

"I thought you only wanted him to support Caleb while he was telling the judge about his father."

"That was one reason. I admit I also wanted him to stay close to both you and Caleb. Doug Harrington isn't the type of man who likes to lose. You know he'll try to intimidate you. Or worse." She squeezed my hand once more before starting the vehicle.

I looked out the window at Riot, who was adjusting his leather vest and seemed to be scanning the area around us before putting on a helmet and closing the tinted visor. I thought it odd, but if the guy was on probation, he was probably doing his best to avoid giving anyone a reason to look at him. Not my business.

There was something primal about Riot. Something dangerous making me both wary and... something else I wasn't ready to examine too closely.

"When you first told me about this, you said Riot had been to prison. It's obvious the judge knew it too. Can you tell me why he was in prison?"

"Does it matter, Vi? You saw how he was today. He's solidly on your side."

"Because you told him to be. For the right price, maybe he takes Doug's side."

Lana scowled at me and shook her head. "Are you not listening to anything I'm telling you? I don't pick bikers at random for my program, Vi. This isn't a volunteer program where you get what's available. Anyone I use in a particular case for victim support understands what it's like to be a victim. He might not have experienced exactly what you did, but he's been in a similar situation, and it changed him." She took a long breath, tamping down her building anger. Lana was the best person I'd ever met, but she was very passionate about people in general. "Look. You know I believe everyone deserves a second chance. Our choices in life sometimes take us down a dark path, but if we work hard enough, when we come out at the end of that tunnel, we're stronger and, hopefully, better for those experiences and consequences. Riot will protect you with his life. That's what his experiences made him into. There is no amount of money in the world that could make that man take Doug's side over yours and Caleb's. Riot is not a man who can be bought in this instance. Not for any price."

"Mom." Caleb leaned forward between the seats. "I think we should let him help us. Just for a little while, until we figure things out."

I turned to look at my son, surprised. Caleb had been slow to trust anyone since Doug's behavior had escalated. The fact that he was advocating for Riot's presence said a lot.

"You're sure?" I asked him.

"Yeah." Caleb's eyes were serious as he held my gaze. I wanted to cry. I wasn't looking into the eyes of a child. Sitting in the courtroom, telling the judge exactly what he'd seen and what had happened to him personally, all while his father stared at him with that accusing gaze, had effectively killed anything left of the child in Caleb. He still had a lot to learn but he was a young man, and he was determined to protect his mother. While I loved him all the more for that protective streak, I wanted to howl at the injustice of his childhood being cut short by a megalomaniac.

"All right," I said, relenting. "If you think it's a good idea and Caleb is OK with him, then we'll accept Riot's help for now."

Lana nodded, satisfied. "Good. Now let's get you both back to your hotel. You're booked under a different name. Right?"

"Yes." I continued to stare out the window as we pulled away. I could see Riot behind us in the rearview mirror. "I paid cash for two weeks." There was something reassuring about his large presence following us, like a shadow that for once meant protection rather than threat.

The small hotel where we were staying wasn't anything fancy. It was a chain hotel for people on a budget, so there were two beds, a bathroom, a small table, two chairs, and a tiny fridge. That was pretty much it. But you had to have a key card to get anywhere inside but the main entrance, so it was more secure than some hotels. I'd chosen a room like this on purpose because Doug would never look someplace like this for me. He thought I was a spoiled, dimwitted trophy wife, but my dad married me off to Doug to bring the rest of my family into Doug's lifestyle. I grew up on ramen noodles and cereal. This hotel was a couple steps up from some places I'd lived growing up.

We parked and Riot pulled alongside us, shutting down his bike. I opened my door and slid out. Caleb followed, putting himself between me and Riot. I thought the big man would take exception or act irritated. Instead, he met Caleb's gaze and gave him an approving nod. The gesture seemed to shock Caleb as much as it did me. Riot moved behind us while I led the way to the side entrance. I swiped us in, then we all headed down the hall.

"Are you sure your husband doesn't know where you're staying?" Riot's voice was soft and low, not quite a whisper but not much louder.

"If he knew where we were, he'd already have us back at the estate." I swiped open our room door. "Whether we wanted to go or not."

Riot nodded, a grim look on his face. Then he entered the room ahead of us, looking in the bathroom and small closet before letting us in. "Even if you're positive he doesn't know where you're staying, I'll feel better checking your room any time you come back here."

Caleb glanced at me, his eyes wide with shock. "Wow. That's just like in the movies."

"Well, I did watch a lot of TV in prison." Riot kept his face perfectly blank, but Caleb chuckled before trying to smother it with a cough. When he looked up at Riot, the man winked at my son before stepping further into the room so we could all go inside.

"You have my number, Violet. Make sure Caleb and Riot have it as well." Then she addressed Riot. "Let me know if you need anything and I'll get it done." He nodded, and Lana pulled me into her arms for a hug. "I'm going to help you through this. You're not alone, as you'll soon find out. Trust Riot, but you can always call me if you need a second opinion. You're not boxed in. OK?"

I nodded. "Yeah. I understand."

"Good. I'll leave you to it. Get to know Riot. Ask him questions. He'll either tell you or he won't, but I believe we've established he doesn't lie." That last was said like a dig at Riot when I knew she was trying to put me at ease. Riot must have known too, because he growled his displeasure.

Caleb shook his head with a wide grin. "That's never gonna get old." He flopped down on his bead and groaned. "That wasn't like I thought it was going to be."

"Oh? How's that?" After checking the door and even attaching the safety chain, Riot sat in one of the chairs while I took the other one.

Caleb turned his head to look at us. "I'm not really sure. I thought it would be harder somehow. Or like I'd feel sad." He turned to me. "I can see now how mean Dad was to you for a long time, but he wasn't bad to me. Not until that night."

"I'm so sorry, Caleb." I could feel the tears threatening again. I thought I'd cried all the tears left inside me, but apparently there were a few more. "I never wanted this for you."

"I don't want it for you either, but here we are." My son moved to the edge of the bed and turned to take my hands in his. "It hurts, Mom. I'm not gonna pretend it doesn't make either of us feel better. But he betrayed me too. Not in the same way he did you, but he made me believe he was a good man when he's really nothing but evil."

I closed my eyes and let out a breath. "You

deserve better than what you got handed, honey."

He shrugged. "Up until now, I've had a good life. Even now, it's not that bad. I'm gonna miss my gaming systems, but I was spending too much time on them anyway. One failed algebra test and all of a sudden he grounded me for my grades." He chuckled, like it was all a big joke.

It was on the tip of my tongue to defend the bastard. He'd ingrained it in me to agree with him. To show a united front. Not just with Caleb, but in every aspect of my life. I was to follow his lead. But he was wrong. And my son was worth fighting that instinct and admitting to him and myself I could form my own opinions and ideas.

"You failed one test. One test. And you failed because you were sick the day before the review. You've never been anything other than a straight A student. When he grounded you, you didn't say a word in protest, yet Doug and Mr. Todd made you sound like a petulant child." I had a good mad building. "If I ever see either of them again, I may punch them in the nose." I rarely got angry because it didn't do me any good with Doug. But when I lost my temper, it was the only time I was ever capable of fighting back.

I stopped to take a breath. I thought Caleb might say something to tease me like he did when I was upset on his behalf if he wanted to diffuse the situation. Instead, neither he nor Riot said anything. Caleb raised an eyebrow as he looked at Riot. Riot looked at me like he was trying to fit me neatly into a box, only to find out he couldn't quite make it work to suit him. There was a spark of something in his eyes, but I wasn't sure what. He was definitely looking at me differently.

"That was, uh…" Caleb cleared his throat before

continuing. "That was a lot of words, Mom." He gave me a solemn look. "And a little violent."

I blinked, looking from Caleb to Riot in confusion. "Violent?"

"Yeah," Caleb said. "I mean, we shouldn't punch people."

Riot snorted out a laugh before coughing like he'd gotten choked. Caleb cracked up too. I wanted to be irritated, but was so happy to see Caleb's smile I found myself laughing at my own expense. I wasn't sure I'd see him smile like this so soon. Sure, I'd seen a few sparks, but mostly when we were around Riot. In the couple hours we'd been around the man, Riot seemed to know what to say to make things, if not better, at least bearable. For that alone I could give Riot the benefit of the doubt.

"So, what do we do now?" I continued to hold Caleb's hand, but I addressed Riot.

He sat back in his chair and sprawled out lazily. "I'm going to go talk to the front desk and see if anyone's taken the adjoining room." He pointed to the door that would open into the next room. "It will simplify things."

"What if it's not available?" Caleb asked.

"I'll worry about that if it comes to it."

Chapter Five

Riot

I *was* able to get the adjoining room next to Violet and Caleb. She shut their door with the promise not to lock it, but I left mine open. As I lay on top of the covers on the bed, I thought about the two people in the other room. Caleb was already a good man. He went out of his comfort zone to help his mother without explanation. Someone had hit his mother. That's all he needed to know. The why or the who didn't matter. Only that she be protected.

Then there was Violet. Something about her drew me like gravity. Maybe it was the vulnerability mixed with that flare of temper I saw from her when she talked about how her husband and his lawyer had spoken about Caleb. She wasn't completely broken despite what her husband had done to her.

I rolled onto my back, my gaze fixed on the open door separating our rooms. I could hear them talking softly, their voices a gentle murmur that somehow made me feel more at peace than I had in years. Prison had a way of hollowing you out, making you forget what it felt like to just exist in normal spaces with normal people.

My phone buzzed on the nightstand. Knuckles.

"Yeah," I answered, keeping my voice low.

"How'd it go? Lana called. Said you're all set up at the hotel."

I grunted in affirmation. "Judge wants me to stick close. Play bodyguard."

There was a pause on the other end. "And you're good with that?"

"It's not exactly hardship duty." I sat up, rubbing a hand over my face. "The kid's solid. Smart.

Mom's..." I trailed off, not sure how to describe Violet. "Complicated."

"Complicated as in a headache for me?"

"Nah. Headache's all the bastard she's married to. Violet's doing the best she can in a bad situation. I have her side of things -- well, Caleb's anyway -- but I'm betting she's had it rough almost from the beginning of her relationship with Harrington."

"I've got Knight going over the files Lana gave me on Harrington, as well as Violet's parents and her homelife before she got involved with Harrington."

"Good. Thanks, prez. Thanks for giving me a chance here."

"You did the right thing for the right reasons, man. You took the consequences like a man and did your time."

"I'm not sure I can look that kid in the eyes and tell him I'm sorry I killed that motherfucker, and I'm really not sure telling him the truth is the best idea. The look in his eyes when he sees his father is the same look I see in the mirror sometimes."

"So, make him understand. Sounds like he's big into takin' care of his mom. He can't protect her from jail."

"He's asked about my past once already. He's not gonna let it go."

"Can't help you there, Riot. You're in a unique position to relate with him, though. What does your gut tell you?" Knuckles always got to the heart of the matter. It was part of the reason everyone in Kiss of Death now followed him willingly and without hesitation. The other reason was Knuckles was ruthless to his enemies. I hadn't learned everything yet. I'd only been part of the club a grand total of three days. But I'd heard rumors while I was in Terre Haute. Knuckles had made sure the traitors in the club were eradicated while he was in prison.

"My gut says if I lie to him, he'll never trust me again."

"Then I guess you have your answer." He sounded smug, which he knew pissed me off. The man loved getting under my skin for some reason. It was the highlight of his day on the inside.

"Bastard."

Knuckles' chuckle was cut off when I ended the call. Rude, but Knuckles wouldn't take it personally. The phone was a burner. I was told that, normally, the only phone any of us had was the one we were required to have for our parole officer to contact us. I was also told by Gunnar not to wait for my phone to ring because Knuckles was the only person I had to be accountable to.

I needed to get some sleep, but I was too wound up and restless to relax. Mainly because I was afraid the woman and young man in the room next to me were about to become the most important people in my life. The kid because he reminded me too Goddamn much of myself at his age, and the woman because she was mine. I wasn't exactly sure what that was going to look like for me because I could never give her a normal life, but I was going to figure out how to win her heart and keep her happy.

There was a loud *bang* followed by a short scream. I was on my feet before I fully registered the noise. I shoved open the door between our rooms. Thank God she hadn't shut that fucking door because, when I burst into the room, two men had Caleb and Violet. One of them was struggling to hold Caleb and keep a hand over the young man's mouth, while the other was dragging a stunned-looking Violet by her hair toward the door.

I saw red. Pure, fucking rage I could barely control filled me. I lunged forward, grabbing the asshole who had Violet by the back of his neck and slamming him face first into the wall. He released her hair with a yelp. I shoved his head against the door twice in rapid succession. The guy dropped and I kicked him in the head hard enough my steel-toed boots caved in his skull. He didn't move.

"Mom!" Caleb's muffled shout came through the hand still clamped over his mouth. He fought against his attacker, but the guy had Caleb in a firm grip.

The second guy's eyes went wide, clearly not expecting to deal with someone my size -- or, possibly, not expecting I'd use lethal force to protect Caleb and Violet. He tried to use Caleb as a shield, backing toward the door. Big fucking mistake.

"I swear to Christ, I'm gonna break every fuckin' bone in your fuckin' body." The deadly calm of my voice belied how much I was seething on the inside. "Let him go and I'll kill you quickly."

"Mr. Harrington wants to talk to his family." The guy was belligerent but also realized his severe disadvantage. He still dragged Caleb backward, trying to get to the shut door. Caleb struggling in his grasp was an added obstacle. "This ain't your business, man."

"Wrong answer." I lunged for the guy just as Caleb lifted his legs, forcing the guy to either take Caleb's full weight or drop him to face my attack. Caleb hit the floor on his ass a moment before I was on the guy.

I slammed my fist into the guy's face, feeling the satisfying crunch of his nose breaking under my knuckles. Blood flowed from his busted nose as he howled in pain, but I didn't let up. I grabbed him by the throat with one hand, using my other to rain down blows on his ribs, feeling them crack beneath my fists. The guy grunted in pain but fought his way up.

"You think you can come in here and grab them?" I snarled, driving my knee into his stomach. "You think I'm gonna let that happen?"

He tried to fight back, throwing a wild punch that grazed my jaw. I barely felt it through the adrenaline. I slammed his head against the wall, then dragged him to the floor. I used my weight to hold him down with both my hands around his throat, effectively cutting off his air. The guy was panicking now, clawing at my hands, his eyes wide with fear.

"Just… doin'… my… job…" It sounded like he was struggling with everything he had to get each word out.

"Your job?" I growled, tightening my grip on his throat. "Your fucking job is terrorizing women?"

Behind me, I heard Violet's ragged breathing and Caleb's frantic movements. "Mom, are you okay?" Caleb's voice was strained.

The distraction cost me.

I barely registered the flash of metal before a searing pain tore through my side. I grunted but caught his knife hand when he tried to arc the blade back into my side. When I twisted his arm backward and shoved him forward, I jerked his arm upward with a sharp jerk. There was an audible pop as his shoulder gave way. This time, the guy shrieked before clamping his teeth shut. Sweat erupted over his face with the pain. His right arm now hung limp.

He struggled to his feet, pain obvious in his features. Stumbling backward, he held up his other arm. "OK! OK! I'm sorry! I'm leaving!"

"Right. And go straight to the police, no doubt."

"No, man! You'll never see or hear from me again!"

I shook my head sadly. "Wish I could believe that, but anyone who'd drag a woman across a room by her hair can't be trusted to keep his word."

"The cops are probably already on the way, with as much noise as we've been making." The guy was trying to maneuver himself between me and the door, but the room was small and I was more than capable of blocking his way.

"If they are, I'll deal with it. But you are not leaving here on your own."

"He always gets what he wants, man. Harrington." The guy looked up at me. Pain still lined his face, but I saw the calculating look in his eyes. When he flipped open a switchblade with his good hand, I was ready.

He lunged, aiming at my chest. I stepped back, avoiding the blade before taking a short jab to his throat. Just so happened, he stepped forward the same time I did and the punch that would have been enough to incapacitate the guy was turned into a death blow.

I felt his windpipe give way when I hit him. He dropped to his knees, eyes bulging, hands clutching desperately at his neck. The crack was even more sickening than when his shoulder popped out. His death rattle as he tried to gasp in a few, futile breaths was worse, and I knew it was going to take at least four to five minutes for the guy to die. Last thing I wanted was Violet and Caleb to witness his death.

"Caleb, take your mother to my room please."

"I..."

"Now, Caleb." I tried to keep my voice calm so I didn't terrify them further, but I needed them out of here while I called Knuckles. I was afraid to look at Violet, trusting Caleb to tell me if I needed to get her to a doctor. If she looked at me with disgust and horror, I wasn't sure I could bear the pain. "Keep the door open between our rooms and make sure the door to the hallway is locked and chained."

"Yes, sir." Caleb's voice shook, but I saw him hurry Violet through the door.

"Caleb." I waited until the boy looked at me over his shoulder. "I promise everything will be all right. I'll protect you with my life."

He looked shell-shocked, but he nodded his head. "I believe you, Riot. You're in charge. All you have to do is tell me what to do to keep Mom safe."

"I'm supposed to be the one keeping you safe." Violet's voice was shaky. She clung to Caleb as he guided her through the doorway into my room but didn't resist him. "I'm the one who put you in danger by defying your father."

"Mom, you left him because I made you. But it's not our fault. It's his for being a fucking bastard."

"Caleb!"

"I'm sorry about my language, but I'm not sorry about disrespecting him. He hurt you, Mom. No one gets to do that. Not even Dad."

His voice faded as he guided her across the room. I heard him following my instructions as I called Knuckles. He answered on the second ring.

"I need clean-up." No need to waste time with explanations yet. There would be plenty of time for that.

"He come after them?" Knuckles was vague while still getting his meaning across. We were both on burners, but old habits die hard.

"Looks that way. If you could pick up a couple

bags of garbage it would help me out. Also need a cage and someone to haul my bike."

"Be there in twenty."

I used the time waiting on Knuckles to move both bodies to the bathroom and into the walk-in shower. Surprisingly, though I'd caved in the one guy's skull, there wasn't as much blood as I'd feared. He had blood from his ears, nose, mouth, and eyes, but his skull had caved in on itself, not breaking much of the skin. There was still a small stain, but it should be manageable. I hoped.

Christ, I was in so much trouble! Now that I wasn't focusing on a task, I was starting to feel the drop after a fight. All the emotions I'd learned to suppress until the crisis was over came rushing at me with a vengeance. I'd nearly lost Violet before I had the chance to get to know her. I'd claimed her in my heart and had failed to protect her. That stark realization hit me to my core. I'd failed at so many things in my life, but I absolutely could not fail at this. Protecting these two people was the purpose I needed in my life. I hadn't been able to protect the person in my life who'd mattered to me most before I'd gone to prison. This time, no matter what it took, no matter what I had to sacrifice, I absolutely would not fail to protect the people I loved again.

I checked my watch. Knuckles would be here any minute. The need to check on Violet and Caleb and assess their injuries was too strong to avoid any longer. I walked into my room with slow, deliberate steps. Both mother and son met my gaze. Violet looked relieved before she swallowed and ducked her head. Caleb gave me a slow nod, never letting go of his mother.

"Are either of you hurt?" I knew I needed to be

gentle, but it was damned hard. Not because I didn't want to be careful, but because I didn't know how to be gentle.

"I'm fine," Caleb answered as he pointed to my side where the cut I'd gotten now burned like fire. "You're bleeding."

"Just a scratch. I'm fine." I'd get Pain to stitch me up when we got back.

"I can get a towel to hold over it if you want."

"No." I winced at my abrupt tone. "Thanks though." Hopefully it was enough not to get the kid's back up. "I'm more worried about you and your mom."

"He wasn't trying to hurt me. But Mom got pretty banged up."

"She was already banged up," I muttered. "When I get my hands on that bastard, there's gonna be a reckoning."

"I'm not hurt. I promise." Violet's voice was surprisingly steady. It was almost like the more stressed she got, the more detached she became. I had to wonder if it was a defense tactic. To protect herself and anyone who might try to help her.

"I've got help coming. You know you can't stay here any longer. Right?" Again, I tried to be gentle, but she didn't have a choice in this matter.

"I don't have anywhere else for us to go." She looked up at me with resigned sadness. "He's going to win. Isn't he?"

"No, Mom!"

"Not a fuckin' chance."

Caleb and I spoke over top of each other. I could see the panic in her face now. While she'd worked hard to keep her head, the adrenaline drop was starting to shake her control.

Caleb had a tight grip on both his mother's hands. "We're not going back to him, Mom. I won't let that happen." I watched the fierce determination in the kid's eyes, the way he placed himself between his mother and anything that might hurt her. It was like looking in a Goddamn mirror. I ached for the kid. As well as for my younger self.

A knock at the door interrupted us. I checked the peephole to find Gunnar and Oktober outside as expected. I undid the locks and let the two men inside.

Gunner and I shook hands before Oktober pulled me into a hug. "Haven't got to talk to you since you got here, but it's good to see you."

"Good to see you, too." We clapped each other on the back a couple times.

"Prez said you had a couple sacks of garbage to take out?" Gunnar took off his backpack and pulled out two black tarps still in their packaging. "Cleaning company this hotel uses is on our payroll. I'll take care of the scrub down after me and Oktober deal with the trash."

"I owe you one, man." I wasn't too proud to admit I needed help.

"Riot, this is part of being in Kiss of Death." Gunnar gave him an incredulous look. "Did you think Knuckles was gonna send you off with a smile and a princess wave into something like this?"

"Like what? Like a situation where Violet and Caleb get attacked? There's no way Knuckles could have known that was going to happen. I'm doing my community service." I stepped closer, trying to keep my voice for the three of us alone. "I'm sure Knuckles never meant for me to kill two guys. I doubt he's gonna be happy about what I did."

"Everything Knuckles does is for a reason,"

Gunnar said. "This community service gig wasn't dropped in your lap by accident. Knuckles wanted you with Violet and her kid to protect them from this Harrington guy. If that means you have to kill, we clean up the mess and make sure nothin' comes back to you or the club."

"What about my parole?"

"As long as you're doing what Knuckles tells you to, we've got your back. You go out there on your own and kill someone, that's a different story."

I nodded. "I can respect that."

"Take them back to the club for tonight. You and Knuckles can get together with Violet tomorrow and decide what she wants to do from there. If she thinks she can be comfortable there, she'll be welcome to stay as long as she needs."

"We don't want to be any trouble." Violet approached us cautiously. It was easy to see how fragile she was, and how hard she was trying to not fall apart.

"You're not," Gunnar said firmly. "Will you go with Riot to our compound? I can give you all the assurances in the world, but you either trust Riot or you don't. But every man in the place will gladly stand between the two of you and any danger."

Violet's pale blue eyes filled with tears that glistened like diamonds. As she ducked her head, one droplet slid down her cheek. "Thank you. I'd appreciate your help."

"Good." Gunnar clapped me on the shoulder. "Take your family home, brother."

Chapter Six

Violet

"I can't stay in the same apartment with you," I said softly. I didn't want to be ungrateful, but I was feeling pretty raw at the moment. I wanted to lock myself and Caleb away for a few hours and lick our wounds before we went to battle again.

"You'll have your own apartment, honey." Riot didn't seem irritated, but I felt guilty for making demands. If I had been by myself in this I'd never have spoken up, only taken what I was offered. But I thought it was bad enough I wasn't putting up much of a fight for us to stay someplace other than a motorcycle club compound. With men I didn't know. Who appeared to have more than one member who'd done time in prison.

The irony of this whole situation was unmistakable. In public, my husband was part of the Nashville elite. He donated to the university's children's hospital and was on the board of directors of several charitable organizations. He kept me behind closed doors most of the time, telling everyone I was a very private person and had anxiety in crowds. Doug had taken Caleb with him a few times, but I got the impression it was more because it benefited him to be seen as Caleb's loving father. The few times he'd insisted I go with him to a social function had felt like I was as much an accessory as his cufflinks. And I knew better than to try to escape him, or defy him. The man he presented in public was a far cry from the man he was in private.

"I should be horrified at what happened at the hotel."

"That make you see me differently?"

"I'd have to be a fool not to see you differently, but I don't think you'll hurt me, and I don't think you're a bad person. In fact, you and Ms. Thompson have done exactly what you promised. Doug would tell me you guys were the monsters when I know the real monster is him."

The men Riot had called in had brought him an older model, big-ass Bronco. It only had two doors, but the back seat was surprisingly roomy. Riot sat on one side of me while Caleb was on the other. The two men in the front had been introduced to me as Tiny -- who wasn't at all tiny -- and Noose. Not really sure there was anything else to say about Noose other than his name. The horror show wrote itself.

"There are so many red flags with you guys I can't even count, but I'd be lying if I said I feel threatened by any of you." I looked up at Riot as I spoke. His features were hard. He constantly scanned outside the vehicle as we rode to the outskirts of the city. He was obviously taking the threat to me and Caleb very seriously, and was determined to protect us.

"Good. I want you guys to feel safe. Before anything else, you need to know you have a secure place to regroup."

"I'm sorry." My whispered apology sounded as broken as I felt. I wasn't sure what Doug had planned for me when he sent those men after us, but I was sure I wouldn't have lived long after he had me. "I didn't mean to sound ungrateful."

"You didn't." To my surprise, Riot found my hand with his. His large fingers closed around mine and gave a gentle squeeze. He didn't look at me or acknowledge the physical contact, but he didn't let go immediately so I curled my fingers around his. If he wanted me to let go, he could easily pull away. He'd initiated the contact, and I craved the security his touch represented.

We drove for a good thirty minutes. I got the impression they were taking a wandering route. No one spoke. Occasionally one of the guys in the front would grunt, but that was the extent of their communication.

Eventually, we got closer to the river and came to several large warehouses surrounded by a chain-link fence. A large gate blocked the road ahead of us but slid open as we approached. I saw two men, one on either side of the road, as we rolled through. The area looked like a shipping storage yard.

"Home, sweet home," Tiny announced as we pulled to a stop outside a warehouse in the middle of at least a dozen warehouses over a larger area. Camouflage netting stretched between buildings. The whole thing was very much like a militia compound. I wondered how they got away with something like this so close to the river and the shipping yard, but these didn't seem to be normal people. I thought maybe the less I knew, the better.

Caleb looked up at the artificial ceiling-like canopy over us, taking everything in. "This is where you live?" he asked Riot.

"Yeah." Riot rubbed the back of his neck, clearly uncomfortable. "Well, sort of. I mean..." He took a breath. "I've only been out of prison, like, three days. I live here, but it's gonna take a while for it to feel like home."

We'd already gotten out of the Bronco. Riot had only let go of my hand long enough to exit the vehicle, then he immediately grabbed it again. I glanced up at him. He raised an eyebrow, daring me to say anything.

Instead, I shrugged and gave him a small smile. I wasn't going to object if the man wanted to hold my hand. I knew the contact grounded me when it really shouldn't have.

"It's not fancy, but it's very secure. No one can get to you guys while you're inside the fence."

"Do we have to stay here?" The stubborn set to Caleb's chin said he was pushing Riot, like he wanted to see if the calm demeanor would crack and how much pressure it took.

Riot shrugged, letting go of my hand as he did. I felt the loss immediately, my anxiety rising at the thought of him leaving us. "No. Up to you, I guess. I'll protect you wherever you go. Just thought it would be easier here with all the guys." I could tell Riot was almost turning in on himself. His shoulders were back, his head high, but he almost seemed defeated. "I have to be careful where I go because of the terms of my parole." He didn't look at either me or Caleb but somewhere over our shoulders. Obviously, he was uncomfortable calling attention to the restrictions he had. Probably because it brought his prison time front and center.

Caleb studied Riot for a long time. "Yeah. It wouldn't be fair to you if you went back to prison because we went somewhere you weren't supposed to go. And I don't want Mom to not have somebody besides me looking after her." He looked around him as other members of Riot's club came our way, then he sighed. "Sorry, Riot. I don't like feeling trapped. Not now. I feel like Dad's trying to box us in or something."

"What happened, Caleb?" Riot asked. "At the hotel."

"They had a key or something," Caleb said. "I was between Mom and the door when I heard the lock whir and click, then they shoved it open and came after us."

"He knew where you guys were." Riot gave me a hard look. "Who else knew where you were staying, Violet?"

I shook my head, trying to think. "No one. I had no one to tell, and Caleb didn't know where we were going. Lana set us up at the hotel."

"You guys still have your phones? Any other electronic devices?" This came from one of the men approaching us.

"No." I shook my head. "We made sure to leave all that behind. I don't have a bank account, so all we had was what cash I'd managed to hide away from Doug."

"What about your clothes, or your handbag? Did you bring anything with you?"

I shook my head. "We left with the clothes on our backs and replaced those as soon as we could." I looked at Caleb. "Did you bring anything you haven't gotten rid of?"

He shook his head. "No. We even got new shoes and underwear."

The man nodded. "Good. You covered the basics and then some. I'll pull the hotel's security footage. See if I can find out how the guy got a key."

"Thanks, Knight." Riot stuck his hand out and Knight took it.

"Any time, brother. We're all here to help each other." Knight gave me a respectful nod. "Ma'am." He turned to Caleb. "I got a bitchin' gamin' system in my command center. You're welcome to stop by whenever you want. I'm usually there. If I'm not, ask one of the guys to let you in."

Caleb's eyes widened in excitement, then he

ducked his head and glanced at me. "I'll think about it."

Knight nodded before turning to go back inside. As he did, I saw another man walk up to Riot and speak softly.

Then the man turned to me. "Hi, Violet. I'm Knuckles. My wife, Hannah, is getting an apartment ready for you and Caleb. She, Pippa, and Carrie are all getting some stuff together for you guys."

"Pippa and Carrie are Gunnar and Hawk's women," Riot explained. "I've only met them a couple times, but the guys all say they're really good old ladies." God, this man. He was such a contradiction. He sounded almost subservient when he spoke to me sometimes. Or maybe shy. Other times, like when he saved me from Doug's men at the hotel, he was a dominant force you didn't dare disobey. Yet, even then, he'd been gentle with both me and Caleb.

Looking up at Riot, I studied his face. "If you trust them, I'm good."

That must have been the exact right thing to say because Riot let his breath out slowly as he nodded his head. He blinked several times then cleared his throat. "I do. I trust them because Knuckles trusts them. I trust Knuckles without question."

"OK, then." I smiled up at Knuckles. "Thanks for helping us."

"Just, if the parole board asks you about anything, tell them Riot went the extra mile to protect you."

I started. It hit me how serious this was for Riot. "Oh, my God! When the cops find those guys, are they going to come after you?" The thought nearly made me sick to my stomach. I didn't know what his past was, but there was no way he deserved to go back to prison for killing those bastards.

Knuckles raised his hands. "Calm down, honey. No one's going back to prison, and certainly not for killing those pissants."

"How can you know that?"

"This is one of those things I want you to trust me on." Riot squeezed my hand so he had my attention. "I won't let you down."

Had he phrased it any other way, I might have insisted they tell me everything. The fact was, I didn't really want to know. I knew in my heart I couldn't handle the raw facts.

I nodded. "You're right. I'm just concerned about it is all. I don't know you, but you've shown me more kindness in a few short hours than Doug showed me in thirteen years of marriage. I don't want anything to happen to you."

Riot's jaw clenched, but his eyes softened as he looked down at me. There was a long moment as we stared at each other. His brow furrowed and I could see him struggling with something. Then he shook his head and gave me a small smile. "Let's get you inside. You guys need rest."

Riot took us inside the nearest building. The door opened into one large room. It looked like a common room or just the place everyone hung out. Kind of reminded me of a sports bar from my college days. He took us to the back, and we stepped into the elevator. He closed the gate and the lift started moving up.

When he stepped out into the hallway, he held out his hand to me once again. I took it without hesitation. Caleb cleared his throat. When I glanced back at him, he raised an eyebrow, looking from mine and Riot's joined hands back to me.

Immediately, a wash of shame crashed over me. I

was still married, for Christ's sake! What was I doing holding this man's hand?

I tried to jerk my hand away, but Riot held fast. He looked down at me and his eyes widened in shock. He let go of my hand and took a step away from me.

"It's all right, Mom." Caleb's face was bright red. "I was teasing. Apparently, it backfired spectacularly."

"I'm still married to your father," I said softly. "I should respect my vows."

"Right," Caleb said, ducking his head. "Like Dad loves and cherishes you. Seems to me he disrespected stuff first."

"That doesn't mean I should --"

"Mom. Stop." Caleb reached out and took my hands. "I'm sorry."

"I'm jumpy," I said, trying to smile when I really wanted to cry. The sad truth was, I wanted to crawl into Riot's arms and let him hold me together while I grieved for a while without shattering into a million pieces. "I'm overreacting to everything. I'd be lying if I said I wasn't more than a little scared. But not of you, Riot. Or anyone here. Doug Harrington is a dangerous man. The very last thing you want is him looking at this place too closely."

"You let me worry about that, honey. I promise none of us will underestimate him." Riot's expression was so earnest there was no way not to believe him. Riot was a funny mixture of violent killer and simple country boy. Of course, most simple country boys could become violent killers if pushed far enough, so I kind of thought the analogy fit him perfectly. As he spoke, two women hurried down the hall. They greeted us with large, welcoming smiles.

"We put you in one of the top-floor apartments." The woman speaking smiled warmly. "I'm Hannah,

Knuckles' woman. Pippa here is Gunnar's. Gunnar is my twin."

"Hello." I managed a small smile, despite how exhausted I felt. "I really appreciate your help. We don't want to be a burden."

Pippa waved my words away with a flick of her wrist. "Honey, you're not a burden. We take care of our own here."

"We're not --" I started to say we weren't part of their club, but Hannah cut me off.

"If Riot's looking after you, you're one of us now." She smiled and linked her arm with mine, guiding me down the hall. "The apartment's not fancy, but it's clean and there's, like, four bedrooms. I honestly don't think anyone has ever lived in any of the top-floor apartments before me, Pippa, and Carrie got here." Hanna opened the door to a huge living area. She waved her hand around the large living area. It was pretty plain and had nothing on the walls or surfaces, but there was a lot of space. Doug's estate was luxurious in the extreme, but even though I'd lived there for thirteen years, I'd never felt comfortable. This place felt like a new start. I knew it wouldn't be a permanent thing, but it represented the beginning for me and Caleb.

"We've put some clothes in there for you both. Basics until we can get you proper shopping time." Pippa pointed to several bags sitting on the table. "We put bedding on all the beds. I'm afraid there's not much more than what you see here." She waved her hand around the room. There was a sectional in front of a TV, a dining room table and a kitchen with the basics in appliances. "The bedrooms all have a bed and nightstand. A couple of them have a desk... I think? We can find more furniture when you're ready. What we don't have, we can buy."

"I'm sure that won't be necessary." I smiled at the two women. "We appreciate what you've already done. This place is huge."

Hannah smiled. "Yeah. I think that's why the guys don't want to use them. They like structure. Some of them don't feel safe sleeping in large rooms."

I glanced back at Riot, who shrugged. "When I had a cell to myself was when I felt the safest to sleep. Large rooms sometimes feel like a dormitory. Sometimes there were a hundred or more guys in one room in bunk beds. It was hard to sleep then because I was vulnerable."

"I could see that," I replied softly. "Where do you stay?"

"Got a room on the second floor. But I can stay in the other apartment on this floor if you want me to."

Caleb followed close to me as Hannah led us to a door at the end of the hall to the master bedroom. "That's pretty much the grand tour." She smiled as she produced a key and handed it to me. "This is yours. No one comes in without your permission. Not even Riot. Hawk has a key to everything in the compound other than personal rooms, so you're in complete control."

The acknowledgment of boundaries nearly made me tear up again. Doug had never respected any boundary I tried to put between us. The more I tried to make myself a safe space, the more he delighted in tearing it down.

Caleb shifted beside me. "Do you have, like, security cameras and stuff here?" he asked, his voice betraying his suspicion despite his attempt to sound casual.

Hannah nodded. "The whole compound is

monitored. There are no cameras in your private rooms or anything. But out in the hallway, the lift, or any areas more than one person -- or family -- has unfettered access. The main floor has cameras everywhere. All the windows have alarms. Knight and Hawk run the security systems."

"But we can leave whenever we want to. Right?" Caleb looked from the women over his shoulder to Riot.

"Of course," Hannah said, her brow furrowed in confusion. "We wouldn't hold you guys here if you wanted to leave."

Caleb nodded, seeming satisfied with her answer. I could tell he was still processing everything that had happened today. The courtroom, the attack, and now this strange new environment. I knew my son well enough to recognize when he was overwhelmed but trying not to show it. Hell, I was overwhelmed myself.

"Is there food? I just realized we haven't eaten since before court."

Hannah brightened. "Sure. It's not much but there are, like, three large pizzas left over from the party earlier. I'll bring them up to you."

"I'll bring them up," Riot said. "I'll bring some drinks too. We can stock you guys up with groceries tomorrow. That way you can have your own stuff if you don't like what the club's having." His eyes met mine briefly, and I saw concern there. "You should rest. It's been a hell of an evening."

I nodded gratefully. "Thank you."

Hannah and Pippa exchanged a look I couldn't quite interpret before Hannah said, "We'll leave you to get settled. If you need anything at all, we're in the building straight across the walkway. Top floor. There are only two apartments on our floor, too, so we're pretty easy to find." She grinned.

After the women left, and Riot had gone to bring back pizza, Caleb went to check out the other bedrooms. I went to the table and started going through the bags. There were two changes of clothes for each of us, toiletries, linens, and toilet paper.

When Caleb wandered back to the main room and the table where I was busy opening packages, he went straight to the fridge. He was too grown up for my peace of mind, but he was still a growing boy. "Did you find anything?"

"I mean, there's some milk, butter, cheese, and eggs." He shut the door. "Date's good on the milk."

There was a knock at the door. Caleb hurried to the door and looked out the peephole before opening the door and stepping back to let Riot inside with three pizza boxes.

"You'll have to heat it up because it was in the fridge, but it was from tonight. I can go get something else if you don't want leftovers."

"Leftovers are perfect." I took the pizza boxes from him and moved to the counter. I found three plates and put two slices each on them before heating each of them in the microwave.

No one spoke in the awkward silence. I turned to find Caleb and Riot both sitting at the table staring at each other.

"Took you long enough." Caleb pinned Riot with an icy gaze.

If Riot took offense, he was good at hiding it. "Pain had to put a quick stitch or three in my side. Figured I'd take care of that before I came back here."

"So," Caleb said after a moment, "you were in prison for killing someone."

My heart stopped. I whirled around from the microwave, nearly dropping the plate I'd just retrieved. "Caleb!"

Riot didn't flinch. He held Caleb's gaze steadily, his expression unreadable. "Yeah, I was."

The microwave beeped, but I couldn't move. The tension in the room was thick enough to cut with a knife. I watched as my twelve-year-old son sized up the convicted killer sitting across from him.

"Did they deserve it?" Caleb asked quietly.

I opened my mouth to stop this conversation, but Riot raised his hand slightly, silently asking me to let this play out.

"I thought so at the time," Riot answered, his voice low and measured. "Still do, if I'm being honest."

"Was it someone like my dad? Someone who hurt people?"

Riot's jaw tightened and for a moment, I wasn't sure he'd answer Caleb. Then he spoke. "Yeah. Someone like that."

Caleb nodded slowly, processing this information. "And you went to prison for it."

"I did. Sixteen years." Riot held my son's gaze and Caleb didn't back down.

"Was it worth it?"

The question hung in the air, raw and complicated. I watched Riot's face, saw the conflict there, the way he struggled with how to answer a child's deceptively simple question. "That's what I wanted to think about," Riot finally said. "I never second-guessed what I did. Not once. My lawyer got me a deal, and I pled guilty." He shrugged. "Because I was."

Caleb's eyes narrowed and he suddenly went pale. "Riot. Who did you kill?"

"Does it matter? I got sentenced to twenty-five years for what I did. It's only because of Knuckles that I'm out now. He pulled some strings and shit that got me out early. The man I killed deserved what he got. No question there. A week ago, before I knew I was getting out on parole, I'd have told you killing that guy was absolutely worth losing all those years behind bars."

Caleb cocked his head. "And you don't know now that you're out?"

"I hadn't really thought about it until you asked me before. The thing is, the *only* reason I'm out is because of Knuckles. If he hadn't been able to get me out, or I hadn't met and impressed him, then I would still be in prison."

"I don't understand." Caleb was paying close attention to Riot, and I knew exactly why he was asking these questions.

"If I was still in prison, I wouldn't be here to protect you and your mom."

Silence stretched between them before Caleb responded. "But if you hadn't gone to prison --"

"Yeah. I wouldn't be here to protect you either. But there would at least be a chance I could be here. If I was still in prison, there's no chance I'd be able to help you."

"Will you tell me what happened?"

"Caleb, I'm not sure this is appropriate. Riot's past is private." I put my hands on Caleb's shoulders. I needed to touch my son, to remind him how much I needed him.

"It's all right, Violet. I rarely do anything I don't want to. Not anymore." He laced his fingers together and rested his hands on the table. "Will you give me until tomorrow? Your mother's tired, and she won't go to bed unless you do."

I held my breath. Caleb had always been highly intelligent and very good at reading people. I thought what he perceived as a betrayal by his father had shaken him. Caleb had always looked up to his father. Though they never had a close relationship because Doug was away much of the time, Caleb loved his father. He'd believed Doug was a good man. To actually see him hitting me had to have messed with the kid something fierce.

Finally, Caleb nodded. "OK. I think that's reasonable."

"Thanks, kid." Riot stuck out his hand to Caleb and my son took it. "Get some rest. We'll talk tomorrow after breakfast."

It was only eleven, but I felt like I'd been run over by a truck. I was tired and my insides were battered from the constant emotional trauma and fear.

"Will you do one thing?" Caleb kept hold of Riot's hand, not letting go when Riot did.

"Name it."

Caleb tightened his grip even more, his knuckles going white as he gripped Riot's hand. "I want you to stay here with us tonight."

Chapter Seven

Riot

I was fucked. I glanced at Violet, who looked as shocked as I did, and I knew I was *totally* fucked. Like *truly and totally fucked* because I knew I'd be staying with her tonight and she'd expressly said she didn't want to stay in an apartment with me. I didn't care if it meant I'd have to be flayed alive and die of gangrene. There was no way I was not staying with her and Caleb. Why? Because the kid put the idea in my head, and now I couldn't let it go. The only reason I was trying to keep my distance was because Violet didn't want me here.

The need to protect them had been riding me hard since the attack at the motel. I was also puzzled as fuck as to why there hadn't been a better effort to kidnap Caleb and Violet. So yeah. I had questions I couldn't answer, a woman I wanted to be mine with every breath in my body, and an angry preteen who was more adult than some of the guys here. So, yeah. Fucked.

"I'm not sure that's the best thing, Caleb." Violet was practically wringing her hands. Why was she so agitated?

"Mom, stop." Caleb wasn't disrespectful. In fact, he stood and wrapped his arms around his mother and hugged her. Violet clung to him the way I wanted her to cling to me. But she didn't know me. She was trusting me now, probably because she had no other options, but eventually she was going to need to pull back to think about what she wanted and what she and Caleb needed.

I stayed in the background while her son spoke to her. I wanted to know his reasons too. I mean, beyond learning my story. I knew that was what he was pushing toward. The full story. My reasons. My fucking feelings about what I'd done. He was probably going to use my captivity in this apartment as an opportunity to grill me.

"We need him, Mom." He glanced at me, a guarded expression on his face. "At least for now. You said he'd been better to you in a few hours than Dad had been since you'd married him."

"Yes, but --"

"You either trust him or you don't." Caleb still hugged Violet. "I can't say I like him yet, but he protected us. He did what he had to do to keep us safe. Just like he promised. I trust him, Mom. I don't know the other guys here, but I'd rather have Riot close in case Dad manages to get to us."

Violet stood there for a long moment. When she finally pushed away from Caleb, she gave him an affectionate smile, cupping the side of his face with her hand. "Don't think I don't know what you're doing here, young man."

"No clue what you're talking about, Mom." Yeah. Judging by the wide grin on his face, the little shit knew exactly what she meant and was enjoying the fact that he'd just won this battle.

"You're managing me and cornering Riot at the same time." She turned her head to catch my gaze. There was no amusement, only a silent plea for me to make my story as kid-appropriate as I could. If she knew what I'd done, she'd kick me out and keep me as far away from Caleb as she could. "I'll leave this up to you, Riot. Caleb's a kid, but he's not a child. I know he can handle a lot. Just... I don't know. Don't give him nightmares or anything maybe?"

"It's not that simple, Violet. Besides, Caleb is

going to give me until tomorrow. Like he agreed to."
The imp just shrugged. "I know this isn't what you
wanted, but this place is fuckin' huge. You'll never
know I'm here."

Violet moved away from her son and toward me
in slow, deliberate steps. She reminded me of a curious
kitten who knew this was a bad idea but couldn't seem
to stop herself.

When she stood in front of me, she stared at the
middle of my chest. I had on a black T-shirt and my
cut, but I got the feeling she was trying to see beneath
all the layers. Physically and metaphorically. She
placed her hand lightly in the middle of my chest. I
nearly closed my eyes and sighed in bliss. That simple,
gentle touch was the final nail in my coffin. She might
never accept me, but I was never leaving her side. If
that meant I had to watch while she found someone
more appropriate to marry and help raise her son,
someone acceptable to society, then I'd do it. If that
man hurt her like her husband had, I'd kill the
motherfucker. I was going to be this woman's shadow
for the rest of her life or until she told me to go to hell.
Even then, I'd probably stick around as long as I could.

"I'm scared, Riot." Her voice was so soft I barely
heard her. "Not of you. I'm scared of what Doug might
do. I'm scared for Caleb. I'm scared of what happens
next." Her eyes lifted to mine, those pale blue orbs
seeing more than I wanted her to see. "I've never been
on my own. Not like this. I've never had to make
decisions like this, and I find I'm ill-equipped because I
know the right thing to do is to shove you out the door
and stick with my original demand that we not share
an apartment." Her hand rubbed gently, up and down.
I got the feeling she was comforting herself in some
way. Like maybe the fabric under her hand soothed

her.

When she met my gaze again, I knew she was going to let me stay. "But my instinct is telling me I need you here. You feel… I don't know. Safe? Having you stay here with us might not be the smart thing to do, but I think it's the right thing." She cleared her throat and gave a subtle lift of her chin. "So I'd appreciate it if you'd be so kind as to stay with us and watch over both of us while we're here."

"You're not alone now." I covered her hand with my own. "Even if I'm not in this apartment, I'm never far away. I promise you that."

She bit her lip, indecision written all over her face. Finally, she nodded. "All right. But I want you to promise me something."

"Name it." Hell, I'd promise -- and deliver -- the moon if she asked it!

"Don't lie to me. Ever. Even if you think the truth will hurt me or make me pull away from you. I've had enough lies, deceit, and pain to last a lifetime."

The weight of her request hit me hard. I'd never planned to lie to her, but I hadn't planned on telling her everything either. Some truths were better left buried. But looking into those eyes, I knew I couldn't give her anything less than complete honesty.

"I promise." The words felt like a vow, heavy and binding.

"Good." She stepped back, taking her hand away from where I had it trapped against my chest. I felt the loss like a physical blow, wanting to cling when it wasn't appropriate. "I think all the bedrooms have bedding and such, but I'm sure you know how to help yourself if you need to." Her smile was genuine, and there was a measure of relief that she wasn't frightened and actually welcomed my presence.

As she walked away from me, my gaze might have lingered places it shouldn't, but what struck me most about this woman was her absolute courage. She was obviously beaten down, but she'd only surrendered ground to gain the battle in the end. I had a long way to go with her, but she was giving me a chance to prove my worth. Once she saw I was useful, maybe she'd start seeing me as someone she could be with.

Or I could be kidding myself. Either way I was getting ready to have to explain myself to the pissed-off preteen from before, because Caleb clearing his throat was what pulled me out of my thoughts. And my gaze away from Violet's ass.

"Sorry," I muttered, shoving my hands in my pockets. Then I pulled them out and put my shoulders back. I might be a criminal, but I was still a man, Goddamnit. There was just something about having a woman's kid catch you staring at her ass to make you feel like a naughty child. "I'm not gonna, you know… I'll keep my hands to myself."

"I never said anything." Caleb might not even be a teenager yet, but he already had an intimidating stare I had no problem interpreting.

"You didn't have to. I'm a convicted felon looking at your mom. But I don't hurt innocents, and your mom and you, and the old ladies, are the only innocent people in this whole fucking place. And a couple of the women ain't as innocent as either of you."

Caleb snorted. "You're weird. You know that?"

"Kid, you have no idea." I rubbed the back of my neck, feeling uncomfortable but not wanting to leave the kid before he was ready. I'd been through this a lot in prison. Caleb was sizing me up. I wanted him to see exactly who I was. "You want to do a round with me? Make sure the place is secure?"

Caleb narrowed his eyes at me. "What do you mean? I thought you said the place was safe."

"It is. But I thought you might like to see for yourself."

He opened his mouth to say something, then shut it, shook his head, and tried again. "No. I wouldn't know what I was looking at." I could tell it took the kid a lot to admit that.

"Maybe not the technical stuff. I don't either. But you could see that the windows were all shut, how they open, where the fire escape is. That kind of thing. I'm the first line of defense for your mom. You're the last. So while I'm at the front, you'll be getting her away from the danger."

The young man stood up straighter, and I could see I'd said the exact right thing. "I hadn't thought about it that way, but you're right. That's exactly what I'd do."

I let out a breath I hadn't known I'd been holding. Maybe I had a chance to at least befriend the kid. If I could win him over, maybe he'd let me stay in his and Violet's lives. And yeah. I sounded pathetic, but this woman and her kid were rapidly becoming an obsession. I just wanted to be in her fucking presence, for Christ's sake!

I showed him the layout of the loft apartment, letting him examine the windows and showing him the fire escape. The kid wasn't very chatty, but he did ask a few questions, none of which were personal.

The only sections of the apartment that weren't completely enclosed were the bedrooms. There was still an industrial feel about them, with high ceilings and tall windows along the outer walls. Each room had its own bathroom and took up half the available space on the top floor of the warehouse. So, yeah, the rooms were fucking big. I could tell Caleb didn't want to be impressed, but he liked the place.

Then he did an odd thing. Caleb stuck his hand out for me to shake. "Thanks for helping me and Mom, Riot. I can't protect her on my own and I can't keep my dad away from her. Thanks for offering a safe place to stay, and for supporting my mom in court."

I cocked my head at him. "I thought I was there to support you?"

He shrugged. "I might have suggested it would be easier for me to testify if there was someone big and scary to have my back, so Dad didn't intimidate me."

"OK. So… I was there for you?"

"I never said I needed it. And I never said *why* it would be easier."

I pinched the bridge of my nose and closed my eyes. "I feel a headache coming on."

"Yeah. Mom has that expression sometimes. Usually when she realizes I've manipulated her into doing something she never intended to do. So, for the record, yeah. I was scared shitless. Not to testify, though. I'm scared of what he'll do now that Mom left and I told the judge I wanted nothing to do with him. He's not coming after me. He's coming after Mom."

"I figured."

"I wanted to make sure she had someone with her. She's more afraid of Dad than I am. I think he's done more to her than she's already told me. She admitted the other night wasn't the first time he'd hit her, but I know it's worse than she let on."

"What do you want me to do, Caleb?"

"I want you to stick as close to Mom as you can, especially when we go out of this compound."

"You trust *me* over your father?"

Caleb stuck his chin up. "You gonna hit my mom?"

"Hell no!"

He shrugged. "Exactly."

"Christ." How many more ways could I be fucked today? "Kid, I'm not sure I'm the man you want in this situation."

"You like my mom?"

I was starting to panic. I felt like I was a kid being grilled by my girlfriend's dad and she wasn't even my girl. Yet. "I'm so not qualified for this mission," I muttered. "Caleb, I don't know your mom."

"You know enough. Stay close to her until this is all finished. Then I can take over again."

I took a breath, my head spinning. There was one question I wasn't sure the kid had considered though. "Caleb, what happens when I don't want to leave her after this is over?" I spoke softly in as calm a voice as I could manage, but I wanted to get my point across.

Caleb didn't flinch. He met my gaze with the promise of death in his eyes. "You will if she wants you to."

Very slowly, I nodded. "Yeah. I think I would. One way or another." I had no doubt that if I refused to leave, Caleb would "help" me. Probably in the form of an unfortunate accident.

"We understand each other." Caleb nodded once, then turned to go to his room. "We can talk tomorrow. And don't bullshit me either."

"No bullshit. Got it." This whole situation would be funny if I weren't so fucked. Did I mention I was fucked?

Chapter Eight

Violet

I woke up with a scream. Sweat coated my body, and I was trapped. I thrashed, trying to get my hands free, but something was restraining my whole body. No amount of kicking seemed to help. "NO!" I screamed again. "Let me go!" I couldn't catch my breath. Sweat made my bindings stick to my skin even worse.

A light snapped on, throwing shadows on the ceiling. I had no idea where I was as I looked around me, searching for Doug.

"Violet!" A male voice cut through my panic. "Hey. It's OK, honey. It's OK." His voice was soft. Quiet. Probably trying to keep me from panicking even more.

I sucked in a breath, then let it out slowly. I closed my eyes and tried to shake off the haze of sleep. Slowly, my mind caught up with reality and I recognized my surroundings. "I'm in an apartment in a motorcycle club compound." I don't know why I spoke my thoughts out loud, but the affirmation helped finish clearing the cobwebs from my head. I met Riot's gaze. He was on his knees on the floor beside my bed. "Riot."

He seemed to let out a sigh of relief. "You're back with me, aren't you, honey?"

I nodded, still trying to catch my breath. I felt like I'd run a marathon. My chest ached, my lungs burned, and I was sticky with sweat. Riot didn't touch me, but kept looking into my eyes, making me focus on him. "Yes. I'm sorry I woke you."

"You didn't." His voice was gruff, but he was looking more at ease the more I spoke. "Can I help you get untangled?"

I nodded, unable to speak without my voice wavering. The last thing I wanted was to show more weakness than I already had. He was gentle as he unwound the sheet from my body, his touch clinical and respectful. When I was finally free, I pulled my knees to my chest, wrapping my arms around them.

He stood, then helped me get the sheet off so I wasn't restrained.

"I must have gotten tangled in the sheets and had a nightmare."

Riot grunted as he stepped back out of my space. I probably should have been embarrassed. I was sleeping in a T-shirt and panties and nothing else. At the very least I didn't want to parade around half naked in front of a strange man. Instead, I was too shaky to worry much about it.

"I need to wash off the sweat." It was an inane thing to say, but it was all I could come up with.

"Do you need help walking to the bathroom? You're trembling."

I shook my head. "I think I'm OK."

Riot nodded and moved farther away from the bed, close to the bedroom door, but didn't leave. As I crossed to the bathroom, I found myself oddly grateful he hadn't left immediately. It was inappropriate at best, dangerous at worst, but Riot fascinated me. He was so protective, but unsure of himself. It felt like he was afraid of doing or saying the wrong thing. So not like any man I'd ever been around.

I snagged a clean shirt and underwear before heading to the bathroom. "Thanks, Riot," I murmured as I opened the bathroom door. "I didn't mean to be a bother."

"You're not. Go take your shower. I'll wait until

you're settled." He sat on a plush chair in the corner next to a matching loveseat. It made a small, intimate area for relaxing.

I should probably have told him I was fine and to leave, but I didn't want to. I wanted Riot to stay. At least for a little while. So, I simply gave him a small smile. "You don't have to, but I won't object if you want to stay." I swallowed, then added, "You know. For a little while." Riot nodded but said nothing.

The door was shoved open, and Caleb appeared in the doorway, his hair sticking up in all directions. "Mom?"

"It's all right, Caleb. I'm fine."

Caleb looked around the room until his gaze settled on Riot sitting in the corner. I thought I saw Riot wince, but I wasn't sure. He looked from Riot back to me, then back to Riot. "He hurt you, Mom? Scare you?"

"No, honey," I said immediately, hurrying to his side. "No. He came when he heard me scream. I'm so sorry I woke you."

Caleb opened his arms and let me hug him. He wasn't like typical teenage boys. He never hesitated to show me affection. It never seemed to embarrass him. "I'd rather you wake me up than not, Mom. You sure you're OK with Riot here?"

"Yes. I'm not scared of Riot. I would never put you at risk. If I wasn't sure about him, we wouldn't be here."

Caleb looked satisfied with my answer, then turned to Riot. Something passed between the two of them I didn't understand but Caleb seemed satisfied while Riot looked even more uncomfortable than ever. It was kind of cute. Not a word I'd ever have associated with a biker or an ex-con. Together? Worse than laughable, yet there it was. When Caleb shut the door behind him, I gave Riot a small smile, then went to the bathroom and shut the door.

I leaned against the door, then slid down to sit on the floor. I let the coolness of the wood at my back ground me as I took several more deep breaths. Nightmares were nothing new, but tonight was the worst ever. Probably because of the fight at the motel. The details were fuzzy, but I was still feeling the edge of panic as the adrenaline left me.

The adrenaline drop was the worst. Not only was I sweating and sticky, but I was also sick to my stomach and my legs were wobbly.

After a few more minutes, I stumbled to my feet and turned on the shower, adjusting the temperature until it was as hot as I could stand it. As steam filled the bathroom, I stripped off my sweat-dampened clothes, then used a hair band the women had supplied to secure my hair into a bun on top of my head. Then I stepped into the shower and let the water beat against my tense muscles. I tried to focus on the soothing sensation rather than the lingering fear. Doug wasn't here. I was safe. Riot was just outside in my bedroom.

That thought nearly made my knees give out. *Riot*. The man was an enigma. A convicted killer who looked at me with such gentleness it made my chest ache. I'd spent so many years flinching at sudden movements, anticipating the next outburst, the next blow. Yet around Riot, despite his size and obvious strength, I didn't feel that familiar dread. I didn't feel threatened in any way by Riot.

Not wanting to inconvenience Riot further, I finished up and dried off. I felt more like myself again, but still incredibly fragile. I pulled on clean clothes and ran a brush through my hair before opening the door and exiting the bathroom.

Riot was still there, sitting exactly where I'd left him. His gaze lifted to mine immediately. "Better?" he asked.

I nodded, sitting on the edge of the bed. "Much." For a while I stared down at my hands, not sure what to say when there were so many things I needed to know. "I appreciate your patience with me and Caleb."

"No need for patience. I'm glad to help."

"You and Caleb seem to be getting on well." This conversation had to happen sometime. Might as well get it over with now.

"We've come to an understanding of sorts, I guess."

"What's that?"

The corners of his lips lifted in amusement. "We agree that if I don't scare or hurt you, he won't cut out my heart with a rusty spork."

That got a surprised bark of laughter from me. "That's good to know."

"Also, he wants me to be your protector. At least, for now."

That surprised me. "Caleb said that?"

"Yeah. I don't think it was easy for him to admit he couldn't do it on his own, but he wants you to be safe. I think that kid would do anything in the fuckin' world to protect you."

I had to smile. "Caleb is a great kid."

"He's a good man, too," Riot said. "Better than most I know. I don't respect many people, but I respect your son."

"Wow. That's high praise."

"Deserved."

Again, there was an awkward silence between us. Riot didn't rush me or even anticipate my questions. He simply sat in that chair, resting his arms on the sides, and waited.

"I'd like to know…" I stopped, unsure how to phrase my question without accidentally offending him.

"I'm not going to pounce on you, Violet. I'm not gonna get mad at anything you ask me. As a mother of a boy Caleb's age, you have every right to want to know as much as you can about the ex-con you're gonna be stuck with for the foreseeable future." He grinned, not repentant in the least. "So, you ask all the questions you want, honey."

It was ridiculous how much I liked him calling me *honey*. A couple of the other guys had used that endearment too, but none of them said it to me in the same tone of voice Riot did. Now was not the time for fantasies about the hot biker. Especially when, first, I was married, and second, I had a preteen son in the next room. Also, there was the fact my husband was probably going to retaliate for the legal victory today.

"I'd like to know what you're going to tell Caleb tomorrow."

He raised an eyebrow. "What do *you* want me to tell him?"

"I don't know." I sat on the edge of the bed, my elbows on my knees and my head in my hands. "I'm handling this all wrong."

"Talk it out as best you can. I hate you had a nightmare, but I wanted to talk with you about this before I spoke with Caleb. Probably for the same reasons you're thinking of right now."

"I'm sorry, Riot. I'm convinced you're one of the good guys. Like the *real* good guys. The kind of guy who does what has to be done, no matter the consequences to himself."

He shook his head. "I'm not sure I'd go that far. But in this case, yeah. I didn't care what happened to me."

"I don't want to hear this, do I?" It wasn't a question I needed answered.

"Probably not. I'll be honest with you, Violet, I don't think I should tell Caleb my story. Earlier I promised him I would, but I should have thought the decision through. Having done that, I'm not going to lie to him. There might be things I omit, but I won't lie."

"No. Caleb would never trust you again."

"I'll tell you the unfiltered version now, if you want. Then you can decide how you want me to present it to Caleb."

"Are you even real?" The question slipped out before I realized I was going to say it. "No man is this patient and understanding." That last was grumbled under my breath.

Riot's warm chuckle filled the room and dispelled the last of my tension. Yeah, the conversation was getting ready to get serious, but there was something about Riot that put me at ease. It was a dangerous thing to trust a man like Riot. I knew that without a doubt. I also knew I trusted him with my life. And my son's. "I hope so. Otherwise, I'm not sure who you're talking to."

I stared at him for long moments. This man was like no one I'd ever met before. I'd been around killers all my life. While I had no doubt this man was as dangerous as any one of them, he was different. He had a moral code. I could also tell he wasn't proud of his past. Or, at least, he thought his past would be something we'd balk at. He'd been correct. Both Caleb and I had both been nervous, but Riot had proved to be more than what was on the surface. So, I decided if he was going to have to spill his guts, I'd go first.

I took a deep breath and began. "My mother was the daughter of a low-level soldier with the Russo family in South Florida. Ritchie, the son of the patriarch, got my mother pregnant. Mr. Russo didn't approve of my mother, but Ritchie was his youngest son and the baby my mother was carrying was his grandson."

"Grandson?" Riot raised an eyebrow.

"Surprise! Granddaughter. Not grandson. My grandfather wasn't impressed. He tried to talk my father into making my mother have a home birth, but he refused. Despite my grandfather's obsession with the family business and blood ties, my father loved my mother. I'm not sure if he ever loved me, but my mother did, so Ritchie let her keep me. Pretty sure my grandfather intended to kill my mother's child if it was a girl."

"Sounds like real winners, those two."

"My father and grandfather?" I snorted a laugh. "Oh, yeah. Parent and grandparent of the year. Anyway, Mr. Russo needed a tie with the Harrington family here in Nashville. As I understand it, the arrangement benefited Mr. Harrington far more than it did Mr. Russo, so when I was offered to Doug, his father jumped at the offer."

"The head of the Harrington family is your husband's father?"

"Yes. But there's no love lost. It's why Doug got saddled with me instead of Nevada. Nevada Harrington is next in line to lead the family and his father's favorite by far. I think Mr. Russo thought Mr. Harrington would marry me to Nevada. As I understand it, that was the plan. There was a rush to finalize their deal for some reason, so Mr. Harrington agreed to the terms before doing his research on the granddaughter no one knew anything about. Once he did, he changed plans so I'd be marrying the misfit brother instead of the one who had the real power. It left Nevada free to secure a similar deal with an enemy of Mr. Russo and get payback for them pawning off a useless woman no one wanted."

"Sounds pretty Goddamned miserable for you."

"I'm surprised I haven't had an accident before now. The only reason is Caleb. I got pregnant really quickly after I married Doug, so they didn't want to do anything until after I had the baby. From the very beginning, Caleb didn't want anyone but me so they let me live. The older Caleb got, the more protective of me he got, which vexed his dad to no end."

"Oh? Didn't like him attached to his mom?"

"No, I think it was that he thought Caleb should follow in his shoes. He should want to be with his father instead of his mother."

"So, jealousy."

I chuckled softly. "Beyond belief. Caleb didn't know what was going on, and Doug was careful to keep it from him. He knew Caleb would always take my side. Caleb had proven it over and over whenever Doug would say anything out of the way to me. Even if I was in the wrong, Caleb would stand up to his father. For whatever reason, instead of turning his anger on Caleb, Doug did his best to win him over. The past couple of months, they'd spent a lot of time together. To hear Caleb talk, they had a great time doing all kinds of different father-and-son type things."

"You think Doug convinced himself Caleb's loyalties had changed?"

I nodded. "Yeah. When he drank, no one could

convince him he was wrong, and he assumed everyone thought he was right. So when he told Caleb to get his baseball bat and punish me, he fully expected Caleb to obey him with gusto."

"Christ, Violet." It was the first emotional response I'd seen from Riot since the nightmare had woken me.

"Well? Now you know my story. Will you tell me yours?"

Chapter Nine

Riot

I'd been dreading this conversation. Sixteen years in prison, and I was practically quaking in my boots because I had to tell a little slip of a woman what I'd done to go to prison. Not only that, but I also had to find a balance between telling Caleb the raw, gritty truth, and shielding him from the harsher aspects of my reality. Not to protect myself, though. To protect Caleb.

"You're a hell of a woman, Violet." Strange way to start this conversation, but that's what popped out. I also didn't miss the slight flush blossoming on her cheeks. "I'm going to give you all the information. Then you're gonna tell me what you want me to tell Caleb."

"All right." She stood from the bed and crossed to the loveseat next to my chair, tucking one leg under her. "You said you were incarcerated for sixteen years." She looked away and took in a shuddering breath. "I had a thirteen-year sentence."

"We're both out now," I said immediately. "And neither of us are goin' back. Get me?" I tried to keep my voice calm, but the way she looked at her marriage as a prison sentence was the final nail in my coffin. And I wasn't altogether certain I could make good on my statement. I had a feeling I might well be going back to prison before this was over.

She gave me a small smile, adjusted her position, and cleared her throat. "I hope that's true. I can't…" She closed her eyes and gave a little shake of her head. "I can't go back to him. I'll do what I have to, to protect Caleb, but I can't take him back to Doug."

"You won't have to." I made my voice as firm as

I could to get her attention. "If you believe nothing else, if there is nothing else I can ever do for you or that boy in this world, I promise, you'll never have go to back to him."

She shook her head emphatically. "No. Don't worry about me. Concentrate on Caleb. That's why you're here." She tried to put a little bite in her voice, but it was wobbly, like she was trying not to cry. I had to focus on keeping myself calm. Meditation was one of the useful things I learned in prison. They recommended I learn discipline to control my temper. Never thought I'd be grateful for learning how to meditate, but I was now.

"He's a little shit who needs someone to keep a close eye on him," I muttered. Then I realized what I said and I met her angry gaze with mine. "That came out wrong! I know that sounds bad," I said, holding my hand out in front of me and moving to the edge of my seat in case I had to get out of her reach. "But that kid is sneaky. And he's manipulating you. Problem is, I can't say a Goddamned thing to him because I'm kind of in awe of him." I rubbed the back of my neck which was flaming hot with embarrassment.

When I glanced up at her there was shock on her face, then irritation. "What do you mean he's manipulating me?"

"Honey, that kid talked you and Lana into bringing in someone to protect him because he was scared of his father. Right?"

"Yeah. So?"

I let out a breath and sat back in my chair. "So, he was scared, but not of his father. At least not for his own sake. Caleb knew that, once he spoke out against his dad in court and you left Harrington for good, that bastard would come after you. He knew you'd have a huge target on your back, and he wanted someone physically capable and willing to protect you through this."

"Little shit," she muttered before realizing what she'd said. Then she froze and found my gaze. I really doubt I kept the amusement from my face, but in my defense, I tried. I knew I'd failed when she gave me an exasperated look. "Not a word."

"Wouldn't think of it."

"For the record, your first priority is Caleb." She gave me a stern look.

I grinned. "You look cute when you make that face." That startled her. "How about I look out for both of you?"

"You can't! You can only be in one place at a time!" She pointed a finger at me. "You will protect Caleb."

"Yep. 'Cause he'll be protecting you."

She seemed to deflate. "That little shit."

"Sometimes it's pointless to resist," I offered helpfully.

"Don't be that person, Riot."

I couldn't help but laugh. She really was too cute. And, oh my God, I was so completely under her spell. When she found out how deeply infatuated I was with her, Violet would likely run the other way as hard as she could and I wouldn't blame her. "I'm not that person. You know I'm right."

"Yeah." She sighed. "I guess I do." For the first time, I thought I saw a genuine smile with no stress. She was sharing a small amusement with a friend over her son.

One look at that soft expression, the ethereal loveliness of her smile, and I saw what I wanted in my future. Moments like these where she laughed softly at something amusing I'd said. I cleared my throat. Past fucking time to get down to business. "So. Yes. I did sixteen years in prison. I was sixteen and my victim was an important person in the community, so they said due to the nature of the crime they wanted to try me as an adult. Because I'd planned on killing the bastard and set him up, the judge had no problem granting the DA's request."

She sucked in a breath, her eyes going wide. I almost sighed in despair. Here it came. She'd be horrified and tell me to leave. I'd be stuck in the background. Just like I had been all my life. But I'd still protect her.

"Oh, my God! You were just a boy!" She looked like she wanted to reach out and touch me, but we were too far away from each other. "Where were your parents? Who was advocating for you?"

I frowned at her. "Did you not hear the part where I planned to kill this guy?"

"Well, yeah. But you were still a kid!" She looked as incensed as she sounded, genuinely upset on behalf of my younger self. "There had to be extenuating circumstances." When I just stared at her, she seemed confused. "What? Do I have something on my face?"

"I'm not sure anyone's ever said that the first time I told them my story." Even my own lawyer hadn't asked why I'd done it. They'd only been interested in getting my confession and putting me away.

"Why the hell not? That's the first thing you want to know!"

I gave my head a little shake, not understanding this woman. "I... don't know. No one believed me anyway. Like I said, the guy was a pillar of the community."

"What did he do?"

"This is the uncomfortable part, Violet." She nodded but said nothing. "The man I killed was my adoptive father. I killed him because I came home from a football game to find my father standing over my mother with a bloody baseball bat."

"Oh, God," she whispered, going pale.

"I couldn't kill him right then. I freaked out initially and hesitated too long. He called his security guy and blamed it on me." I shrugged. "My instinct was to run, and that's what I did.

"I came back the next night. The bastard thought he'd locked me out, but I'd lived there my whole life. Being a mischievous teenage boy, I knew how to bypass the security system and break into and out of that house at three different places. So I got in, waited until he was getting ready for bed, and I beat him to death. Same as he'd killed my mother."

Two tears slid down Violet's cheeks and her fingers were laced so tightly together her knuckles were white. She stood slowly, releasing her fingers and rubbing her palms on her shorts. With one cautious step at a time, she approached me and crouched beside me on her knees. With trembling hands, she reached for my hand resting on the arm of the chair. She gripped it in both of hers. "Caleb." She swallowed. "He reminds you of you. Doesn't he?"

"Are you going to push me away now, Violet?" I hated that it mattered what this woman thought of me. I'd survived in prison and become a man under harsh conditions. Even though I probably had a bit of a morally gray streak, I wasn't a bad person. I had a strong sense of right and wrong, so yeah. Even though I'd had a shitty start, I was proud of the man I'd become.

She shook her head. "No, Riot." She smiled at me, even though tears continued to flow down her cheeks. "I'm not going to push you away. In fact, I think I understand now why Caleb is so willing to trust you, even if he doesn't fully realize it himself. I think he sees something in you."

I tried to swallow past the lump in my throat. Her grip on my hand tightened. "You aren't afraid of me?"

"I'm not afraid of you. I'm afraid *for* you," she whispered. "What you did... I can't imagine how much pain you were in."

"The truth is, I don't regret it. Not then, not now." I met her gaze squarely. "I'd do it again in a heartbeat, though Caleb made me rethink that sentiment. It's a miracle I'm here to protect the two of you and not still in prison. But you said Caleb threatened to kill Harrington if you didn't leave. Right?"

"Yes," she whispered.

"What if he thinks --"

"That your confession is the go ahead for him to kill his father anyway?" She finished my thought. "That's what you're worried about."

"Yeah. Your kid's smart. Too smart. He reads people better than anyone I've seen in a really long while. And Caleb's got the same protective instinct I had."

Violet nodded slowly. "I could see that. But I don't think so. He trusts you, Riot. If you tell him not to, he won't."

"Do you really want to take the chance? It's not wrong to want to protect someone you love," I said softly. "But there are consequences. Harsh ones. And that's why I never asked why my lawyer didn't fight my sentence. I did it. I killed the motherfucker. If society needed to punish me, fine. I was man enough to kill someone. I could be man enough to deal with the consequences."

She released my hand and stood, moving back to perch on the edge of the loveseat. "I think he feels helpless. Like he's alone in this. And no, I don't count because Caleb has always tried to take care of me, ever since he could first toddle around the house with me. You are quite possibly the only person we know who understands his feelings."

"Christ, Violet." She was fucking killing me with how fucking *kind* she was. No wonder Caleb wanted to protect her. Violet had absolutely no sense of self-preservation, but she had a bigger heart than almost anyone I'd ever met.

"You tell him what you would have wanted someone to tell you before you went back to your house the next night," she said with absolute confidence in her voice. "If you'd have wanted someone to tell you to kill the son of a bitch, I'd prefer if you were gentle in your expression of that point of view. But be honest with him. That kid can smell a lie while it's still forming in your head."

I moved to sit beside her on the loveseat. Turning my palm up, I reached out to her. To see if she would take it. She did. I covered her hand with my other one so hers was sandwiched between mine. "I swear to you, I will protect Caleb. Even from himself."

"I met you less than a full day ago," she said, putting her other hand on mine. "When I said you'd shown me more kindness in a few hours than Doug has during our entire marriage, it was the absolute truth. He doesn't see us as family. We're possessions. I think maybe in his own twisted way, he loves Caleb, but his animosity toward me -- the physical and verbal abuse -- got worse the more Caleb insisted on staying with me. It was kind of expected as a child, but as he got older, he insisted on staying with me as my protector. He said he liked playing bodyguard. So that's what he did."

"Probably had a feeling something wrong was going on." I grunted. "I know I did. I think I was angrier with myself for not preventing what happened to her than I was with him for actually killin' her."

"Oh, Riot!"

The next thing I knew, Violet threw her arms around me and sobbed against my shoulder. At first, I stiffened, not sure what to do. It didn't take me long to wrap my arms around her and pull her more securely against me.

Her scent filled me with warmth and peace and a sense of homecoming I hadn't felt since my mother had died. This was where I was supposed to be. And I was convinced with all my heart this woman was meant to be kept and protected by me.

She didn't pull away, and I didn't rush her. I knew I'd sit there and hold her the rest of the night if that's what she wanted. When she shifted like she was uncomfortable, I pulled her across my lap so she sat with her feet to one side. I was rewarded for my efforts with a soft sigh from Violet as she relaxed into my embrace. And I'll be Goddamned if my heart didn't swell three sizes.

We sat like that for a long time. I rested my chin on her head and occasionally rubbed my beard-roughened cheek over her silky hair. Violet was so still I thought she might have drifted off to sleep.

I was reluctant to move, worried I might disturb her if she was asleep. But after a moment, I felt her shift slightly against me. "I'm sorry," she whispered, her voice soft against my chest. "I didn't mean to fall apart like that."

"Nothing to be sorry for." I stroked her hair, letting my fingers trail through the silky strands. "You've been through hell, Violet. You're entitled to a breakdown or two."

She pulled back just enough to look up at me, her eyes still wet with tears but clearer now. The vulnerability in her expression knocked the breath right out of me.

"Why are you being so kind to me?" she asked, her voice barely audible.

I considered lying, giving her some bullshit about community service or doing my job. But I'd promised her honesty. "Because from the moment I saw you when you got out of Lena's car, I fell for you. Fuckin' hard." I swallowed hard, knowing I was treading dangerous ground. "And the more I know you, the deeper I'm getting."

Her eyes searched mine, like she was looking for the catch, the hidden agenda. I held her gaze steadily, letting her see whatever she needed to see.

"I don't understand," she finally said. "You barely know me."

"I know enough." My thumb brushed away a stray tear on her cheek. "I know you've survived years with a monster and still have kindness in you. I know you've raised one hell of a kid, one who would give his right arm to protect you. To have a kid love you that much, you have to be a good person." Two more tears slid down her cheeks. "I'll never deserve a woman like you. I won't pretend to think I will. But if you'll give me a chance to prove myself, I promise you'll never have someone treat you better than I will."

"I'm still married." She stated the fact like it physically pained her. Then she met my gaze with longing and maybe even a small measure of hope. "I've never had such an instant pull to someone in my life. You feel safe, Riot. I'd like to know what it's like to have that security. It might be throwing myself at you for selfish reasons, but I think I'm weak enough to accept that about myself without reservation if it means that maybe we could see where this goes."

"I'm sure relationships have been built on less."

"You know Doug isn't going to let me have a divorce without a fight. Right?"

"Knuckles told me to let him know if you wanted him to take care of the paperwork. He says he'll get your divorce, and there won't be a Goddamned thing anyone can do about it."

Her eyes widened and she sat up straighter. I didn't like the distance but managed not to growl. Too much. "What do you mean? He can't just make a divorce happen."

"He can, because he knows the right people. All you have to do is say the word, honey."

"I don't want to take advantage of your club's kindness, but I'll get on my knees and beg if someone here can get me divorced from Doug and have it be completely legally binding."

"What about Caleb?"

She tilted her head. "What about Caleb?"

"I heard him in court. He said he didn't want anything more to do with his father. Would you want me to ask him if he wants us to terminate his father's rights?"

She shook her head hard. "There's no possible way you could do that. Nope."

I couldn't help the slow grin that spread across

my face. "Like I said, honey. Anything is possible if you know the right people and if those people owe you something."

"Yes. Ask him. That's his decision." She didn't hesitate. "If you guys can really make all this happen and it be real, then he gets to make that choice on his own."

"I'll talk to him tomorrow when I tell him my story."

She looked up at me, hope and longing and hunger in her gaze. Now that she wasn't trying or wasn't able to disguise her emotions, I recognized the expressions on her face. I'd seen those exact same emotions but with no real expectation I was what she wanted me to be.

Then she did something I wasn't expecting. Violet raised her hand to my face, cupping my cheek and stroking my beard a couple times. Then she leaned up and pressed her mouth to mine for a soft, lingering kiss. That simple touch of her lips against mine altered my world forever. Violet was mine. God have mercy on anyone who tried to hurt her, because I would have none.

Chapter Ten

Violet

This man.

This dangerous, shattered, wonderful man.

I felt him shudder around me when I kissed him. His arms tightened briefly, then he seemed to make an effort to relax. As for me? My world burst into a million pieces. Some of those pieces were emotions and emotional restraints I needed rid of, but some of them were so dangerous I was completely and utterly terrified.

I pulled back, trembling at the intensity of feelings this simple kiss had unleashed. How was it possible to feel so much for someone I barely knew? I'd spent my entire adult life in a marriage devoid of genuine affection, where every touch held the potential for pain rather than pleasure. Yet here I was, melting into the arms of an ex-convict I'd known for less than a day.

"Violet," Riot whispered, his voice rough with emotion. His eyes searched mine, looking for any sign of regret or hesitation. He held me securely, but I didn't feel trapped. One big hand moved in a comforting slide up and down my back, gentling me like he might a nervous filly.

"I shouldn't have done that," I said, but made no move to leave his lap. "I'm still married. And you're --"

"I'm what?" he asked softly when I didn't continue.

"You're too good to be true," I confessed. "Men like you don't exist in my world. Men who *protect* instead of harm. Men who *ask* instead of take."

He laughed, a short, humorless sound. "Honey, I'm nobody's idea of a good man. I've got blood on my hands and sixteen years of prison behind me to prove it."

"And yet you've shown me more respect in one day than Doug has in our entire marriage." I touched his face again, marveling at how he leaned into my touch like a man starved for affection. Maybe he was. "I don't know what this is between us, but I know I don't want it to stop."

"It won't," he promised, his eyes sparked with fervent promise. "Not unless you decide you don't want me."

His words wrapped around me like a vow, and I found myself believing him despite all the warnings in my head. I'd been lied to for so long that I should have been immune to pretty words and promises, but something about Riot's blunt honesty cut through my defenses.

"I've got a man with some power in this city after me, Riot. Are you sure you want to put yourself in his crosshairs like this? The very last thing in this world I want is for you to get hurt or get your parole revoked or whatever." I let my fingers tunnel through his short beard, the rough, bristle-like strands a soothing sensation against my palm. I looked up at him and more of those vile tears slid down my cheeks. "You're too good a person to go back to prison, Riot. You didn't deserve to be there to begin with."

"I absolutely deserved to be there, Violet. Don't ever doubt that. I killed that motherfucker. Then I pissed on him for good measure since I knew I wouldn't be there to piss on his grave."

His declaration should have scared me, and maybe in a way it did. But there was a part of me -- a larger part than I was comfortable admitting -- that took great pleasure in imagining something similar happening with Doug. Just not with Riot or Caleb. I wanted to be the one to kill Doug. God knew I'd earned the right to end that monster.

"I'm married, Riot. I have a husband who's not going to let me go willingly simply because, in his mind, he owns me."

"No, he doesn't." His simple declaration was said in a rough voice filled with sorrow and anger. There were times this man was an open book. Other times, like at the court hearing, I couldn't read him at all. "No matter what happens, there is no scenario where you go back to him if you don't want to. Even if you wanted to, I'd have to be sure you knew Caleb was safe and not in danger because I know you'd walk back to him willingly if he threatened your son."

I smiled up at him. "Seems you already know me."

"I do."

"Thank you," I whispered, resting my head against his chest. His heartbeat was strong and steady beneath my ear, and I found myself matching my breathing to the rise and fall of his chest.

"For what?" His voice rumbled through me like a giant cat purring.

"For jumping into this situation the way you did. You didn't need this complication in your life. I'm sure it brings up bad memories."

"Honey, my whole life has been about those bad memories. Every fuckin' day in prison, I thought about what I'd done. What I could have done differently. Everything I lost. Thing is" -- he looked over my shoulder, his brows knitting together --"I never regretted a single Goddamned thing I did. Not the first time I got the shit beat out of me in prison by a guy twice my fuckin' size, just because he could. Not when the guards saw me as an easy target to work out their anger issues on. Not the first time *another* guy twice my size tried to rape me. Not once." Then he met my gaze and the intensity I found there took my breath. "Not until I met you and Caleb."

"Riot."

He shook his head. "You can always call me Riot. That's kind of who I am now, I guess. But my name is Quinn Devereaux. You need to know that, because I want to claim you." I opened my mouth, but Riot lay his fingers over my mouth gently. "Shh." He leaned in and rubbed my nose with his and my heart pounded. Oh, God, what was he doing to me? "I want to claim you so that my club will be honor bound to protect you. That ain't the *only* reason, but that's the reason I'm gonna give Caleb."

"What's the other reason?" I was terrified of his answer. I knew in my heart there was no way I could resist this man.

For several moments, I didn't think he was going to answer. Then he closed his eyes for a moment, letting out a pent-up breath. It was almost like he was getting ready to confess his worst sin and knew I'd condemn him for it.

"The other reason is because I want what you and Caleb have. I want that." His gaze shifted away, his features hard. I thought I saw what he wanted to hide. That fear of rejection. Longing for something you wanted with every breath in your body, afraid it was right in front of you only to have someone snatch it away. "I want... a family. And I want that family to be you and Caleb."

"Quinn," I whispered, testing his real name on my tongue. His eyes darkened at the sound, and I felt a thrill run through me at the power of that simple intimacy. "I want that too. I want to have something real. Not the facade I've lived for the last thirteen years."

His arms tightened around me, and I could feel the tremor that ran through his powerful body. "Good. Then it's settled. I'm claiming you and Caleb. You'll be under my protection, and by extension the club's. Once we get your divorce fixed or whatever, we'll make it official."

I waited for the panic to hit me. Waited for the doubt and fear of putting Caleb into a worse situation than we were already in. There was none. I took a long breath, staring into his face. Then I exhaled. When I did, a smile tugged at my lips, and I found I wanted to laugh. Was that relief I felt?

I nodded. "Yeah. I think we will."

The smile on this man's face... There was that same look of relief on his face that I was sure had been on mine moments before. And he was so freaking gorgeous when he smiled!

Once again, I leaned up and brushed my lips over his. Riot didn't need further encouragement. He gripped the back of my neck and held me steady as he licked the seam of my lips, daring me to open to him. I did, surrendering to him with a grateful sigh.

His tongue swept into my mouth, hot and demanding yet gentle. A rush of heat blew through me and I gasped. Moaning softly against his mouth, I welcomed the thrust of his tongue. I curled my fingers in the fabric of his shirt as I clung to him. His scent, a heady mix of gasoline and beebalms, soothed me like nothing ever had.

This kiss was nothing like the first one. Riot's kiss was possessive, a claiming. A physical manifestation of the promises we'd just made to each other. His hand at my neck kept me anchored to him while his other arm tightened around my waist, pulling my form firmly against him.

I'd never been kissed like this before, like I was precious and desired. Doug might have wanted to fuck me, but he'd never *wanted* me. Not in any meaningful way. Riot kissed me like a man with something to prove.

When he finally pulled back, we were both breathing hard. His gray eyes reminded me of storm clouds, intense, dangerous, but paralyzingly lovely. I had no hope of breaking his stare, no hope of resisting him. And I wasn't broken up about it.

"Christ, Violet," he murmured, his voice a rough rasp that sent shivers down my spine. "You're gonna be the death of me."

I couldn't help the small laugh that escaped me. "That would be counterproductive to your promise to protect me and Caleb."

His answering smile was slow and devastatingly sexy. "True enough." He brushed a strand of hair from my face, his touch feather-light. "You should get some sleep. Tomorrow's gonna be a long day."

"Have you talked to Lana?"

"I have but only briefly. I gave her what she knew was the bare minimum of information." He shrugged. "At the end of the day, Lana Thompson is still an honorable officer of the court. Unlike some of her colleagues, she does her best to work for justice and still adhere to the law."

He helped me to stand, then followed, leading me to the bed and urging me into it. When I'd crawled between the sheets, he pulled the covers over me and sat on the edge. With gentle fingers, he brushed my hair off my forehead and out of my eyes.

"You're beautiful, Violet. The most beautiful woman I've ever seen. I understand why Harrington would want to keep you, but he can't have you. Not anymore."

"I don't want to go back to him. Not ever."

"You won't." He kissed me once more, this time lingering only a moment with a soft kiss. "You good by yourself, or do you want me to stay?" He waved at the couch. "It's pretty comfortable. I can get a pillow and a blanket."

I took a deep breath and smiled. "Why not sleep next to me? Get a quilt and sleep on top of the covers."

The wonder on Riot's face was heartbreaking. "You'd let me sleep with you?" Sweet God, this man was breaking my heart!

"Yes. I think I'd like that. If I have a nightmare, you can wake me before I disturb Caleb." Then I felt the familiar burn of tears behind my eyes, and I gave Riot a watery smile. "Maybe, with you next to me, protecting me, I won't have any nightmares."

Riot swallowed, nodding several times. I smiled and scooted over in the bed. He snagged a blanket from the back of the couch and lay on top of the covers next to me. The blanket covered him from the waist down. He was dressed in gym shorts and a T-shirt because he'd been asleep before he'd come to rescue me from my nightmare. That curiously comforting scent of gasoline and beebalms surrounded me.

I had time to register how warm Riot was at my back. Then his arm dropped over my waist. Somehow, his other arm ended up under my head, pillowing my head.

I sighed...

And surrendered to sleep.

Chapter Eleven

Riot

Someone was in the room. I knew it the second I woke, even with my eyes closed. It took me a moment to remember where I was. Then Violet curled sweetly against me, and I remembered I wasn't in prison. I was in the Kiss of Death compound with my brothers, so whoever was in the room with me and Violet right now wasn't a threat. I breathed a small sigh of relief before opening my eyes.

Standing over me, giving me a death stare, was Caleb. Instinctively, I tightened my arms around Violet fractionally. She sighed and snuggled deeper into my embrace, burying her face in my chest before she settled once more.

Caleb didn't speak, but he stared at me for a long time. I could see a mixture of anger, surprise, and relief on the young man's face. He nodded at me once, then took a step away from the bed.

"Caleb," I murmured. "I swear I won't hurt your mother. Not in any way."

"You'll be faithful to her?"

"Always."

"You'll stand between her and danger? Especially my dad?"

"I'll protect both of you. No matter who or what the danger is."

"I'm never letting anyone hurt my mom again, Riot. I will always be watching you."

I lifted my chin in acknowledgment. "I consider myself warned, then."

Caleb's gaze shifted from me to his mother. Violet chose that moment to sigh, a soft smile tugging her lips for a brief moment. Like she was in the middle of a happy dream. "You keep that look on her face, and you and I won't have any problems."

"Caleb, nothing would make me happier than being able to keep that look on your mother's face for the rest of her life. She deserves better than me, but she's letting me claim her. I have no intention of making her ever want to leave me."

"But if she does want to leave you," Caleb pressed, "would you let her go?"

"No." I didn't hesitate with my answer.

"You'd keep her against her will?" Now his gaze was narrowed on me. If looks could kill, Caleb and I wouldn't be having this conversation.

"I didn't say that." Violet mumbled something and lifted her face so that she nestled between my neck and shoulder before she settled once again. "If she ever wants to leave, I'll find out what I fucked up and fix it. Understand me, Caleb, I would do anything to keep you and your mom in my life."

"*Me*?" he asked incredulously. "You actually want me? Not just my mom?"

"I do. You're going to be a great man, Caleb. You're going to be a man other men want to follow because you admit when you're wrong. You're willing to do anything you have to for the people you care about. I don't know many men brave enough to go outside their comfort zone the way you did with me. You made hard decisions based on information you trusted, and you did what was best for your mom. I want to watch you grow into that man, and be your friend. That way you know I'll always have your back."

Again, Caleb studied me closely before nodding his head. "If all that's bullshit, it's really good bullshit." He tilted his head. "But I don't think it is. I think you mean every word you're saying."

"I do, Caleb. With everything I am."

"Good." He put his shoulders back. "She's always looking out for everyone else and forgets to take care of herself."

"You can count on me. I swear it."

He gave me a curt nod and turned to go. "Caleb?" When I called, he stopped, turning his head in my direction. "First thing in the morning. Unless you want to talk now."

"About your past? Why you went to prison?"

"Yeah. I had to tell your mom first."

"So she could censor you?" The kid was a master at interrogation. At least, interrogating someone who cared about the information he was spilling and the people involved.

I winced. "Well, I wouldn't put it quite like that…"

"But you wanted her to approve of how you worded what you told me."

Again, I winced. Christ, this kid! "Look. I promised I wouldn't lie to you, and I won't. But I will always defer to your mom on shit like this. I hope you and I can be the best of friends, but mother trumps friend in this case."

"I hear you. But don't worry about it." He actually smirked at me. "I heard you talking to Mom before you guys went to bed. I know all of it. And I do mean *all* of it."

"Christ, Caleb." I wanted to be horrified and part of me was. What came out was a clipped laugh.

Violet snorted awake, looking around her with confusion but not fear. "Caleb?" Violet's voice was slurred with sleep. She tried to open her eyes but only managed to get one eye open for longer than a couple of seconds. Part way.

"Everything's good, Mom," Caleb leaned in and kissed Violet on top of her head. "Go back to sleep."

"Love you, squirt." Violet stretched and held her hand up to her son even as she laid her head back on my chest.

Caleb took her hand and squeezed lightly before letting go. "Love you too, Mom."

We both waited a few minutes for Violet to settle. I doubted she'd remember this. I *hoped* she didn't remember this…

Caleb stared at me as I lay there with his mother in my arms, cuddling her against me. What the fuck else was I supposed to do? The kid had this whole intimidation thing down pat. In a fight, I could take the kid. Easy. The problem was, there was no way I'd fight Caleb. If he thought I needed a beating, I'd take it like a man.

Finally, Caleb glanced down at his mother. In the dim light from the clock on the nightstand, I saw his features soften before he looked back at me again. Instantly his expression changed to one of menace. Then he pointed at his eyes with two fingers, then pointed the fingers at me. He did this a couple times, raising his eyebrows when he finished. I nodded my acknowledgment. He was watching me. Good to know. The young man finally nodded back at me before turning to leave.

Once Caleb had closed the door behind him, I let out a long breath. Christ, that kid was going to give me a heart attack before this was over.

I glanced down at Violet, her face peaceful in sleep against my chest. The weight of her trust crushed me in the best possible way. I'd spent sixteen years in prison with nothing but my rage and regret for company. Now I had this woman and her son in my life, and I'd kill anyone who tried to take them from me.

Just as I suspected, Violet didn't move afterward. Apparently, the woman was exhausted. And, honestly, I was surprised she hadn't crashed already. Probably because she didn't have a safe place to let her guard down. I'd be lying if the thought of her being comfortable enough with me, safe enough with me, to get the rest she needed didn't make me feel ten feet tall.

I kissed the top of Violet's head before closing my eyes again. She didn't move.

I must have dozed off because the next thing I knew, the room was flooded with sunlight from the open curtains. Violet was still sound asleep in the same position. Her hand rested lightly on my chest. There was a soft, contented look on her face. My heart melted. Never in my life had I felt so proud and important. This woman needed me. I knew better than anyone who'd never been to prison how rare a truly, peaceful sleep was when you didn't feel safe.

I had no desire to move. I didn't care how uncomfortable I was becoming, only that Violet didn't seem interested in moving, and I wanted her to sleep as long as she could. She needed it. Unfortunately, my phone buzzed. Several times. I'd initially tried to ignore it, but after the fifth time someone tried to call, I knew I was going to have to answer.

Carefully, I extracted myself from Violet's sleeping form. Once I'd gotten up from the bed and made sure Violet was still settled and asleep, I picked up my phone from the nightstand and stepped just outside the door to her bedroom.

Just as I shut the door, the fucking phone started

buzzing again.

"This better be fuckin' important," I grumbled when I answered the fucking thing.

"Nice to hear your voice too, Riot." Knight was deceptively cheerful. Mainly because Knight was typically reserved. Sure, he had a wicked sense of humor, but it wasn't often that side of him came out to play. Of all of us, Knight had been in prison the longest and had had the worst time of it. How he'd managed to have a grip on the latest technology and could manipulate it to serve his needs, I had no idea. But the man wasn't just smart. He was fucking smart. "Get your ass to my office if you want to know the latest on your girl."

"Tell me now." The second the words left my mouth, I knew I'd fucked up. I hastily added, "Please."

"Uh-huh." I could almost see the tic next to his eye indicating how pissed off he was. "I could do that." There was a long silence while I waited for him to continue but he didn't.

"Well?"

"I said I could. Not that I would. You want shit delivered to you in a manner convenient for you, my suggestion would be to answer your phone a little nicer."

"Sor --" I stopped speaking when the phone beeped, indicating the call had been terminated. "Temperamental asshole," I muttered before opening the door to Violet's room again and glancing in. She hadn't moved. Good. Because it looked like I was going to see Knight.

I went to my room and got dressed, throwing on a pair of jeans, a T-shirt and my cut. When I opened the door, it was to a scowling Caleb.

I raised my hands in a defensive gesture. "I

swear to God, I didn't touch her last night other than to kiss her." I'd blurted out the information without intending to, but honestly, the kid had this whole intimidation thing down. Or it could be I knew how important it was to earn Caleb's trust. Not just for my sake in winning over Violet, but for Caleb's sake. He'd never feel safe if he didn't trust me. If he didn't feel safe, Violet wouldn't either.

His gaze narrowed. "You kissed her. My mother." His voice was cold and deadly.

"Are you sure you're twelve?" I suddenly realized I'd taken a step backward, retreating when I hadn't intended to. He said nothing, so I scrubbed a hand over my face, opening the door further so Caleb could come inside my bedroom and we could talk without disturbing Violet. "Yeah. I kissed her. But only because she kissed me. I was kissing her back." Again, Caleb just stared at me. "OK, I'd have kissed her anyway if I'd known she wanted me to." Still nothing. "If I say I liked it, are you going to hire someone to kick my ass?"

"You saying you don't think I can beat you on my own?" Finally, the kid spoke. And yeah, he sounded as angry as I'd first thought.

"No. I'm saying you'd want someone you knew could kill me because Violet wouldn't approve of you killing me." I smirked because we both knew it was true. Not because she liked me or anything. She'd be against her son killing anyone. Regardless of if they needed killing or not.

Caleb's expression didn't change. "Who said she'd ever find out?"

Fuck.

Yeah. Mic drop moment.

"Jesus Christ," I muttered, running my hand

through my hair. This kid was something else entirely. "Look, I get it. You're protective of your mom. But I'm not your dad. I would never hurt her."

"Heard that before," Caleb said flatly, his gaze boring into me, probably trying to see into my soul. "Men make promises they're unable to keep."

I stepped closer to him, keeping my voice low but firm. "I'm not asking you to trust me blindly, Caleb. I'm asking you to watch me. Judge me by what I do, not what I say. Your mom deserves someone who treats her right, and I intend to be that man."

Something flickered in Caleb's eyes. Maybe uncertainty, maybe grudging respect. It was hard to tell.

"Knight called," I continued, changing the subject. "He's got information about your situation. I need to go see him."

"I'm coming with you," Caleb said immediately. Not a request.

I considered arguing but thought better of it. "Fine. But you stay close to me, and if I tell you to do something, you do it without question. Got it?"

He nodded once, a sharp jerk of his head.

"We should leave your mom a note," I said, glancing toward her bedroom door. "I don't want her to wake up and panic."

"Already done," Caleb said. "I left one on the kitchen counter. Told her we were checking out the compound."

I sighed. "I realize you're pushing me and I'm fine with you testing the boundaries. But there are some things you don't get to decide. Hell, there are some things *I* don't get to decide, and this is my home."

Caleb gave me a patient look. Like he was bored

with the whole conversation. "Look." Caleb sighed. "I get what you're saying. I just don't give a fuck. If it involves my mom, I'm going to be there. End of story. Someone doesn't like it, they can tell me to my face."

"Yeah. I don't think you're really twelve."

Caleb followed me to Knight's office. The door, which was always open, was now closed. A quick check of the handle revealed it was locked too. "Fucking grumpy bastard," I muttered before knocking. "Knight! It's me! Open up!"

There was a long enough pause I knew he was making a point. When he opened the door, his glare was unmistakable.

I sighed. "I apologize for being rude on the phone." Sometimes it was best to admit you were wrong. "I didn't want to wake Violet." It was a low blow, but I couldn't let the bastard think he'd won the war instead of just the battle.

He rolled his eyes but stepped back and let me and Caleb inside his office. Instead of talking to me, he offered Caleb a seat in front of his desk before perching on the edge himself.

"I've filed the paperwork that officially finalizes the divorce between your mother and father. She's free, but she got nothing from him in the way of monetary value." Knight got down to business, but he completely ignored me. Yeah, he wasn't giving up on the war just yet. "I have everything ready that will free you from him as well, but I hadn't talked to you about it."

"Mom told Riot I should have a choice." Caleb didn't flinch at the news. Any of it.

Knight shrugged. "Didn't realize that, but I wouldn't have done anything permanent without checking with you first. You're old enough, and severing legal ties with a parent isn't a trivial matter."

That seemed to surprise Caleb. I wasn't sure why, but he clearly wasn't expecting Knight to ask his opinion on something like this.

"I figured you'd do what Mom and Riot thought was best no matter what I wanted." He glanced at me.

Two things struck me at Caleb's statement. First, he was clearly shocked Knight was taking his feelings in the matter into consideration and wasn't doing anything until he had the answers he was looking for. Second, Caleb included me in what he thought the decision-making process would be. That surprised the shit outta me.

Knight waved his concerns away. "Doesn't matter what they want. This decision affects you in very intimate ways. Cutting someone's father out of their life isn't something I'd ever do if the person was able to make that decision rationally. You're clearly in possession of your faculties, so it's your choice."

"Then my choice is to never see that son of a bitch again."

Caleb's fierce assertion was all Knight needed. "Consider it done."

"Dad's gonna be pissed," Caleb stated. I swear to God, the kid could have been one of the patched members of Kiss of Death the way he adapted to the situation at hand. He hadn't flinched no matter what we threw at him, however unintentional. "What happens next?"

"That's part of the reason I called Riot. Your dad's hired some really nasty people to come after your mother."

"Kill him," Caleb said without pause. "If he's dead he can't pay anyone. If there's no money, there's no danger. Problem solved."

Knight gave me a look. I shrugged. If he was looking for a clue as to how to deal with this kid he was going to have to look at someone else. I had no fucking clue.

"That's certainly one option," Knight said carefully. "Maybe we could look for another deterrent?"

"I want him gone," Caleb insisted, his voice steel. "He'll never stop otherwise."

I stepped forward, finally inserting myself into the conversation. "We need to think strategically, Caleb. Killing your father might solve one problem but create ten more."

Knight nodded. "Riot's right. Your father has connections -- financial, political, and criminal. First rule of being in a club like Kiss of Death is to never kill if it can be avoided. Why? It makes people look. Especially someone like your father. The more connected someone is, the more questions people ask and the more they demand answers."

"So, what then?" Caleb demanded, frustration evident in his tense shoulders. "We just wait for him to try again? Maybe succeed the next time?"

I placed a hand on Caleb's shoulder. "No. We make it impossible for him to come after you. We make the cost too high."

Knight tapped a few keys on his computer. "I've been digging into Harrington's business. There are... irregularities." A smirk crossed his face. "Significant ones. Your father appears to be under investigation already. Has been for months, and probably has no clue."

Caleb's eyes widened. "By whom?"

"Seems your father's business dealings have attracted federal attention," Knight replied. "FBI, DEA, and IRS. The unholy trinity."

"Can we use that?" I asked.

Knight's smile was cold. "Oh, I think we can do better than that. In fact, if we play our cards right, there's every possibility Doug Harrington's unspoken associates will do him in."

It was hard to tell what Caleb was feeling, but I thought there was a sense of frustration. This was a kid who had some big feelings, and I couldn't read him for shit.

"Knight." I gave him a wary look. "Is this something you want to discuss now?"

"What?" Knight asked, not looking confused in the least. "Killin' the kid's father?" He shrugged. "The way I figure it, the kid's got just as much a right as anyone other than maybe your woman to decide what happens to the bastard."

"Mom would never condone this." Caleb's expression still didn't change, but I could tell how he felt about it. "So you don't say anything to her."

That got my attention. "Uh, maybe this isn't the best conversation to be having?" I gave Knight a hard look.

"If I'm not keeping this from you, Caleb, I'm not keeping it from your mother. You both get to have a say in this."

"Are we really fuckin' talkin' about this?" I felt like someone had to be the voice of reason here.

Knight shrugged. "Honestly, it's probably all moot. Harrington has been laundering money through several businesses for years. He's also been skimming from his bosses, which is never a good idea, but especially not with the people he's working for. In any case, the Feds have been building a case for months. If they don't get him the cartel will, since that's who he's been working for."

"Can we use that to keep him away from us?" Caleb's voice had lost some of its hardness, replaced by genuine curiosity.

"That's the beauty of it," Knight said with a satisfied smirk. "We don't have to do anything illegal ourselves. We just need to make sure the right information reaches the right people." He glanced up at me before turning his attention back to Caleb. "Both the Feds and your father's associates would be very interested in certain files I've uncovered."

"So either the Feds get him or the cartel does." Caleb looked thoughtful. "It'll take the Feds forever."

"Maybe. Maybe not." Knight crossed his arms over his chest. "Either way, all we have to do is sit tight and wait."

"Except I'm sure my dad will find a reason to drag Mom back to court. Any time she goes outside this compound, she'll be at risk."

Knight stared at Caleb for a long moment. Then he looked at me. "You sure this kid's twelve?"

"Twelve?" I snorted. "Heard he was gonna be forty his next birthday."

"I will totally tell my mom you guys ganged up on me." The smirk on Caleb's face would have made me laugh out loud if I hadn't been slightly wary of the kid. "I'm not stupid. I'm also not about to let anything happen to my mom. No matter what has to be done."

"Give me a few days, Caleb." Knight moved from the edge of his desk to the bank of computer screens behind him. "No matter what happens, I promise your mom will be safe."

I wasn't sure Knight's promise satisfied Caleb, but he didn't raise any more objections.

"How long before I'm not legally Doug

Harrington's son?" The sudden change of topic was welcome as far as I'm concerned.

"Give me twenty-four hours. I'll have to contact a couple of people, but I swear to you, Caleb, when I'm done, Harrington will think every signature of his connected with your mom's divorce or your parental custody change might actually be legit. Even though he knows he didn't sign anything."

"Won't people be able to tell it's not his signature?"

Knight gave Caleb an evil grin. "Nope. In fact, if he contests anything, there will be a string of experts already consulted who will swear his signature is spot-on."

That seemed to satisfy Caleb. The kid stood and held out his hand to Knight who immediately stood and took it. "Thanks. Now. You've just got one more thing to do."

"What's that?" I could tell Knight couldn't wait to hear what Caleb had to say.

"I want you to legally make Riot and Mom married."

Chapter Twelve

Violet

For a moment, I thought I'd misheard what Caleb had said. I stood frozen in the doorway of Knight's office, my hand still gripping the frame. I'd woken up alone, found Caleb's note and decided to do a little exploring myself. I ran into Hannah and she said she'd seen them in Knight's office. I followed her directions to Knight's office where, sure enough, I found them.

And I'd arrived just in time to hear my twelve-year-old son ask a man I barely knew to forge marriage documents between me and Riot.

"Caleb!" I gasped, finally finding my voice.

All three males whipped around to face me. Knight looked mildly amused, Riot looked like he'd been caught with his hand in the cookie jar, and Caleb... my son simply gave me a steady look, not in the least repentant.

"Mom, it makes sense," he said, his voice perfectly reasonable. "If you're legally married to Riot, Dad can't touch you."

I stepped into the room, my legs shaky beneath me. "That's not how this works, Caleb. You can't just decide who I marry."

"Why not?" Caleb crossed his arms. "You didn't decide who you married the first time."

His words hit me like a physical blow. I flinched, and immediately Riot was at my side, his hand warm and steady at the small of my back. "That's enough, Caleb," Riot said, his voice gentle but firm. "Your mother deserves to make her own choices, especially about letting another man in her life."

Caleb didn't back down. "Are you telling me you

don't want to be with Riot, Mom?"

"I don't know what I want, Caleb." I tried to keep calm, but the fact was I was reeling on the inside. Not because Caleb had, apparently, found me a husband, but because I wasn't as opposed to the idea of marrying Riot as I should be. Not because I loved him. I didn't know Riot well enough to love him. Riot represented safety and security and all the gentle, tender things I'd needed for so long but had never had. He was also unfailingly kind to me and seemed willing to give me anything he thought I needed.

"Yes, you do." Caleb didn't flinch. "Or are you telling me he climbed into your bed without your knowledge or consent? Because if he did, Dad's not the only one I'll make sure has a miserable life."

"OK, this is really getting out of hand." I tried to use my sternest voice.

"Mom, it was out of hand the first time Dad put his hands on you. Now it's time for you to belong to someone who protects rather than hurts."

"Caleb --"

"No, Mom." He was more forceful now, an Alpha male in the making. "I heard every conversation you've had with Riot. I know the best way for the rest of the men in this club to get involved in making Dad stay away from us is for them to see you as Riot's woman."

"We can't expect these people to risk everything to help us. They've done more than enough already."

"Then do it for me, Mom. Marry Riot. I don't know if Knight could do something to have Riot adopt me and make it all legal and stuff before Dad catches on or not." He gave Knight a sneaky glance. Knight narrowed his gaze. I wasn't sure if it was because he knew he was being manipulated or if he was incensed that Caleb would doubt his skills. Could be either. "If he can't, at least he's making it so Dad has no rights to me."

"I can do any fucking thing with a computer," Knight said stiffly, straightening to his full height. "Anything."

"Then marrying Mom and Riot and making Riot my legal parent shouldn't be a problem for you." Caleb didn't back down, giving orders like he was not only an adult, but *the* adult in charge.

"I don't know whether to strangle you or be proud of you," I muttered.

"Be proud," Riot said with a grin, giving my shoulder a little squeeze.

"I'm assuming you ain't supposed to be given the opportunity to protest this union, Riot?" Knight turned to his keyboard and started doing computer shit without looking in our direction.

"Nope," Caleb said. "He lost that right when I caught him in my mother's bed. *Cuddling* her." He made a face. "That's just gross."

I couldn't help but laugh despite myself. "We were just sleeping, Caleb."

"Uh-huh." His skeptical tone made me want to simultaneously hug him and ground him for life. I never had been able to get the upper hand on this kid. Mainly because everything the child did, and I mean everything since he was old enough to realize something might be wrong with me and his dad, was to make my life better. How the hell did you argue with a kid who was that observant and empathetic?

Riot cleared his throat. "I think we need to slow down here." His voice was steady, but I could feel the tension in his body where his hand now rested against my back. "Marriage isn't something you rush into."

"You don't want to marry my mom?" Caleb challenged Riot, his eyes narrowing.

"Not what I said, kid." Riot's jaw tightened. "I happen to think your mom deserves to be wooed properly before she gets hitched again."

Knight leaned back in his chair, clearly enjoying the show. "Notice he didn't say anything about having met her less than twenty-four hours ago." Then he shrugged. "I could have the paperwork ready within the hour. I backdated your divorce papers six months just in case getting married was what you needed to keep him away. So I can have a marriage properly filed, witnesses accounted for, even signed by clergy. No one would question it."

"That's not the point," I said, finding my voice again. "The point is that decision like this should be made by the people actually getting married! Not a twelve-year-old with delusions of grandeur!"

"So, you're saying you don't want to marry Riot," Caleb pressed.

I felt my face flush. "I'm saying that's between me and Riot to discuss. *Privately*. Which means you don't get to eavesdrop or manipulate the narrative." I actually shook my finger at him before I realized what I was doing and quickly put my hands behind my back.

Caleb grinned. "You forgot to add 'young man'."

Just like that, all my outrage disappeared. "I give up," I said, opening my arms to hug my son. "If all men were as protective of their families as you, Caleb, the world would be a much happier, better place." I looked up at Riot. "I really hope you know what you're doing. Because *that* is what you have to live up to," I said, pointing at Caleb. "He'll make sure you do."

"'Cause if he doesn't live up to my standards, he

may not live long." Caleb gave Riot a bright smile and a big thumbs-up before scowling at him.

Riot shot Caleb an exasperated look, then held out his hand to me. "Why don't we go talk about this?"

"Not sure why," I grumbled. "Seems to me the three of you have taken matters into your own hands."

"Paperwork isn't done yet, Violet," Knight said softly. Where before I thought maybe he'd been playing along, enjoying Riot's discomfort, now Knight was sober and very serious. "No matter what I said before, I was only teasing. If you really don't want to do this, I won't do it."

"I have the feeling I should have stayed in bed." This was happening. I knew it like I knew my own name. Knight was going to get everything properly dated and filed, and I was going to be Riot's wife. Mrs. Quinn Devereaux. How did I know this? Because my son said that's what he wanted.

Caleb's smile was radiant. "Awesome!" Then he turned to Riot. "You know there's no way my dad can belong to an MC and not teach his son to ride a motorcycle. Right?"

"Nice try," Riot said, without hesitation. "That's one hundred percent up to your mother. And I have a feeling I know how she feels about you riding a motorcycle."

Caleb shrugged. "I'll get her there."

"Christ, my life," I muttered.

"Go talk this out." My son plopped down in a gaming chair in the corner of the room. "I'm gonna be here for hours and hours." He pushed off the desk to make the chair spin. "Gotta supervise. Make sure Knight gets everything done the way I want it."

"You sure you can handle this?" I asked Riot.

The big man grinned. "Nope. Still not letting you

back out." He snagged my hand. "Come on. We got some things to discuss."

Riot led me out of the office with Caleb calling after us, "Don't do anything I wouldn't do!"

I was so nervous and excited and keyed up I thought I was going to puke. Somehow I made it through the lift ride. We didn't get off on the fourth floor, however. Instead, Riot led me by the hand halfway down the long hallway to the door to another apartment. We passed a couple of guys on the way, but they greeted Riot and acknowledged me with a nod and a "Ma'am."

The second he opened the door and I stepped inside, I knew it was his room. His living area. He'd brought me into his private space, and I was going to get to see a little more of what he was really like.

Soon. We had more important matters to discuss first.

Riot shut and locked the door, then turned to me. There was such longing and need on his face, it took my breath. I knew the second we left Knight's office what was going to happen. Caleb had practically signed his consent for us to have sex, so I really had no other objection. The only reason I hadn't already fallen into this man's arms was Caleb. Caleb would always come first. No matter how old he got or pretended to be.

I'd never had a lover other than Doug, and he was about as far from a "lover" as he could get. He was a man who fucked me occasionally. Nothing more. I'd never experienced sexual arousal before Riot. I'd never experienced any kind of pleasure during sex. I'd grown to loathe the thought of anything to do with sex. Now, I wanted to explore everything I'd been denied, and I wanted to do it in the arms of a man of my choosing. I wanted Riot.

"We don't have to do this, Violet." Riot's voice was rough, strained with the effort of restraint. "Marriage, I mean. I'll protect you no matter what."

I shook my head, taking a step toward him. "I know that. But I think I want this. All of it." My heart hammered in my chest as I closed the distance between us. "I've never had a choice before. Not with Doug, not with anything. But I'm choosing you, Quinn."

His eyes darkened at the sound of his real name on my lips. "Are you sure? Once I have you, I won't let you go."

"That's exactly what I'm counting on."

With a growl, he pulled me to him, his mouth finding mine a little desperately. This wasn't the gentle kiss from last night. This was hunger and need and promise all wrapped into one. His tongue demanded entrance and I gave it willingly, meeting his passion with my own awakening desire.

He backed me against the wall, his powerful body pressing against mine. I could feel every hard muscle playing under his skin, the heat of him burning through my clothes. One hand tangled in my hair while the other gripped my hip, holding me steady.

"You deserve better than me," he murmured against my lips. "But I'm too fuckin' selfish to walk away."

"I don't want *better*," I whispered. "I want *you*."

His hand slid from my hip to the small of my back, pulling me closer to him until I felt his hard cock against my stomach. The sensation sent a thrill through me. Not fear, though. Anticipation. "Christ, Violet," he groaned, his lips trailing down my neck. I thought he inhaled like he was taking in my scent. "If you want me to stop, tell me now."

Instead of answering, I tugged at the hem of his shirt, wanting to feel his skin against mine. Understanding immediately, Riot stepped back just enough to take off his vest and pull his shirt over his head in one fluid motion. The vest he carefully draped over the back of a nearby chair, the shirt he dropped on the floor.

I gasped at the sight of him. His chest and arms were covered in intricate tattoos, a beautiful canvas of art that couldn't hide the scars beneath. Some scars were thin and white with age; others were puckered and angry -- the physical reminders of his time in prison. There was also the bandage along his side where he'd been hurt defending me and Caleb. Without thinking, I reached out to trace where that curved around his ribs.

"Does it bother you?" he asked, watching my face carefully.

"No," I whispered honestly. "Well, only that you were hurt. This is part of who you are. These scars helped make you into the man you are. And my son, the kid who, because of how he'd hurt me, threatened to kill his own father if I didn't leave the bastard, wants you to be my husband."

"He wants me for your protector. I can be that without marrying you. Or fuckin' you." Something in his expression shifted, a vulnerability I hadn't seen before.

"You're worth more than simply being a protector, Quinn. You're a good man. A kind man. You're also a man who protects people important to him."

"Christ, woman." Then he kissed me again. His hand slid underneath the hem of my shirt, skimming up my side around to my back. "You better be fuckin' sure about this."

"I've never been surer of anything in my life."

I knew this experience would be different than what I'd been through before. Doug liked to hurt, not pleasure. I thought I'd been kissed before, but what Quinn did to me was something entirely different. It was possession and tenderness wrapped together with a need so intense it stole my breath. He ran his hands over my torso anywhere he could reach, learning my body with reverent touches that made me shiver. When his palm cupped my breast through my bra, I gasped against his mouth.

"Too much?" he murmured, already pulling back.

"Not enough," I whispered, surprising myself with my boldness. I'd never been a demanding lover. Couldn't be. Now I was going to make damned sure I enjoyed myself. And the only way to do that was to make Goddamned sure Riot knew what I wanted.

Something dangerous flashed in his eyes. He lifted me effortlessly, and I wrapped my legs around his waist. He carried me toward his bed in the far corner of the open room. The whole time, his mouth never left mine, kissing me like I was oxygen and he was drowning.

He laid me on the bed with unexpected gentleness, his body covering mine. His weight should have frightened me after years with Doug, but instead I felt sheltered, protected. Quinn propped himself on one elbow, studying my face.

"I went to prison when I was sixteen. Before, I was with one woman. She was three years older than me. I lasted a minute and a half." I couldn't help but smile. Before I could say anything, he continued. "Even back then, I'd never wanted a woman the way I want you," he said, his voice rough. "I swear to you, I will protect you and Caleb with my life."

I felt small beneath Riot, but instead of fear, all I felt was an overwhelming sense of relief and expectation. He was so gentle, yet fine tremors racked his body and sweat erupted over his skin like he was stressed. I leaned up to kiss his neck, needing to give him whatever he needed. His confession and the careful way he treated me only affirmed my belief he was the perfect man for me.

He inhaled sharply at the touch of my lips against his skin, a shudder running through his powerful frame. "Violet..." He breathed my name like a prayer, his hand sliding beneath my shirt again, this time pushing it upward. "Can I see you? All of you?"

I nodded, suddenly shy but determined. He helped me sit up just enough to pull my shirt over my head, tossing it aside. His eyes darkened as they took in my simple cotton bra, nothing fancy or seductive about it.

"You're fucking gorgeous," he murmured, his fingers tracing the edge of the fabric. "So fucking beautiful it hurts."

No man had ever looked at me this way, with reverence and hunger mingled together. Doug had always treated my body as something to use, never to appreciate. The way Quinn looked at me made me feel beautiful for the first time in years. Maybe ever.

I reached behind me to unclasp my bra, letting it fall away. His sharp intake of breath sent a thrill through me. When his calloused palm cupped my breast, his thumb brushing across my nipple, I arched into his touch with a gasp.

"Tell me what to do, Vi." I couldn't imagine any other man in this position asking that question. Not because I expected him to know, but because no other man I knew would care more about making this good for me than protecting his ego.

"Whatever you want. Touch. Explore. Taste. Then you let me do the same."

Riot's eyes flashed with heat at my words. "I want everything," he growled as he lowered his head to my breast. The first touch of his mouth on my nipple sent electricity shooting through me. I gasped, arching into him as he sucked gently, then with more pressure, his tongue circling the sensitive peak and making me cry out.

I tunneled my hands through his hair, my fingers tangling in the dark strands, holding him to me. He switched to my other breast, giving it the same attention while his hand kneaded the one his mouth had abandoned. All the while, he growled and snarled against my chest. Though he was obviously a man on the edge, his touch was still gentle, almost reverent.

"Quinn," I moaned, squirming beneath him as heat pooled between my thighs. I'd never felt anything like this before, this desperate, clawing need building inside me. It was frightening and exhilarating all at the same time.

"I've got you," he murmured against my skin, his mouth trailing down my stomach. His hands moved to the waistband of my pants, hesitating there. "Still okay?"

Christ, this man! It was obvious how much he wanted to fuck me. And maybe any woman would do. But he was still stopping to check with me. He wasn't moving and counting on me to stop him, he was forcing me to make the decision myself so he knew he wasn't scaring me into submission. No one had to tell me that's what he was doing. This was who Riot was.

A protector through and through.

"Yes," I breathed, lifting my hips in invitation. "I'm more than OK. Don't stop, Riot. I swear I'll tell you if you scare or hurt me. Just do what feels good."

He must have needed the encouragement because he groaned and sat up on his heels, sliding my pants and underwear down in one smooth motion. I was completely naked beneath him now, and Riot's gaze ate me alive. I fought the urge to cover myself as his gaze traveled over me, hungry and appreciative. "Fucking perfect." He scrubbed a hand over his mouth. "If I could have made a woman for myself, she'd look exactly like you."

"Where have you been all my fucking life?" I whispered.

He snorted out a laugh. "In prison. But not anymore."

I smiled, reaching for him. "No. Not anymore."

"I got lost time to make up for." He raised his eyebrows as if challenging me.

"I know a double-dog dare when I hear one."

Riot moved from the bed and stripped off his jeans and boxer briefs. His cock stood out proudly from the thick curls at its base. He was long and thick, his fist circling the base. He gave a slow pump, and I saw pre-cum glistening on the top.

My mouth went dry at the sight of him. I'd never seen a naked man and actually wanted to look at him, never wanted to reach out and touch, taste, explore. But now I couldn't look away from Quinn's powerful body, scarred and tattooed and utterly magnificent.

"See something you like?" he asked, his voice deep and rough.

"Everything," I whispered honestly. "I love everything I see."

He climbed back onto the bed, his movements predatory and controlled. When his naked body covered mine, skin to skin, I gasped at the sensation. The weight of him, the heat, the incredible feeling of his hard cock pressed against my belly, it was overwhelming in the best possible way. I wanted more.

"I want to taste you," he murmured against my neck. "Every inch of you."

Before I could respond, he was moving down my body, pressing kisses along my collarbone, between my breasts, across my stomach. His hands gripped my thighs, gently spreading them as he settled between them. The first touch of his tongue against my pussy had me arching off the bed with a sharp cry.

"Christ, you taste good," he growled, his hands holding my hips steady as he explored me with his lips, tongue, and teeth. "Worth the Goddamned wait."

Riot fastened his mouth on my pussy, his tongue making a long, slow sweep. I fisted my hands in the sheets as pleasure unlike anything I'd ever experienced rocketed through me.

"Oh my God!" I whimpered as he continued his relentless erotic assault. He circled his tongue over my clit before dipping lower to tease my entrance.

One large hand splayed across my stomach, holding me in place as I writhed beneath him. He slipped two fingers of his other hand inside me, petting my pussy until I was bucking my hips, desperate to come.

"Fuck, you're so wet," he groaned against my thigh, his fingers curling inside me to find that perfect spot. "So fucking perfect."

When he returned his mouth to my clit, he sucked gently while working his fingers inside me. There was something building, a tension coiling tighter and tighter at my core. I'd never felt anything like this before, this rising, desperate need for release.

"Quinn," I gasped, my hands finding his head, tangling in his hair. "I'm gonna come!"

"Fuck, yes," he urged, his voice rough with desire. "Come for me. Wanna feel you come on my tongue."

His words pushed me over the edge. The orgasm crashed through me like a wrecking ball. I thrashed beneath him, my body arching upward, thighs trembling as pleasure unlike anything I'd ever known consumed me. I cried out his name, over and over, as he worked me through it, gentling his touch but not stopping until the last tremor subsided.

When I finally collapsed back on the bed, boneless and breathless, Riot crawled up my body, pressing kisses against my heated skin as he went. His eyes were dark with all kinds of emotion. Pride, eagerness, anticipation, but most of all raging desire shimmered in his gaze.

He reached into the nightstand and took out a condom. Stood to reason. He'd only just gotten out of prison. No way he didn't have condoms handy. He ripped open the packet and rolled the bit of latex over his shaft.

When he laid on top of me once again, he gave me a brows-drawn look of longing. Stroking my face with one fingertip he leaned in to rub his nose against mine. "Are you sure, Vi? Last chance." Instead of answering, I pulled him down for a kiss, then guided him inside me.

Chapter Thirteen

Riot

The feeling of her guiding me into her body nearly broke me. I'd never felt anything like this. The wet heat of her wrapped around me, taking me inch by inch. I had to clench my jaw to keep from coming right then. Sixteen years without a woman, and now I was buried inside the only one who'd ever mattered.

"Fuck," I groaned, my forehead pressed against hers as I fought for control. "You feel so Goddamn good."

She trailed her hands over my back, nails digging into my skin as I began to move. I started slowly, giving her time to adjust, watching her face for any sign of discomfort. Also, I thought it might be a good idea for me to calm the fuck down or this would be over before it really began.

"More," she whispered, lifting her hips to meet mine. "Please, Quinn."

The sound of my real name on her lips pushed me further toward the edge. I drove into her, holding myself deep to keep from coming. I couldn't take my eyes off her face. The flush on her cheeks, the way her lips parted with each thrust, the absolute trust in her gaze were all so satisfying I wanted to howl in victory.

"You're mine now," I growled, tangling one hand in her hair. "I can see it in your eyes."

She gave me a tremulous smile. "I know. I can feel it too, Quinn." Reaching up, Violet stroked my beard, letting her fingers sift through the strands. "I'm supposed to be yours. And you're supposed to be mine."

Her words hit me like a punch to the gut. The raw honesty, the welcome and complete acceptance were everything I'd never dared hope for. I captured her mouth in a desperate kiss, my hips moving with more urgency now. Each thrust drove me deeper, claiming her in the most primal way possible.

"You have no idea what you do to me," I panted against her neck, inhaling the sweet scent of her skin. "How long I've waited for you and didn't even know it."

She wrapped her legs around my waist, changing the angle and taking me impossibly deeper. The little gasp that escaped her lips told me I'd hit something good inside her. "There," she breathed, her eyes widening. "Oh God, right there!"

I kept the angle, driving into her with measured strokes, watching as pleasure transformed her face. Her eyes fluttered closed, her head thrown back against the pillow. I'd never seen anything so beautiful in my life. This woman coming undone beneath me, because of me, was the most awe-inspiring thing I'd ever seen. Her face was flushed with pleasure. A little puff of air left her parted lips with every forward stroke I made inside her body.

"Look at me," I commanded softly. "I want to see your eyes when you come again."

Her eyes opened, hazy with pleasure but focused on mine. The connection between us in that moment was more intimate than the joining of our bodies.

I slid my hand between us, finding her clit with my fingers. The second I did, Violet screamed. Her body seized around me and my world detonated.

"Oh God, Quinn!" Her eyes locked with mine, pupils blown wide as another orgasm ripped through her. The sight of her completely undone pushed me over the edge.

I buried myself deep inside her and let go with a

hoarse shout, my release hitting me like a freight train. Every muscle in my body tensed as I pulsed inside her, the pleasure so intense it bordered on pain.

"Fuck, Violet," I gasped, collapsing beside her and pulling her against me. I couldn't bear to be separated from her, not even for a second. "Just... *fuck*."

She giggled as she nuzzled against my chest, her breathing gradually slowing. "Yeah. I guess that's a good way to describe it."

I rolled us over so I was on my back and Violet cuddled against my side. We lay there in silence for several minutes. I traced lazy patterns on the bare skin of her shoulder. I kept waiting for regret to hit her, for her to pull away and start making excuses. But she just sighed contentedly and pressed closer.

"So," I finally said. "I guess we're getting married."

She laughed, the sound vibrating against my chest. "Apparently. My twelve-year-old son has arranged it all."

"Are you okay with that?" I needed to hear her say it.

Violet propped herself up on one elbow, looking at me with those clear blue eyes. "I should be terrified. I should be telling you this is crazy, that we barely know each other." She traced a finger along my jaw. "But nothing about this feels anything but *right*. I believe that *this* is right where I'm supposed to be. With you. With your club." She grinned. "I don't even know what motorcycle clubs like this do. And, quite frankly, I don't care. You all came to my rescue, and you didn't even know me." She leaned in and kissed my lips. There was so much wonder and affection in her gaze it nearly made me tear up. You know. If I was the kind of guy to do that kinda shit. "And that, Quinn, is all I need to know about you and your club. You helped a stranger and her son when you didn't have to. I think you've all earned my trust."

I couldn't help the grin that spread across my face. There was something about this woman's trust that felt sacred, like I'd been handed something precious and fragile.

"You're takin' a hell of a chance on me, honey," I said, tucking a strand of hair behind her ear. "But I swear I won't let you down."

She settled against me again, her warm breath fanning across my chest. "I don't think you could if you tried. It's not in your genetic makeup."

We lay in comfortable silence for a few minutes. Part of me couldn't believe this was happening. Twenty-four hours ago, I was just another ex-con trying to figure out how to navigate life on the outside. Now I had a woman who was going to be my wife and a kid who, despite his threats, seemed to think I was worthy of his mother.

"I just have one thing to tell you, and I need to do it now. While I'm sure we're alone."

"Oh Lord," she said with more than a hint of humor in her voice. "Here it comes."

"Caleb scares me. If you even hint that I've done something he doesn't much approve of, he will slit my Goddamned throat in my sleep. I'm not ashamed to admit I'm worried for my safety."

"Simple solution."

"Oh? What's that?"

"Don't do anything he doesn't approve of."

I thought about that for a moment, then grunted. "Yeah. Can't argue with that logic."

"He's the best thing to ever happen to me," she

admitted softly. "But I think you're the best thing to ever happen to me and Caleb." She looked up at me, stark vulnerability in her gaze. "Please be that man, Quinn."

"On my life, honey. On my life."

Chapter Fourteen
Riot

The following week and a half were tense, but I've never enjoyed life more. Every morning I woke up with Violet in my arms, her warm body curled against mine like she'd always belonged there. Each day, Caleb tested me with probing questions and suspicious glances that gradually softened into something resembling respect. By the third day, he'd stopped threatening to kill me in my sleep, which I considered a major victory.

Knight had worked his magic, creating a paper trail of our marriage that would hold up under any scrutiny. According to official records, Violet and I had been married for a week. Her divorce from Harrington was finalized six months before. Sure, Harrington was gonna pitch a bitch fit when this got presented, but Knight guaranteed no one would be able to prove their divorce, our marriage, and Caleb's adoption were anything other than legit. Lana assured me Judge Whitmore wouldn't bat an eyelash. In fact, Knight had already been in touch with her. Apparently, she'd had a confrontation with Mr. Todd about the discrepancy and, as far as the court was concerned, the divorce and adoption was "an oversight the court deeply regrets filing incorrectly." That's how she put it.

Knuckles had called a meeting with the full club to announce Violet and Caleb were under Kiss of Death protection. No one questioned it. Even before they heard what Harrington had done, every brother in the room was ready to ride for my new family simply because they were mine.

"You look happy," Violet said, leaning against the doorframe of our bedroom. She was wearing one of my T-shirts, the hem hitting her mid-thigh. The sight of her in my clothes did things to me I couldn't put into words.

"I *am* happy," I admitted, setting down the gun I'd been cleaning. When she raised an eyebrow, I shrugged. "Better to be prepared. None of us are supposed to have guns so we keep them in a weapons locker, hidden away. We don't have them out much, but I'm not taking chances with you and Caleb."

"You think he's going to use physical force?" Violet looked worried, but I could tell she trusted me.

"I don't know, honey. When did you last talk with Lana?"

"Yesterday," she said. "She just said nothing new had developed and to stay with you until she said it was safe to leave."

I frowned. "She hasn't heard from Harrington's lawyers?"

"I don't know. If she has, she didn't say."

I put my arm around her and led her to the little oasis we'd created in the very center warehouse in our territory. We'd hollowed out the thing and put in a swimming pool. It wasn't really fancy or anything, but it was a safe place to grill out and have a party if we wanted. Since the guys had started acquiring old ladies, they'd quickly taken over this place.

There was camo netting over the ceiling, but sunlight still filtered down. Sometimes, the girls had us remove the net to let in direct sunlight, but since Violet and Caleb got here, we decided it was best to hunker down. Which actually made this place all the better. Maybe because the enclosure was so big, or the way the sun hit the windows around the perimeter, but more sunlight came through here than anywhere else on the property inside the camo netting. This was by far Violet's favorite place on the whole property.

"Good afternoon, Violet."

I spun around, putting myself between Violet and the newcomer. Which was when two things happened. First, I realized it was Doug Harrington speaking. He'd somehow gotten inside the compound and hunted us down.

Then, he shot me.

"Riot!" Violet screamed as I spun around. Harrington had fired at the same time as I'd moved and managed to only graze my arm. I grunted and jerked but didn't go down.

With a roar of fury, I launched myself at Harrington. He got off another shot but missed. I heard Violet scream and looked over my shoulder. "Vi!" If that bastard had hit her, I'd tear him apart.

The second I took my eyes off him, Harrington attacked, tackling me to the ground. The impact slammed me hard against the concrete, but I barely felt it through the adrenaline. Harrington's face was twisted with rage as he tried to bring the gun down toward my head. I caught his wrist, straining against his surprising strength.

"You think you can take what's mine?" he snarled, spittle flying from his lips. "The bitch belongs to me! So does the boy!"

"Like hell," I growled, twisting his wrist until I heard the satisfying crack of bone. He howled, the gun clattering to the floor. I shoved him off me, scrambling to my feet. Blood soaked my shirt sleeve from the graze, but I barely noticed. My only thought was getting to Violet.

She stood frozen several feet away, her face pale with shock. "Quinn!"

"Get out of here!" I yelled, gesturing toward the

exit. "Find Caleb!"

Harrington dove for the gun, but I kicked it away, sending it skidding across the concrete. He turned on me with a vicious growl, pulling a knife from his belt. "You're nothing," he spat. "Just some ex-con piece of trash. You think she wants you? She's just using you for protection."

I circled him warily, keeping myself between him and Violet. "So?"

That seemed to catch him off guard. "Are you willing to die for a little whore who'll never love you?"

"Absolutely."

Harrington's face contorted with rage. He lunged at me, his knife slashing toward my chest. I sidestepped, grabbing his wrist and using his momentum to slam him face first into a steel post. The knife clattered to the ground but he recovered quickly, spinning and landing a solid punch to my wounded arm.

Pain exploded through me, but I'd endured worse in prison. I drove my fist into his gut, then his face when he doubled over. Blood spurted from his nose as he staggered backward. "How the fuck did you get in here?" I demanded, advancing on him.

He spat blood onto the concrete. "Money opens all doors."

"Not here it doesn't," I growled.

"Quinn, behind you!" Violet screamed.

I whirled to see another man entering from the far door, gun raised. I'd seen this man at court. He hadn't been in the courtroom with Harrington and his lawyer. He'd been outside. Had to be one of Harrington's bodyguards.

I crouched and dove for Harrington just as a shot rang out. I swear, I could feel the wind from the bullet on my cheek. Violet screamed again as I slammed Harrington's head against the concrete, knocking him out.

There was another shout. The newcomer raised his gun again, and this time he had a good bead on me. Another shot exploded and I flinched... but there was no pain.

The man jerked, a red stain blossoming on his chest, then he collapsed. That's when I realized it hadn't been the newcomer who'd shot. Violet had the gun Harrington had dropped. She clutched it in shaking hands, eyes wide but determined.

"Violet?" I put myself between her and the two men.

"Is he dead?" Her voice was surprisingly steady, all things considered. If she trembled a little, I'd never mention it. She still clutched the gun in one hand at her side.

"I don't know. How about we get you out of here, then I'll figure that out."

"I'll make sure you get sent back to prison, you son of a bitch."

Doug Harrington wasn't dead. I thought I'd knocked him out for a while, though. Guess I was wrong.

"No, you won't." Violet sucked in a breath. Standing in the doorway was Caleb. He had a gun in his hand, finger on the trigger.

"Caleb. Good. Get rid of this asshole. He's a criminal. Probably killed a bunch of innocent people, so you'd be doing the world a favor." Harrington looked like he fully expected his son to shoot me.

"Riot's taking care of Mom now. You don't get to touch her ever again." Caleb's voice was steady, though I could tell he realized he'd bitten off more than he could chew. The reality of what he was poised to do was far different from the daydream. Caleb fully understood that killing a man wasn't a trivial matter. Not when it was your father you were killing.

"Caleb. Come on." The patronizing look Harrington gave Caleb had my hackles rising for a multitude of reasons. Mostly because I was afraid it would be the thing to set Caleb off. "Be reasonable. You're not going to kill me."

My heart pounded, but I didn't dare move. Not until I knew Caleb wasn't going to pull that trigger.

"He'll never stop," Caleb said, his voice eerily calm. The gun didn't waver in his grip. Yet another red flag. "He'll always come after Mom. Not because he loves her. Because he can't stand to lose."

"You're not a killer, Caleb." Harrington tried to adopt a soothing tone, but it came out calculating and manipulative. "Don't do something you can't take back."

Caleb's eyes flickered between his father and me, the internal struggle clear on his face. Then his gaze settled on me, searching for something. "You killed your father when you were sixteen."

"I did," I acknowledged, taking another step toward him. "You know the whole story."

"And you didn't regret it."

"You heard what I told your mom. No. I didn't. But the cost was high, and you've got a future here. Once my mom was dead, I had nothing." I tried to keep one eye on Caleb and the other on Harrington, but I was going to keep Caleb from killing his father, no matter what happened to me. Hell, I'd rather the kid accidentally kill me than intentionally kill his father. "Your mom still depends on you. She needs you. I do too, so I don't screw things up for Violet."

"Listen to your mom's criminal boyfriend. He knows what happens to murderers."

"Christ, Doug. Know when to shut up," Violet snapped.

Caleb's hand trembled slightly now. "You know I'm right. He'll never stop. You know he won't."

"I'll take care of it. You know I don't lie. So I swear to you, I *will* take care of him."

Caleb pulled the hammer back. He was going to do it. I could see the exact moment he made the decision. Recognized it deep in my soul. I'm pretty sure I had the exact same expression on my face the second before I swung that bat at my father and beat him to death.

I lunged for Caleb, grabbing his hands and shoving them over his head away from Violet and Harrington. The instant we hit the ground, there was a deafening *BOOM* as a gun went off.

Harrington dropped to the ground. I wasn't sure where he got hit, but I knew by the way he hit the floor the bastard was dead. I rolled me and Caleb, keeping the gun over our heads as I put our backs to Harrington's body.

I looked up at the gun. It hadn't been fired. Tugging the weapon away from Caleb's limp fingers, I scrambled to my feet. Violet stood with her gun still pointed at Harrington. The gun she'd picked up – Harrington's gun -- was a .357 Magnum. Looking from Violet back to Harrington, my guess was he had Critical Defense rounds loaded, because Violet had shot him in the face. Now Harrington had no head.

"Huh," Violet grunted. "I guess Dirty Harry was right."

"The Christ happened here?" Knuckles and five other brothers charged into the room, guns in hand.

Knight was right behind Knuckles.

"Oasis. Need heavy clean up," Knight said into his radio. I knew the rest of the club would be on the way. We banded together like that. No one would ever find those bodies or any evidence that either man had ever been within ten miles of this place.

"Get Caleb and Violet out of here, Riot." Hawk spoke softly as I handed him the gun I'd taken from Caleb. "We'll take care of this."

"The gun Violet shot Harrington with was his." I didn't know if they needed to know, but I'd rather err on the side of caution.

"Got it." Hawk gripped my shoulder. "Go on. Take care of your family."

My family. Caleb had hurried to his mother. The pair clung to each other. I kept myself between them and Harrington. I wasn't sure what Caleb had actually seen, but I didn't want to take a chance on him seeing more if I could prevent that.

I put my arms around both of them, shielding them from the gruesome scene behind us. Violet was shaking, adrenaline drop setting in as her body calmed. Caleb's face was buried against his mother's shoulder, his body rigid with tension.

"Let's get out of here," I murmured, guiding them toward the exit. As we stepped outside, the bright afternoon sunlight felt surreal after what had just happened. I could hear the efficient sounds of my brothers already at work behind us, securing the scene, removing evidence. Kiss of Death MC took care of its own, and Violet and Caleb were now family.

I led them to our apartment, keeping my arm around Violet's shoulders. Caleb walked stiffly beside us, his face pale and jaw set. The kid was in shock, processing what had just happened. Hell, we all were.

Violet held Caleb's hand in a white-knuckled grip. No one spoke until we were safely inside with the door locked behind us. Violet collapsed onto the couch, her body still trembling. Caleb sat beside his mother, putting an arm around her slim shoulders.

I went to the fridge and dug out a couple bottles of water, handing them each a bottle before I sat on the coffee table in front of them.

"He's gone," Violet whispered. I was afraid she was have trouble processing, but she actually sounded relieved. "He's really gone."

"Yeah, honey. He's gone. He can't hurt either of you ever again."

Caleb looked up at me. He was stunned but shaking it off quickly. "I was gonna kill him."

"You didn't have to." Violet tightened her grip on her son. "I did what I had to do to protect you both. He would have killed Quinn and taken us back."

There was a knock at the door. "Riot. It's Knuckles and Gunnar."

I stood and squeezed Violet's shoulder as I passed her on the way to the door to let the men in. Knight was there too.

"Everything OK?" I asked, searching Knuckles' face for a sign something was wrong.

"We've got everything under control."

I snagged a couple chairs from the kitchen table and pulled them closer to Violet and Caleb so everyone could sit.

"Lana Thompson called me a little bit ago." Knuckles said without preamble. "She said everything was filed properly with your divorce and marriage, as well as Riot's adoption of Caleb. Apparently, Harrington's lawyer is livid but can't find anything to overturn any of it. She said Harrington might come after you."

"Well, I guess she was right." Violet seemed to be coming to life the longer she sat there. She was still trembling, but some of her color was back at least.

"No one will ever find him, Violet," Gunnar said softly. "Even if the law investigates you or Caleb or us there will be nothing tying any of us to Harrington since the last court appearance. That's why Lana avoided talking to you. She wanted to be able to say she'd had minimal contact with you in case things went south. She's our biggest alibi."

Violet nodded slowly, understanding dawning on her face. "She knew he'd come after us. She was protecting herself legally while still helping us."

"She's a smart woman," Knight confirmed. "She's been around this club, and others, long enough to know how we operate."

Caleb's jaw tightened. "So that's it? He just... disappears, and we get to go on with our lives?"

"That's exactly it," Knuckles said, his voice gentle but firm. "Some people might ask questions for a while, but without a body, without evidence, it'll eventually be forgotten. Just another rich asshole who went missing. And to be honest, with the Feds after him, who's to say he didn't leave the country?"

I watched Caleb's face carefully, trying to gauge how he was processing everything. The kid had been ready to pull the trigger on his own father. That kind of moment changes a person forever, even if they don't follow through. "You okay, kid?" I asked softly.

"Yeah." He nodded slowly. "I think I am." And yeah. I'd seen that same look on my face. He might not have killed his father in truth, but in his heart, he'd been the one to blow his head off. "I just hate it had to be Mom who killed him."

"Don't be sorry about that, Caleb," Violet said, gripping her son's hand. She smiled at him. "It wasn't something I'd have done under any other circumstance, but I would do anything to protect my family. And that's you and Quinn."

"I'm going to need therapy for years after this," Caleb muttered. "Or maybe I can con Knight into getting me a set up like he has and I can do a first-person-shooter gaming marathon or something."

There was a beat of silence before Violet let out a small chuckle. Then we all started laughing. Inappropriate? Absolutely. The way I saw it, sometimes it's either laugh or cry. I'd rather laugh any day of the week.

Chapter Fifteen

Violet

Both Caleb and I had nightmares for weeks after Doug's death. Gradually we both healed mentally and physically. Caleb had been sleeping much better. In fact, it had been at least two weeks since I'd heard him up in the middle of the night, and he was looking much better rested. He was also acting more and more like his old self -- the person he was before he'd found me in the middle of the floor with his father hitting me. We still didn't know how Doug had gotten into the compound, but I knew Riot would find out. Once he did, God help whoever was responsible.

The door opened and Riot stepped inside, shutting the door carefully behind him. He watched me warily, like he knew he'd sprung a trap and was waiting for the jaws to close around him.

"I just want to say I had nothing to do with it. I didn't even know what had happened until it was done." Riot looked as guilty as any teenager I'd ever seen. If I didn't know the man was actually three years older than me, I'd swear he and Caleb were the same age sometimes. He played like a kid and seemed to have this driving need to win my approval. I supposed I understood. He'd been robbed of his childhood and his family. I tried my best to give him any emotional support he needed and then some. Honest to God, the man was a once in a lifetime find.

"I see." I wouldn't have to pry to get him to tell me. The man couldn't keep secrets from me for shit, much to Caleb's dismay.

"I swear, honey." He was actually pleading with me now. "He already had it here before I could stop it."

"Did he?" I had no idea who or what he was talking about, but I was guessing it had something to do with Caleb.

"Vi, the bike was already here when I got back from the shop. Swear to God." He was working for Tiny in his motorcycle garage. He built custom bikes for high-end customers. Which was used to launder money. Among other things. Me and Quinn both were finding out Knuckles was way the fuck more resourceful and connected than Quinn had thought. Which was good because it seemed Knuckles had half the police department and state police working the Nashville area on the payroll. Also, that was two oaths to God almost back-to-back. He must feel really guilty.

"Riot," I said, using his road name to get his attention. "Is Caleb all right?"

"What?" He looked confused, then his eyes widened. "Yes! Caleb's fine. Nothing happened to Caleb." When I merely raised an eyebrow, he ducked his gaze, toeing the edge of the rug with his shoe. Then he sighed and I knew I had him. "He bought a motorcycle."

I blinked. "Come again?"

"I swear --"

"To God. Yes. You said that," I snapped. "What the fuck is going on, Quinn?" This... was alarming. For multiple reasons.

"Caleb bought a motorcycle. He had it delivered to Tiny's this afternoon after he got out of school."

"A motorcycle."

"Uh, yeah. Kind of a nice one too. A Harley Breakout." He swallowed, trying to smile but failing.

"OK. So, my first question is how did a twelve-year-old buy a motorcycle? Without an adult present at the time of the buying." Oh, the guilty look just got worse and worse.

"OK, it's my fault. I'm sorry! But the kid practically double-dog dared me!" He hung his head like a naughty child. I also knew the old double-dog dare scheme from Caleb all too well. "I'm sorry I lied. And I'm sorry I swore to God and still lied."

I tried to keep a straight face. I really tried. It was simply impossible with Quinn sometimes. "I'm going to ground you both for this."

"It's my fault. Don't ground Caleb." Riot actually stuck his lip out. *Pouting*!

"Oh, so you didn't take that double-dog dare?"

"OK, so that's not true either. He did double-dog dare me and I couldn't help but take it, but I still don't want you to get him in trouble."

Yeah, the asshole was playing me, making me laugh so I'd forgive him and my son. I knew he was managing me, and I didn't give a good Goddamn. "You're incorrigible! Both of you!"

"Oh, yeah?" Instantly, his demeanor changed. Instead of cute and contrite, he now looked wicked and corrupt. "I'll show you incorrigible."

In a heartbeat, he was on me, his mouth claiming mine with a hungry intensity that stole my breath. My back hit the wall as his powerful body pressed against mine. He gripped my hips with a possessive heat that had me melting into his touch. "You think I'm bad?" he growled against my lips. "You should see what I'm about to do to you."

I gasped as his teeth grazed up my neck. I was already tugging at his shirt, needing nothing between us. "Caleb --"

"Is at Knight's for the next two hours learning computer shit." He slid his hands up my shirt, his rough palms skimming over my bare skin. "Which means I have you all to myself, Mrs. Devereaux."

The way he said my name sent a shiver down my spine. Three months of marriage and I still wasn't used to it being so wonderful. Quinn had shown me what it felt like to belong to someone who treasured rather than possessed.

"Quinn," I moaned as he lifted me, and I automatically wrapped my legs around his waist.

He carried me to our bedroom, kicking the door shut and locking it behind us even though we were alone. Better safe than sorry. He laid me on the bed with the same gentleness I'd come to crave like a drug before standing back to strip off his shirt, revealing the tattooed expanse of his chest and abs.

"You're still the most beautiful thing I've ever seen," he said, his eyes dark with desire as he watched me pull my own shirt over my head.

I smiled up at him, no longer shy about my body. "You're not so bad yourself."

Quinn undressed me, tossing my clothing aside before lowering his mouth to my breast. He circled my nipple, sending an electric zing straight to my clit. I arched beneath him, tangling my fingers in his hair.

"I love the sounds you make when we fuck," he said, his voice gruff with lust. "Drives me fuckin' mad!" He shoved at his pants, getting them over his hips before leaning in to swipe his tongue through my pussy.

I cried out at the first touch of his tongue, my body already conditioned to respond to him. Every swipe, every delicious lick sent pleasure coursing through me. He gripped my thighs, holding me open for his hungry mouth.

"Quinn, please," I gasped, my hips lifting off the bed. "I need you inside me."

He looked up at me with those storm-gray eyes, his mouth glistening with my arousal. "Not yet," he growled. "Want to taste you first. Want to feel you come on my tongue."

He returned to his task with renewed vigor, his tongue circling my clit before dipping lower. When he slid two fingers into me, curling them to hit that perfect spot, I nearly came off the bed.

"That's it, baby," he murmured against my sensitive flesh. "Let go for me."

My orgasm crashed through me with stunning intensity, my body shaking as pleasure enveloped me. Before I could recover, Quinn was moving up my body, positioning himself between my thighs.

"Never get tired of watching you come," he said, his voice rough with need as he guided himself to my entrance. He pushed inside with one smooth thrust, filling me completely.

I moaned at the delicious stretch, wrapping my legs around his waist to take him deeper. "You feel so good," I whispered, running my hands over the hard planes of his back.

Quinn started to move with slow, deep strokes that had me gasping against his shoulder. His powerful body covered mine completely, making me feel sheltered and cherished even as he claimed me with increasing urgency.

"Fuck, I love you," he groaned, his forehead pressed against mine. The words fell from his lips so naturally, so honestly that my heart stuttered in my chest.

"I love you too," I whispered back, and I meant it with every fiber of my being.

His rhythm faltered for just a moment, his eyes searching mine with wonder and disbelief. It was the first time either of us had said those words. We'd shown our love in countless ways over the past months, but neither had dared speak it aloud until now.

"Say it again," he demanded, his hips driving harder now, pushing me toward another peak.

"I love you, Quinn Devereaux," I gasped, cupping his face between my hands. "I love everything about you."

He captured my mouth in a searing kiss, swallowing my cries as he thrust deeper. His hand slipped between us, finding my clit with unerring precision. The dual sensations of his cock inside me and his fingers against my most sensitive spot had me spiraling toward release again.

"Come for me, Vi," he urged, his voice strained with the effort of holding back his own climax. "Wanna feel you come around my cock."

My second orgasm hit even harder than the first. I shattered around him, crying out his name as I thrashed helplessly underneath him. Quinn soon followed me, burying himself deep as he found his own release with a hoarse groan against my neck.

For several minutes, we lay tangled together, our breathing gradually slowing. Quinn's weight pressed me into the mattress, but I welcomed it, the solid reality of him anchoring me to this moment, this life we'd built together.

"Did you mean it?" he finally asked, lifting his head to look at me.

"Every word," I whispered, tracing the line of his jaw. "I love you, Quinn."

His smile was breathtaking in its intensity. "I've loved you since the moment I saw you, I think. Just took me a while to understand what I was feeling." He rolled to his side, taking me with him, so we remained connected. His fingers traced lazy patterns on my back as we basked in the afterglow.

"So," I said after a comfortable silence. "About that motorcycle…"

Marteeka Karland

International bestselling author Marteeka Karland leads a double life as an action romance writer by evening and a semi-domesticated housewife by day. Known for her down-and-dirty MC romances, Marteeka takes pleasure in spinning tales of tenacious, protective heroes and spirited heroines. She staunchly advocates that every character deserves a blissful ending.

Marteeka finds joy in baking and gardening with her husband. Make sure to visit her website to stay updated with her most recent projects. Don't forget to register for her newsletter which will pepper you with a potpourri of Teeka's beloved recipes, book suggestions, autograph events, and a plethora of interesting tidbits.

Marteeka at Changeling: changelingpress.com/marteeka-karland-a-39

Wanda Violet O. (Teeka's Dark Erotica side) changelingpress.com/wanda-violet-o-a-226

Bones MC Multiverse

Contemporary MC and Crossovers
    Bones MC
    Shadow Demons
    Salvation's Bane MC
    Black Reign MC
    Iron Tzars MC
    Grim Road MC
    Bones MC Legends
    Kiss of Death MC

Print and Audio
    Bones MC Audio
    Salvation's Bane MC Audio
    Iron Tzars MC Audio
    Bones MC Print Duets
    Grim Road MC Audio

Changeling Press LLC

Contemporary Action Adventure, Sci-Fi, Steampunk, Dark Fantasy, Urban Fantasy, Paranormal, and BDSM Romance available in e-book, audio, and print format at ChangelingPress.com – MC Romance, Werewolves, Vampires, Dragons, Shapeshifters and Horror -- Tales from the edge of your imagination.

Where can I get Changeling Press Books?

Changeling Press e-books are available at ChangelingPress.com, Amazon, Apple Books, Barnes & Noble, Kobo, Smashwords, and other online retailers, including Everand Subscription and Kobo Subscription Services. Print books are available at Amazon, Barnes and Noble, and by ISBN special order through your local bookstores.

Changeling Press. LLC

ChangelingPress.com